Tin Roof Rusted

Jeff Zwagerman

The final approval for this literary material is granted by the author.

First printing

This is a work of fiction. Names, characters, businesses, places, events and incidents are either the products of the author's imagination or used in a fictitious manner. Any resemblance to actual persons, living or dead, or actual events is purely coincidental.

ISBN: 978-1-61296-947-3
PUBLISHED BY BLACK ROSE WRITING
www.blackrosewriting.com

Printed in the United States of America
Suggested Retail Price (SRP) $19.95

Tin Roof Rusted is printed in Book Antiqua

This book is dedicated to my dear friends and winter companions, BJ and Marcia. I wonder if I would have had the courage to write my first novel if Marcia hadn't said, "I always thought you would have written a book." Thanks for the motivation my friend.

Prologue

Tin Roof Rusted

Prologue

De waarheid wilniet altijd gezegd zijn
All truths are not to be told.
— Dutch Proverb

The rabbit died.

It seemed like an archaic way to announce a pregnancy.

Sara Jane's childhood experiences in Iowa should have been the first clue. Nobody ever used the word pregnant. It might be whispered among woman, but no one with any upbringing said the word out loud, and never in mixed company.

She had heard all of the clichés: "bun in the oven," "knocked up," "in the pudding club," "up the duff," "pea in the pod," "eating for two," "slipped one past the goal line," "ate a watermelon seed," "preggers," and "she's glowing," just to name a few.

Sara Jane wondered what she was.

Her mother had been more discrete and just said: in the family way or with child. Later, it would be acceptable to say PG.

The strangest phrase, Sara Jane had encountered, however, was from the eighties song, "Love Shack." Near the end of the song, the female singer cries out "tin roof rusted." It meant she got pregnant in their little love shack. Maybe it should have happened that way with Zander when they were younger. It might have changed both of their lives back then.

There was always a great deal of baggage connected with an unmarried pregnancy. Things weren't like they were in the 50's, but there still seemed to be that same old stigma among many.

She would not let that bother her. What did bother her was that she got herself into the situation in the first place.

Her little affair with Avon didn't require birth control, so she went off the pill. Zander hadn't even entered her mind. After all, he wasn't in Florida, until he was.

That little ill advised tryst would end up costing her much more than it was worth. It wasn't even satisfying, in the end, for either of them.

It wouldn't do much good to relive this mistake. It couldn't be changed. Now the thing to decide was where to go from this moment on.

It was coming on two months, but Sara Jane could feel her body changing. She had never considered childbirth. She wasn't opposed to it. It just never entered into any of her schemes or plans. She had been too busy trying to wring out the most in her life.

Now she would have to decide if this were one of those things that would be value-added or if it would hinder her future.

The thoughts were ponderous, as she sat on the beach of her hotel in the Grand Caymans. It was at least a pleasant place to ponder all the considerations.

Where would she go? Who should she tell? The more questions she asked herself, the more confused she became. One thing was painfully apparent; she had very few people in this world that she could trust.

One of those people was her sister back in Iowa. The other one was her childhood friend, part-time lover and father of this future child, Zander. But he made it quite clear that he didn't want to continue the relationship. If that's what you could call it. It was never much of a relationship from her perspective.

Sara Jane supposed it was her fault. Her selfish decisions had come home to roost.

She pushed her drink glass off the armrest of her beach chair. Her drink, "Sex on the Beach" ran into the sand and disappeared. There was a life lesson there, but she was too preoccupied to consider it.

With that one simple act, she had made her first decision. She would quit drinking, because it made her sick to her stomach.

That was the surface decision, but it also sparked the deeper predetermination. A conclusion she wouldn't even comprehend until later.

She was going to keep the baby.

1

Zander had every intention of finding his way to Cedar Key, so he could spend the holidays with his friends Gail and Herbie. That was the plan anyway.

But his travels through the Keys slowed him down. It was by design. He wanted to take in as much of the area as he could. Traveling the country had been something missing in his life, and he was bound to make up for it.

Everything might still have worked out, but he made the decision to turn off Highway 41 and explore Everglade City. That's when he met Aubrey Moreno. She looked like his favorite actress, Natalie Wood. He just couldn't get himself to leave after that.

Aubrey had told him that she was of Cuban descent. She had the dark hair and eyes to be certain, but her first name didn't seem to fit.

"Where did you get the name Aubrey?" he wondered.

"My parents wanted to name me something more American. I think the name is English. I read somewhere that it means "fair ruler of little people."

"Sounds about right," Zander said. "You could rule people with just your smile."

"You are so cheesy, makes me want to urp."

"I just can't help myself around you."

"Try to get a grip," she said, gruffly, but her eyes were twinkling.

"So, did you start your life in Cuba, or have you always lived here?" Zander asked.

"My parents emigrated from Cuba when Baptiste was overthrown. There was too much unrest to suit them. I guess they wanted a better life. I was born in Miami. My father and mother worked all their lives trying to bring Cubans to this country. They both worked as translators for the government."

"What did they do in Cuba?" Zander had always been fascinated with the little island ninety miles off Key West.

"They both worked for the university. My father was a professor of natural history and my mother worked in the business office. That's where they met. Of course here in the states, his degree didn't mean anything, and he couldn't get a job teaching."

"That's just not right." Zander meant it.

"They didn't seem to mind. They were free. They loved this country and they hated Castro, so their government jobs were a good fit."

"Do you see them often?"

"They're both gone now. That's why I left Miami and came here. I wanted to start over and make some new memories. Those had become too painful." Aubrey's voice never wavered, but there was something in her eyes that told Zander she wasn't telling the whole truth.

"Have you ever been to Cuba?" Zander asked, trying to change the subject.

"No I haven't. My parents said it would be too dangerous. I guess I never had much of an interest in going there."

"I think it would be fascinating. Everything I've read points to a country stuck back in the 50's. It amazes me how they can keep all the old cars running."

"Cars are just a way to get around." Aubrey didn't seem interested in old cars.

"But old cars from the 50's and 60's have so much style. They are things of beauty. Besides, you drive a '68 Opal Olympia. That's almost a one-of-a-kind work of art. How do you keep that old German vintage running?"

"It's not mine. It belongs to someone else. I'm just using it to get around. I don't even like the looks of it."

"It is peculiar looking, I'd agree. It's why they didn't catch on much in the US."

"This conversation is boring me."

Zander decided to worm his way into another subject.

"If I could find a way to get to Cuba, I would love to make a visit. Would you be interested in coming along?"

Aubrey thought about the proposal for a moment. "Possibly. I do have some interest about where my parents came from, and I want to know more about any relatives I might have."

"Let me do some research. Maybe there is a way for us to visit educationally."

"I said, possibly. If I did agree, there would be no discussing of cars."

"Agreed." Zander said.

He didn't have the slightest idea of how he could accomplish getting permission. He had some contacts in the educational world. Maybe he could start there. It would be no easy task.

"If we went, would you smoke a Cuban cigar with me?" Zander asked, trying to lighten the mood.

"If you bought me their best rum. I'm told they have some good stuff."

"Deal."

Zander didn't actually like cigars. He remembered smoking a few on Jasper's patio in Omaha. He never saw what the big draw seemed to be for Cuban cigars. They all tasted like a camel took a shit in your mouth the next day. He decided not to share that thought with Aubrey.

~

After the holidays were over, Zander decided to get rid of his Mustang rental car. He didn't need wheels in Everglade City. Most places were within walking distance and if he did need to go somewhere else, he could always use Aubrey's Opal. The fact that it wasn't hers bothered him just a little.

Tin Roof Rusted

The closest Hertz rental car agency was located on Marco Island. One Sunday in January, the two went to the island. Aubrey followed in the Opal and once they dropped off the Mustang, they were free to make a day of it.

Aubrey wanted to go to the beach, and it was fine with Zander.

When they found a spot, Aubrey pulled into a parking space. She got out of the car and began taking off her clothes.

Zander was a little disappointed, when he saw she had on a two-piece swimsuit underneath. He was wearing his cargo shorts, so that would be just fine. He could take off his tee shirt if it got too hot. It was a pleasant day but not overly warm. It didn't seem to bother Aubrey in her skimpy suit. It didn't bother Zander, and he made sure to get his fill of looking at her. If his gawking bothered Aubrey, she never let on.

Aubrey went to the trunk, pulled out two short beach chairs, and handled them to Zander. She reached in again and pulled out a cooler. She was prepared. Zander liked that.

"What's in the cooler?"

"A few beers, some water, and two ham and cheese on rye."

"Perfect."

The day sailed by. Zander got a terrible sunburn, and he cried about it all the way back to Everglade City. Aubrey told him to shut up. She would rub aloe all over his body when they got back.

Zander thought that might be quite satisfying, and he shut up.

2

By day, Zander was a student of history, with the Everglades being his major. By night, he went back to what he knew best, being a bartender.

Aubrey Moreno got him the job at the Rod And Gun Club. She just couldn't stand seeing him "buying cotton." It was a southern term. Zander found out later that it was just a polite way of saying, "doing nothing."

He told Aubrey that he liked the Midwestern one better, "Big hat-no cattle."

"Either way, it fits you. I got you a job. You start tonight," Aubrey said, already moving on.

That was the end of it. Zander went to work that evening. The truth was, he was starting to get restless. He needed some sort of a schedule. When that schedule involved working with Aubrey, so much the better.

He had found a rental house in Everglade City and moved into it right after the first of the year. That had been two months ago. He was pleasantly surprised that there was a Cushman scooter at his disposal. It would be the transportation he would need. He could even get Aubrey on the back if she would agree to look like a dork.

The rental came furnished with everything Zander needed. That included Aubrey. She moved in shortly after Zander took possession. Zander wondered where she was living before they met. When he asked her, she just told him she had a small room in Chokoloskee. She wasn't anxious to return to it, and that suited Zander just fine.

Zander had discovered Chokoloskee by accident. One day he just kept driving south on the only road that led out of Everglade City and he stumbled on it. The locals pronounced it "Chuck-a-lusk-key" and it took him a while to get used to the pronunciation. The south was always doing things like that to trick the rest of the country.

He was especially interested in the Ted Smallwood Store. The actual building was built in 1917. It was one of the oldest buildings in Collier County. The store and trading post served the Seminole Indians and early pioneers. It now served as a museum, and Zander was enamored with the whole thing.

He met a working author there by the name of Rick Magers, who in turn, introduced Zander to Totch Brown. Totch was one of those colorful characters from old Florida who was just plain interesting. Zander couldn't get enough. He bought his book at the Smallwood museum and read the whole thing in one sitting. Zander was beyond impressed, after he found out Totch had been in a movie in 1958 called *Wind Across The Everglades*. The cast included Burl Ives, Christopher Plummer, Gypsy Rose Lee, Peter Falk and Emmett Kelly just to name a few. There seemed to be no end to what Totch had experienced in his lifetime.

Zander was most amazed by the freedom these early settlers experienced. When he shared those feelings, Totch became somewhat amused and told Zander that it sounded better than actually living it.

That's about the time Aubrey got Zander the job. She told him he was embarrassing himself. Worse than that, he was acting like a tourist.

Zander didn't want to play the fool, but he had the same excitement for the area that he had when he first discovered musical theatre. It was a quandary to be sure.

"You know, this place is almost perfect. I can see why you stay," he said to Aubrey one slow evening at work.

Aubrey started to laugh. "You've barely been here two months. You know absolutely nothing."

"How much more can there be?" Zander asked.

"It's the winter months. This is the best time to see the

everglades."

"What's wrong with summer?"

"Everything. Heat and humidity are bad enough, but you haven't had the joy of experiencing the mosquitos and the no-see-ums."

"I guess I'll find out," Zander said, smiling.

"Next time you go over to Smallwood's, check into the history of the schools back then. Mosquitos were so bad, they couldn't keep teachers longer than a few weeks."

"But that must have been decades ago."

"Hasn't changed much. You'll see." Aubrey softened her voice. "I'm happy to hear that you are at least considering staying."

"I couldn't leave if I wanted to."

"Why's that?" Aubrey stopped, and looked at Zander.

"Love. I'm in love."

She snorted. "You are in lust. And you are in lust with a dead actress. Natalie Wood has been dead for quite a while."

"I know. That's why I'm with you."

Audrey socked him in the arm as hard as she could. There was a glint in her eyes, however. Zander caught it and put his good arm around her waist.

"Let me take you from this mosquito-infested hell. Name the place and it is yours." He kissed her lightly, and she returned the kiss lightly as well.

"Good start, but I'm not the moving type."

"Once a south Florida girl, always a south Florida girl?"

"Something on that order." She broke loose from his one-arm hold, and he used his good arm to rub the muscle she had slugged.

"Pretty good right cross you've got there."

"From my boxing days." Aubrey said, and left for the storeroom to get provisions for the bar.

Zander just watched her go. He never knew if she was telling him the truth or just making things up. She did both so convincingly.

When she came back with a few bottles, Zander jumped into action.

"Why didn't you tell me the booze needed to be restocked? I would have done it."

"It doesn't really. I'm just being proactive in case we get busy. It is

Saturday night, after all."

Zander hadn't thought about what day it was for quite some time. It just didn't seem that important any longer. On Saturday night, many of the locals came into the bar late to finish their night of drinking. They had worn out their welcome at the other places. Generally, they were a raucous crowd but fun loving and without much violence.

Zander enjoyed watching them for the most part, and they were always respectful toward Aubrey. They were just blowing off steam in a place where it was difficult to make much of a living, let alone get ahead in the world. Some of the locals were guides, while others were commercial fishermen. Zander thought that a few of them might be involved in some illegal activities as well. He knew that poaching was a big problem, and so was drug running. He had never witnessed it, and when he had asked Aubrey about it, she had become serious and told him he'd better not be asking about things like that down here. When he pressed her for more information, she just stopped and gave him a dark look. Zander took the hint and kept his questions to himself. It merely served to make him more curious about the entire area. He would have to find more books on the subject. Maybe he could find a few authors who were working on stuff like that and talk to them. He found that writers liked to talk about their work.

Some of the locals had already made an appearance and were gathered at a bigger table. Zander recognized most of them. Aubrey had been talking them up and taking care of their drink orders. They would tip her well at the end of the night.

It was late in the evening when three strangers casually made their way into the bar area. They sat at a table near the entrance. Zander didn't recognize any faces. Aubrey was busy with the locals, so he decided to go over and take their order.

"What can I get you guys?" Zander asked.

The three just stared at him. Finally one of them spoke.

"Looks like we got us a Yankee pushing drinks. Don't that beat all?"

Zander didn't like his tone but decided to try to keep things pleasant.

"I didn't know my accent was quite so obvious," he said, smiling.

"You just act like one of them northern swishy boys."

Zander didn't know what he meant, but he knew it wasn't meant to be a gesture of friendliness. No doubt, these guys were jackasses.

"Can I get you something to drink?" Zander said, still trying to be pleasant.

The main jackass must have felt he was wasting his time, because he lost interest in Zander when Aubrey turned around.

"Tell the woman to come here. She can help us." Zander was dismissed.

When he looked up at Aubrey to tell her that these guys wanted her to wait on them, he could see she had frozen in place and was looking at The Jackass who did the talking.

She tried to skirt the table to return to the back of the bar, but The Jackass reached out and grabbed her by the wrist and pulled Aubrey in front of him.

Zander started to reach for his boot but stopped when The Jackass spoke.

"Nice to see you. I wondered what happened to you when you stopped visiting. Then to my surprise, I see that all your stuff is gone. You moved out without so much as a goodbye."

Aubrey didn't say a word but just looked at the floor. The Jackass put his other hand around her waist and pulled her close. He said something to her that Zander couldn't make out.

Zander didn't like the scene at all. There were too many variables in the room for him to try anything. He just didn't know where any of the alliances ran with the local crowd. It wouldn't be much of a fight if everyone were on the same team but him.

Zander walked over to the table with his stun gun and switchblade still in his boots. He put his hand on Aubrey's shoulder and said, "Hey Aubrey, the boss wants to talk to you."

Mr. Jackass let her go and focused on Zander. It gave Aubrey the time she needed to move away. She went from the table, to the back of the bar and then to the storeroom.

"Sorry boys, duty calls. Can I be of service until she returns?" Zander was as pleasant as could be, under the circumstances.

The Jackass was trying hard to come up with something to say but finally gave up. He turned to the other two.

"Three bourbons straight up."

Zander wasn't finished. "Any preference on the bourbon?"

"Old Crow."

"Whoa. Pretty harsh. I would have pegged you three for something a bit smoother."

"Just get the drinks," he said, through clenched teeth.

Zander thought it would be best not to provoke them any more than he had. He could tell they thought he was stupid and didn't want to waste any more time on him. It was a new tack for Zander. He thought about how he could try to perfect it to his advantage in the future, as he poured the drinks.

When he returned with the drinks, one of the other men had thrown a twenty on the table. Zander returned with their change of eight dollars.

"Pretty high-priced drinks," the one with the money grumbled.

"I don't set the prices. Just charge them." Zander said.

"No tip," The Jackass replied.

Zander shrugged it off and took the opportunity to go back into the storeroom to find Aubrey. She was nowhere to be found. It puzzled him for a moment because there was no other door leading from the room. Then he saw an open window. Audrey had crawled out of the window and left the premises.

He went back into the bar, and the three were looking at him.

"Send the woman back here," The Jackass yelled.

"I'm not hard of hearing. You don't need to shout. She's not around. I don't know where she went."

The three pounded down their drinks, got up and brushed right past the bar. Out they went. They seemed to be in quite a hurry.

Zander wondered where Aubrey had gone. He hoped she had gone back to his rental. The way the three had acted, they didn't know about Aubrey and Zander being together.

3

Two long days went by, and Zander hadn't seen anything of Aubrey. In fact, no one at The Rod And Gun Club had heard from her. He was getting worried. He hoped that The Jackass hadn't found her the night she disappeared. Her Opal Olympia was still sitting in the parking lot where she had left it.

Whatever was going on, Zander knew it wasn't good. It wasn't like him to worry about things he couldn't control, but he knew Aubrey was someone special, and he just couldn't help himself.

He had been working double shifts trying to cover for her. It wasn't like he couldn't handle it, but he couldn't help but worry when he was at work, because the place reminded him of her.

On the third evening when he arrived at work, he noticed that her car still hadn't moved. Panic almost set in. He had a hard time focusing and was happy that it was a slow Tuesday. The boss sent him home around 10:00.

When he pulled into the driveway on his Cushman, he could see the blue light of the television coming from the living room window. Zander cut the motor and reached for his stun gun. He knew he hadn't left the house with the television on.

He climbed the steps to the main level. The house stood on pilings, and Zander liked how it shook when someone climbed the stairs. Feeling the vibrations inside, he always knew when someone was coming.

He didn't like it very much right now, however, when he was that someone.

When he was almost to the top of the stairs, the blue light of the television was suddenly gone. Someone had indeed felt his presence. He didn't want to go in blind and realized there was one choice.

"I know someone is in the house. Turn on the lights and come out with your hands up," Zander called out, realizing how stupid it sounded as he said it.

The door opened just crack.

"Get in here, it's me Aubrey," she whispered.

Zander pushed his stun gun back into his boot and charged into the room. She was already sitting on the couch.

"Aubrey, are you okay? You had me very worried."

He picked her up and gave her a huge bear hug. She hugged him back.

"I am now," she said, and put her cheek next to his.

"Where have you been?" Zander asked, half peeved.

"Long story. One that would go better with some beer and popcorn."

"Okay. I'll get the beer, you make the popcorn," Zander grumbled.

Zander was more relieved than upset, but he wouldn't let Aubrey know it until she told her story.

They both settled on the couch with the beer and popcorn. Some mundane sit-com rerun was on the television.

"It appeared you were afraid of that jackass from the bar. Is that right?" Zander asked.

"There's more to it than that."

"Well, here we sit. Nothing better to do than talk about things."

"Jackass might be closer to what he should be called, but his name is Corey Prescott." She paused, and looked at Zander to see if the name meant anything to him.

"I don't know that name."

"The Prescotts are huge real estate developers in southeast Florida. They have a large presence in Miami as beachfront property developers."

"Okay. So, how are you involved?"

"Corey and I used to be an item."

"I think you'd better give me the entire story. Start from the beginning."

Aubrey told Zander that Corey was a player, with money and fast cars. He was relatively good looking and made the party circuit nightly.

Aubrey met him at a club at Miami Beach. He was always a real gentleman and had permission from her father to date Aubrey. He and her father had become friends, because Corey knew all the right things to say. Her mother was more guarded, not trusting the things he was saying.

"Eddie Haskell?" Zander asked, trying for some humor.

"I don't know who that is." The humor was lost on Aubrey. Apparently "Leave It To Beaver" was before her time.

They were together for five years, and everyone assumed they would get married. Aubrey assumed it as well. He always treated her with respect, unless he had been drinking. Then, something dark brewed beneath the surface.

Things were going well. Aubrey was in college, and she assumed Corey was working in the family business. She found out later, that Corey wasn't working at anything but the party circuit.

Then one day, Corey showed up drunk, wild-eyed and yelling about getting screwed. His father had given him an alternative. He either needed to get a job, or he was cut off. Corey offered to work with the family's real estate business, but his father told him "that ship had sailed."

"Were you in love with him?" Zander asked.

"I don't know. I guess I thought I was. It was my first real relationship. I didn't have anything else to compare it to."

Zander knew all about those feelings. He hoped she didn't have to experience what he had gone through with Sara Jane.

"So what happened?"

"I didn't see him for a while. It was almost three or four weeks, and then one day, he just showed up and asked me to go with him."

"Where?"

"Right here. Everglade City. He told me he would show his father and start his own business. He would have more money than his entire family when he was finished. He asked me if I wanted to go along for the ride."

"You're here, so I guess you said yes." Zander said, trying to sound matter-of-fact.

"Well sure, it sounded like an adventure. I was almost finished with college, and Corey said I could drive back and finish the semester and graduate."

"Did you?"

"Yes. It's the one thing I promised my father."

"I can't believe they let you go."

"They weren't happy about it. My mother begged me not to go. But I was impetuous and knew way more than my parents." She dropped her head. "A decision that has haunted me to this very day."

Zander waited a few moments.

"Well, if there is a plus to all this, it would be that if you hadn't come here, I would never have met you."

Aubrey smiled at that.

"Things went pretty good for the first year. Corey still had quite a bit of money and was able to buy a house in Chokoloskee. He let me use his Opal to go back and forth to school. I had to go a few times a week. He had a 'Vette that he drove around trying to be a big man. I had no idea what kind of business he was looking into, because he never shared anything with me."

"So what did you find out?" Zander wondered.

"Let me tell this at my own pace. I don't want to leave anything out."

Zander liked that. He would be patient.

"One day his Corvette was just gone. When I asked him about it, he told me he sold it. I couldn't figure it out. He loved that car. Luckily, it was after I graduated because he took over the Opal, and I had to walk everywhere."

Aubrey explained that she had volunteered to work at the museum in Everglade City a few days a week for something to do. It didn't pay anything, and Corey told her she had to get a job until his business took off.

"I didn't complain, because I was bored and needed something to do. That's when I got hired at The Rod And Gun Club. Some days he would give me a ride, but most of the time I had to walk or hitchhike. It's just over four miles, so it wasn't that bad unless it was raining. It always seemed like it was raining when I had to come home from work. I hated that."

Zander wanted to cut to the chase, but Aubrey wanted to relive the whole experience for some reason.

"One day he picked me up after the lunch shift and told me he wanted to show me something. He drove me to the marina at Chokoloskee and pointed out a new boat he had purchased. I assumed it was from the money he got from selling the Corvette. I was confused, because he had never had much interest in being out on the water."

"Sounds strange to me," Zander said

"He told me he had been going out with some of the charter boats learning the trade. He decided to become a charter fisherman."

"That's how he was going to get rich? Is he that stupid?" Zander asked.

"That's what I thought, and when I started to laugh, he hit me. It was just the beginning of many beatings."

Zander was incensed. He couldn't imagine anyone hitting Aubrey. He could feel his forehead getting red, like it always did, just before he got angry.

"You stayed with him even after he hit you?" Zander asked, in a way that made Aubrey stop and look at him.

Her eyes had a hurt look to them. "I was trapped. I wanted to leave but had nowhere to go. I had the money from my job, but that was going toward our living expenses. I found out later that Corey had a second mortgage on the house to help pay for the boat, and we were barely making expenses."

"Why didn't you go back home?" Zander asked.

Aubrey stopped talking and looked away for a few moments. Zander could see that this would be something difficult for her to speak about.

"My parents were killed by a drunk driver, while they were taking a walk not far from our home. It was a hit-and-run, and they never found the driver," Aubrey said, and put her face into her hands and began sobbing.

Zander put his arm around her shoulders and pulled her close allowing her to let out her emotions. They sat there for some time in that position. Zander was looking at the TV not seeing the program, and Aubrey had her head on his chest.

Aubrey sat up and looked at Zander. "You can't begin to know the pain I suffered from that."

Zander thought for a moment, and decided to share with her something he hadn't told another living soul.

"I think I can. My parents were killed in a car accident as well."

"But it wasn't like what happened to me."

"Just let me finish. My father ran his car into an eighteen wheeler on purpose."

Aubrey looked at him with her mouth open. "Why would he do something like that?"

"My mother was dying of cancer, and my father just couldn't fathom the thought of living without her. He felt suicide was his only choice."

"How do you know all that?"

"He left me a letter in his safety deposit box. You are the only other person I've ever told."

Aubrey hugged him hard and wouldn't let go. Zander wasn't about to stop her.

"We are kindred spirits. I knew it when I met you."

Zander smiled. She was sounding a lot like his friend, Fats.

When she let go, Zander asked her to continue with her story.

"It was pretty tight for a while. It seemed like I was the one with the income. Corey was spinning his wheels. Then, it all changed. He started coming home with fistfuls of cash. He was giving me some it and having me put it into the bank."

"What about the rest of it?"

"That's when I became suspicious. He was hiding it around the place. He was putting it in the walls."

"Sounds like drug money."

"Exactly. Corey had decided to revive the drug running trade in the Ten Thousand Islands area. I guess this whole area used to be a high traffic smuggling arena."

"I read about that in some of the books at the Smallwood Store.

Totch Brown used to run bales of weed."

"Corey must have read the same books, but he was pushing the harder stuff. It was more profitable, I guess."

"What did you do?"

"I was stuck. I hated what he was doing and told him so. That's when the beatings got worse. I left just in time. Moved in with a friend in Everglade City who worked at The Rod And Gun. Shortly after that, the D.E.A picked him up."

"So he's been in prison?" Zander wondered.

"He got two years. Became an informant to reduce his sentence. They put away quite a few people and basically broke up the ring."

"I wouldn't want to be in his shoes right now. The drug trade doesn't hold informers in very high esteem. I'd say his life wouldn't be worth much."

Aubrey smiled. "I hadn't thought of that." Then she frowned. "Most of his buddies are in prison for a long time. He might be able to outlast them."

"What about his foreign connections? They can't be very happy about losing their contacts."

"I don't know anything about that. I tried to stay away from all of that stuff."

"I'm surprised the Feds didn't drag you into the mix."

"They tried. They followed me for quite a while but must have figured out I didn't know anything."

"What about all the money he hid in the house?"

"They found most of it."

"Most of it?"

"There's quite a bit buried around the center piling of the house. He rolled a bunch of the money into plastic water bottles and put concrete over them. It looked just like concrete footings around the beams. You would need a sledgehammer to break it up. The D.E.A. never even looked there."

"Did you know about this?"

"No." She was emphatic. "He always did it when I was at work. I didn't find out until I visited in him in jail in Naples."

"What did he want you to do?"

"I don't really know. I think he just told me for something to talk about. He would have known I didn't want anything to do with that kind of money."

"But you still visited him in prison?"

"It's not something I'm very proud about. I was just kind of lost. I didn't know what to do. After I visited him a few times, I knew I had to get away from him. I was living in his house and driving his car, but I wasn't taking a penny from his drug money. I stopped visiting him and decided to leave this place."

"But you never did."

She looked out the window at nothing. "I know. I like it here. I decided I'm not about to let him push me away. I decided to stand up to him. I just didn't know it would be so hard."

"Maybe I can be of some help."

"I don't know. He's dangerous. You shouldn't be involved with something we both could regret later."

"I think we're already there. Besides, it's what I do." He pulled out his billfold and found a card and handed it to her.

She looked it over, and then looked at Zander. "I had no idea."

"I know. We both have things we don't know about each other. If this is going to work, we need to be totally honest with each other. No more secrets about anything. Agreed?"

"Agreed." Aubrey stuck out her hand to shake.

Zander grabbed it and pulled her close and kissed her. He could feel her relax and almost melt into his arms.

By the time they had finished talking, it was four in the morning. They decided to go to bed. Work didn't start until later, so they could sleep in. They both seemed to be too wound up to think about sex.

Zander lay on his back looking up at the ceiling trying to think about their next move. He liked this woman, and he wanted her to be safe. He had to get her away from the area.

Those thoughts were running through his head, when he felt Aubrey's hand on his shoulder. She was drawing clockwise circles on his chest starting from his neck and moving down. She never made it past his navel.

Maybe they were just too wound up to sleep.

4

When Zander woke up, it was almost 10:00. He had slept longer than he had wanted. Of course, they had gone to bed at 4:00, but didn't get finished and fall asleep until after five.

He could smell coffee and heard Aubrey taking things out of the cupboards. He assumed she was making breakfast, so he decided to lie there until he was called. It gave him time to think without being interrupted.

Having sex with Aubrey was a new experience. He was trying to decide how it was different from Lilly, Ingrid, and even Sara Jane. Sex with them had always been wild and animalistic. It was almost a rage. It wasn't just sex with Aubrey. It was slower, with great passion. The old sixties term "making love" came to mind. It wasn't about his compulsion any longer. Zander wanted Aubrey to have her needs fulfilled. Maybe that was the beginning of some kind of love. He didn't know. He just knew he liked caring about someone else for a change.

He tried to compare his last experience with Sara Jane, with what he had experienced just a few hours ago with Aubrey. There was no resemblance. It shook him. Did he have the compassion for her that was absent in his other relationships? He thought so. At least he hoped so.

The last sex with Sara Jane had been a terrible experience, and he was ashamed of himself for giving in. If nothing else, it brought closure. He wouldn't be dealing with her again.

"Get up, get your breakfast before it gets cold and the afternoon gets here," Aubrey called. There seemed to be a sparkle in her voice that wasn't there the night before.

Zander got up and went to the bathroom. He decided to put on some gym trunks and walked out into the kitchen. Aubrey was in a white terry cloth robe. It looked fabulous against her dark skin and dark hair. She was gorgeous. He couldn't believe someone so beautiful would want to be with him. Zander hoped it just wasn't because she was on the rebound.

Zander poured some coffee in both cups. Aubrey came over with a pan and put a glob of oatmeal on Zander's plate. Zander made a face.

"Don't give me that look. You don't have much of anything around here to eat. This was the best I could come up with. Besides, oatmeal is good for you. It's good for your colon."

Zander thought he could go forever and not talk about his colon. He decided to keep his mouth shut. Aubrey put a few other bowls on the table. Zander merely watched.

Aubrey put some canned peaches and cinnamon on Zander's oatmeal and folded everything together. Then she stopped and looked at Zander. It was his cue to try it. He took a bite. He was never much of a fan of oatmeal, but this tasted pretty darn good.

"Hey, I like this." His mouth was full, but he didn't care.

Aubrey laughed. "I can do a lot with little."

Zander liked that comment. She was grounded. After he thought about it, he hoped she wasn't talking about him being little.

"You talked about finishing college. What was your major?" Zander asked, making conversation.

"I started out as a business major, but I hated it. I tried some different things, but in the end, I decided I wanted to follow in my parents' footsteps and work with languages. I have a degree in international communications, but you can see how that worked out for me. I suppose I should go back and get some advanced degree. It would make me more viable in the workplace."

Zander just nodded. He didn't know what to say.

"You haven't told me much about your past," Aubrey said.

Zander figured it was more of a demand rather than an observation.

"Not much to tell, really. I graduated from a small Iowa college with a degree in music. I even taught for a few years."

"You didn't like it?"

"No, I did enjoy it. I think I just got restless and wanted other things." There was just too much other baggage, that Zander didn't want to share, let alone, relive.

"So what did you do after that?"

"I tended bar in Omaha, and then later, in both Frisco and Breckenridge, Colorado."

"I always wanted to go to Colorado. The pictures of the mountains seem so big. I've seen the Smoky Mountains, but they're just overgrown hills."

Zander smiled. "You might just get your chance. I own the bar with a friend of mine right in Frisco. That's in the heart of the mountains."

"You own a bar?"

Zander nodded.

"What are you doing here?"

"Just taking some time off. I wanted to see the country while I still can."

Aubrey messed up Zander's hair.

"Let's go. Let's just get away from here."

Zander paused and looked at her. "You can't always run away from your problems. Sometimes you need to face them and put an end to them."

Aubrey wasn't sure Zander was actually talking about her.

"You talking about me?"

"I think I was talking about myself, but if the shoe fits…"

Aubrey stood up and took the empty dishes to the sink. It looked like she was finished with the conversation for now. Zander wanted her to think about what he said.

"I'm going to take a shower. Let's talk more about this later."

Aubrey just shook her head.

When Zander was finished in the bathroom, Aubrey took over. Zander went to the living room and found a pen and a sheet of paper.

He wanted to list some options for Aubrey to consider. It always helped him to write things down and see how they sounded when he read them aloud. When he was almost finished, Aubrey came back into the room dressed and ready for whatever the day would bring.

"I've thought about what you said. You may be right. I need to face this thing with Corey. I just don't know how to go about it."

"I've been writing a few things down for you to consider."

"Okay. I'm listening."

Zander listed his ideas for her:

1. Confront Corey, tell him it was over and he would need to leave her alone.

2. Just leave the area and not come back.

3. Zander could handle the situation without Aubrey getting involved.

4. Do nothing and hope it would just go away.

5. Make Corey pay, with Zander's help, and put him away for a long time

6. Run off to the mountains together.

Zander included the last item to lighten up the situation. He knew that it wouldn't be confronting anything.

Aubrey grabbed the list from Zander's hands and studied it for quite a while. Zander got up and got some more coffee. The burner had shut off so he put the cup in the microwave to heat up the coffee.

When he sat down next to Aubrey, she was ready to discuss her options.

"I don't like any of them except maybe the last one. But you already said I needed to face up to this."

Zander nodded.

"Okay. Let's look at each one. Maybe we can do number six after we resolve this whole thing."

Zander liked it when she said "we." It meant she was including him in the solution.

"I don't have the stones to confront Corey on my own. I know he would beat on me or maybe do something worse. He's used to getting his way and doesn't handle the word 'no' very well. So item one is out."

Zander nodded.

"If I tried to run, he might find me. He's got too many resources at his disposal. So number 2 is out as well."

"Check," Zander agreed.

"I suppose I could let you handle this, but that's not how I was raised. It's my problem, I should be a part of the solution." She didn't give Zander time to reply, "Number four is just plain dumb."

Zander had to agree.

"So, I like five the best. It would make me quite happy seeing him back in prison again."

"I think that might be the best plan, especially if you want to be able to come back here and not have to run away forever."

"Do you have any idea how we can get this done?"

"Not really. I'll do some thinking on it and let you know the plan when I come up with something."

"Let's get this thing going. I'm sick of living like this."

"You have to promise me that you'll do what I tell you. If I say you need to leave or go somewhere else, you need to do it. No arguments, okay?"

Zander knew that would be a difficult promise for Aubrey. She was a strong woman in many respects and didn't like being told what to do. He also knew she was afraid of Corey, so that might help tame that independent spirit just a little.

"I can do that as long as you tell me everything. No secrets, remember?"

"Agreed," Zander said, but he didn't know if he could keep that promise. It would all depend on how things progressed. He wasn't about to put Aubrey in harm's way, no matter what the circumstances.

"So, now what do we do?" Aubrey asked.

Zander could tell she wanted to get the show on the road.

"We need some intel. I'll have to look around and find out what Corey is planning."

"I liked it when you called him The Jackass much better."

"Duly noted."

"Do I have to stay cooped up here all day?"

"I don't think that it's safe here, especially after you shared that they've been watching me. Where were you staying before?"

"My friend Julie has a place, but it's for sale. She used to work with me at The Rod And Gun Club, but she went back to Tampa. She said I could stay there until the place sold if I would keep an eye on things for her."

"Does The Jackass now about her?"

"Aubrey smiled. "I don't think so. He was already in prison when she worked with me. I've never mentioned her to him."

"The Jackass?" Zander asked, winking.

She winked back. "The Jackass."

"All right, you wait until dark, and then go back to her place. I'll go back to work and keep up the appearance that you're just not around."

"What will we do until then?" Aubrey smiled.

Zander got her meaning but unfortunately had other plans.

"I've got to do some reconnaissance today. We can't have The Jackass following me without some repercussions."

"What are you going to do?"

"I'll take the Cushman, drive around Chokoloskee and try to find out what's going on. You'll need to give me directions."

"His house isn't really in Chokoloskee."

Zander just stared at Aubrey.

"I didn't exactly tell you the truth, because I didn't want you to get involved with my problem. His place is on Plantation Parkway. It's just outside of Everglade City but not in Chokoloskee either."

"I remember driving on that road. A lot of houses hidden away back there."

"That's what he liked. He doesn't like people nosing around in his business."

"I guess it's too late for all that now. Why don't you give me the directions?"

Aubrey scribbled the street and house number on the back of the paper Zander had given her earlier. Below that, she listed some grocery items she wanted Zander to pick up.

"If I have to stay here, at least I can cook for you."

"Do you need anything for the other place? I can pick up

whatever you need."

"You and that scooter? I hardly think you could manage a big grocery order."

"You're right. I've been thinking about that. It's time I purchased some wheels. The scooter is no longer practical."

She was interested. "What would you get? Where would you go?"

"I was thinking about a four-wheel drive pickup. I've seen a few with a vinyl covering over the bed. I like the look of them. I think I might have to go to Naples to find something I like. They've got a lot of used car dealerships there."

Aubrey seemed disappointed. "A used vehicle and a pickup, could you get anything more boring?"

"We don't want to draw attention. Besides, a pickup is practical, and used car dealerships don't ask a lot of questions if you've got the money."

"Practical. Spoken like a man. What color would you get?"

"I would look for something white. It would be like almost every other truck around."

"God, you are so boring," Aubrey said, but Zander could tell she didn't mean it.

"Boring, in this case, is absolutely what we want."

"How will you get over to Naples?"

"I can take highway 41 with the Cushman and after I buy the truck, I can load it in the back for the return trip."

Aubrey started to laugh.

"What's so funny? I just can't ask anyone for a ride. I don't need to draw anymore attention to this situation than necessary."

Aubrey laughed even harder.

Zander didn't see the humor. He decided to wait until she calmed down before finding out the joke.

Finally, when she gained some control, she spoke.

"Can't you imagine how you'd look driving the scooter all the way to Naples?"

Zander was confused.

"Zander, you're six foot seven. You look like a clown driving that thing. It's way too little for you."

Zander hadn't considered his appearance while driving the

Cushman. He couldn't argue with what she found so funny. It even made him smile.

"I see your point, but it's all we've got. We can't take the Opal, and you can't be seen with me driving around."

She decided she couldn't argue with him either. It was difficult for her to imagine how things would turn out, as she watched him leave the house.

5

Zander got on his Cushman and made his usual loop around Everglade City. It was part of his daily ritual. He wanted to know what was going on in the little community. When he went past The Rod And Gun Club, he stopped. Aubrey's Opal was gone. He drove into the parking lot and went inside. His boss was in the office, and Zander barged right in.

"What happened to Aubrey's Opal?" Zander blurted out.

"Good morning to you, too." His boss was just as terse in replying to Zander's outburst.

"Jees, I'm so sorry. I just thought maybe you heard from her." Zander was playing the game, trying not to get anyone else involved in the problem. If people didn't know anything, The Jackass couldn't lean on them.

The boss smiled. "I thought I could tell there was something between you two." Then he frowned. "I don't know what happened to the car. It was there when I left last night. It was gone this morning. If she hasn't contacted you, then something must be wrong."

"I'm on my way to check out her place. Maybe she came back late and didn't want to bother anyone."

"Came back from where?" The boss wanted to know.

"I just don't know. Everything about this is strange."

"Agreed. Let me know what you find out when you come to work this afternoon."

Zander said he would. He liked the fact that the Opal was missing from the parking lot. If it were around the area, it would be easy for him to spot.

Back on the Cushman, he made his way south toward Chokoloskee. It was a small island and in ten minutes, Zander could drive all the streets on his scooter. He made the left turn onto Plantation Parkway. It didn't take long and he spotted the Opal. It was next to a house on pilings. The house didn't look like much, and Zander figured it belonged to The Jackass from the description Aubrey had given him.

Zander rode around the little community trying to decide what his next move should be. He stopped and sat on the Cushman. It was a sunny day just like every other day in southern Florida.

Something had to happen soon, or Aubrey's life would be a very miserable existence. Hiding in the shadows never appealed to Zander. His nature had always been confrontational. He decided to make the first push.

Within minutes, he was parking next to the Opal. He walked around the house and noticed every side had a sign that said, "no trespassing." He looked around, before he ascended the steps. He looked at the pilings and found the center timber. There was a concrete pad around it. Zander looked at the other pilings and noticed they were grown over with weeds. He couldn't see any of their footings. The center footing was completely visible. Someone had disturbed the area recently. He would return later and check it out.

Zander hammered away at the door, hoping there was no one home. He wanted to go back down and check out the center post. He was almost ready to take the steps, when he heard the door opening. There stood The Jackass in all his glory.

It looked like he hadn't slept much and wasn't very pleased to be disturbed. Zander could see he didn't recognize him at first.

"Well?" he croaked.

"Hi, my name is Zander. I work at The Rod And Gun Club. I was wondering if you have heard anything of Aubrey? She hasn't been to work for a few days, and we're all just a bit worried."

Zander could see the recognition flood into Corey's eyes.

"You're the bartender." Corey growled.

"That's right. You remember me." Zander smiled.

Corey wasn't having any of this good humor.

"Get the fuck outta here, you queer."

He started to close the door, but Zander blocked it with his foot.

"I'm just asking for any information you might have. Her friends and co-workers are worried."

The Jackass flung the door open.

"I told you to get the fuck outta here." He started to raise his fist to hit Zander.

Zander calmly reached over and grabbed his protruding Adam's apple and squeezed hard. The Jackass went down to his knees making some choking sounds. Zander hung on for a few seconds and let him go. The Jackass started coughing trying to take in air and clear his throat at the same time. Zander knelt next to his face.

"You're not much of a fighter, I'd guess."

Zander gave him some time to reply but seeing that he was speechless, continued.

"You know, I don't mind being insulted at my workplace. I just figure it's part of the job, and I don't pay much attention to it. Most of the time people say things, when they are drinking, that they wouldn't dream of saying normally. I can forgive that. But when someone insults me when I'm merely asking for some information, well, I just can't tolerate that." Zander slapped him hard on the side of the face. "Are you listening to me?"

There was rage in Corey's eyes. He wanted to scream at Zander, but he couldn't even talk at the moment. Zander saw the hatred and was pleased with the outcome. He stood up.

"I wouldn't have thought to stop here, but I saw the Opal that Aubrey was driving out in front on the drive. It's a hard car not to notice. With your past, I would think you'd want to drive something less conspicuous."

Zander could see he was confused.

"Aubrey told me all about you. How did prison go for you? You're kind of a pretty boy. I'll bet you were popular with the rest of your cellblock. Is that why you felt the need to call me a queer? I think you may be just trying to run away from your past."

Zander decided he had kicked the beehive enough. If this didn't get a reaction, he didn't know what would.

He leaned over and lightly touched The Jackass's adam's apple once again.

"I'll be keeping my eye on you." Turning the tables was always a good strategy, Zander thought.

He bounded down the stairs two at a time. It had been a good start to his morning.

~

When Zander left work for home that evening, he saw an older gray pickup parked in front of the bar. When he left the parking lot, the pickup followed his Cushman. Zander decided that the idiots in the truck hadn't had much experience in surveillance, or they didn't care if he knew they were following him. He decided it must be the latter.

Zander arrived at his rental and turned on all the lights except for the bedroom. He turned on the television, and made sure he walked in front of the windows from time to time.

The pickup parked in front of his house. Zander couldn't believe the stupidity. It was apparent that they meant to intimidate him, or worse. Zander figured they wouldn't do much while he had the lights on. They would wait until they thought he was asleep and then make their move. They would have two choices. They could either leave at that time, or they could come in the house and beat the shit out of him. At least they could try. He was betting on a beating.

Zander was happy for one thing; Aubrey was tucked away safely at her friend's house. She wouldn't be a factor in what was about to happen.

He found a bag of potato chips and decided to wash them down with a bottle of Key West Sunset Ale. He had developed a taste for the beer, when he and Herbie had explored Key West.

The Tonight Show wasn't of much interest, and Zander made sure to get up and walk around briefly. He kept the bedroom dark, so he could watch the pickup. It hadn't moved. It was almost 12:00. Time to "fish or cut bait."

Zander started to turn out the lights. When everything was off, he turned off the television. They would assume that if the blue light of the TV was off, he was going to bed. He went into the bedroom, turned on the lights and went over to the blinds and closed them.

Zander sat on the bed for exactly five minutes. It was about the time it would take him to undress and get ready for bed.

Before he turned out the bedroom light, he arranged some pillows under the sheet and blanket. At first glance it would look like someone was sleeping. When everything was to his liking, he took his place at the kitchen table and waited. He thought he might have a good half-hour. He was wrong. These guys must be impatient. Barely fifteen minutes had gone by; when Zander heard the two pickup doors slam shut. Subtle, he thought.

Zander stood up and took a position behind the refrigerator. Even if they turned on the lights, they wouldn't see him at first glance. He could see the beams of flashlights coming up the stairs. He took "old sparky" from his boot. It was ready to go to work. Earlier, he grabbed a cast iron frying pan from the drawer in the stove. It could be both a shield and a weapon of some destruction. Zander liked the feel of it.

The door handle was moving. Zander purposely left the door unlocked. He didn't want to have to repair any damage. A front door replacement could be quite costly. The door opened, and Zander saw the beams from the flashlights racing around the room. None of the light caught him directly.

The two guys went right for the bedroom. Zander saw they both had something in their hand. He hoped it wasn't firearms. They crashed into the bedroom and flipped on the light, hoping to blind the sleeping lump in the bed. Zander moved and came up behind them. They were already swinging what looked like two huge rubber hammers. Zander realized they were there to maim, not to kill. That was an instant relief.

After the first swing, the two flunkies knew they had been had. Zander swung the frying pan and beaned the first guy on top of his head, dropping him right to the floor. He zapped the second guy with the stun gun right in his neck. One, two second burst, was enough. These guys were far from professional. They must have been some locals Corey had working for him.

Zander sat on the bed. The fry pan guy was out cold. The other guy was moaning something Zander couldn't understand. He gave him another short burst from "old sparky."

Zander was tired. The excitement of the day had concluded and finally cut off his adrenaline. He got up, went out to the kitchen, got some duct tape and returned to bind their hands and feet. They wouldn't be moving for a while. It was late, and he wanted to call the police to remove the two, but he didn't have a phone. He wished now he had purchased another cell phone, after he got rid of the old one in the ocean. He would add it to his "to do" list.

He decided to get rid of the two on his own. He dragged both of idiots down the stairs and put them in the bed of the pickup. He would drop them off at Corey's. Then he would drive the pickup back and ditch it someplace.

He drove to Corey's house. The Opal was gone. At least that was something good. The two idiots had been easier to take down his steps than they were bringing up Corey's. His door was locked, but Zander gave it a good kick and it sprung open. He arranged the two nicely on the living room floor and left.

Before he got back into the pickup, he decided to have a look at the middle piling Aubrey had told him about. He grabbed one of the flashlights; the two guys had used at his house, and went to the center post.

There was no doubt that someone had disturbed the area. Zander began feeling the concrete pad and felt it move under the palm of his hand. The top was loose. He grabbed the edges and moved it up the post. It slid quite easily and when he got it a few feet up the post, he tilted it so it wouldn't slide back down. He shined the flashlight into the hole.

It was a little bunker, really, a concrete hole. The top had been poured later so it could be moved. There were seven water bottles in the hole. Zander picked up one and screwed off the top. It was jam packed with rolled up money. Mostly bigger bills from what he could tell.

This might be too good to be true. He saw an old bucket near the step and filled it with the bottles of cash. He started to move the concrete cover back into its place but thought better of it. It would be more effective if Corey saw that someone had been messing with his stash when he drove in. Zander wished he could stay and watch his reaction.

He decided he needed to share what had happened with Aubrey.

It was late but he needed to talk to her. He put the bucket into the pickup next to him and drove back to Everglade City. When he reached the house, he saw she still had a light on.

They needed to plan things from here. He needed another set of eyes to examine the different scenarios.

The game was on.

6

Zander didn't even get to knock on Aubrey's door. She opened it before he could raise his arm. She had been waiting for him.

"Where have you been? I've been worried."

"Something came up that had to be dealt with immediately. Sorry."

"Well, you could have at least called."

"No phone." Zander could see Aubrey was about to say something, so he just preempted her. "It's on my list of things to do."

She paused and looked at his hand holding the bucket.

"What's that?"

"You'd better sit down. I've got quite a bit to tell you. Some of it you will not like," Zander said, and led the way to the couch.

Zander explained in detail what had happened earlier in the evening. He could tell Aubrey was enjoying the story, until he came to the part of the contents in the bucket.

"My God. You took his cash? He'll go absolutely crazy. He'll kill you."

"I hope not. I just wanted to get his attention."

"You're going to get way more than that. So, now, what are we to do? Or haven't you thought that far ahead?"

"I have actually. It's Sunday tomorrow. I'll take the Cushman to Naples and buy us a nice used pickup. Then I'll look for someplace, away from here, where I can stash you until this thing gets settled."

"You are planning to use his money to buy the pickup?" Aubrey asked, with concern in her voice.

"I have to admit I considered it, but no, I'll use my own money. I would think law enforcement would want to get their hands on this."

"So, what happens the rest of the night? You can't go back to your house. It's the first place Corey will look for you."

"True. A bigger problem is the old pickup parked out front. I need to get rid of that before I do anything else." Zander stood and moved toward the door.

"I'm going with you."

"Aubrey, I don't think that's such a good idea."

"I don't care. You are not leaving me here to worry about you."

Zander could see her mind was made up. He shrugged his shoulders and took her by the arm. Together they walked out the door.

"What are you planning to do with this thing?" Aubrey pointed to the pickup.

"It's a surprise. At least I'm hoping it will be a big surprise to the two guys that jumped me."

Aubrey smiled. "I like surprises."

Just down the street from The Rod And Gun Club, the street angled right next to the Barron River. There were quite a few short docks with boats on lifts. Zander figured it would be a good spot to launch the pickup into the river. It was late and most homes were dark. The locals had all turned in for the night. Zander drove the street, until he found where the road jogged left. If the pickup went straight, it would make a nice little splash into the river.

They both got out of the truck, and Zander noticed the engine idled at a fairly high rpm. He wouldn't need to do anything with the accelerator. After all, he didn't want to hide the pickup, he wanted to disable it and make the owners angry. Angry people usually didn't think straight.

Zander pulled the gearshift into drive and walked along, steering the truck toward the river. When he felt it was taking the right route, he let go and closed the door. They both watched as the pickup ran over some reflectors that were placed to warn motorists of the angle of the road.

The pickup ran itself right over the edge and into the river. Zander had expected the front end to hit the shallows and stop with the hood and engine submerged. It didn't quite work out that way. The river was a great deal deeper than Zander had imagined. The pickup went in and started to float. Then the front end started to dip down, the cab filled with water and it was gone. It took less than three minutes for it to disappear without a trace.

"Damn. I wasn't expecting that," Zander said, rubbing his head.

Aubrey started laughing hysterically. Zander put his hand over her mouth.

"Quiet, we don't want to draw attention to this."

Aubrey nodded her head and pulled Zander's hand from her mouth.

"I told you I like surprises. This was a great one. Don't you think?"

Zander couldn't argue. He didn't know how deep the river was, but he hoped no one would ruin a good prop on a boat motor by hitting the submerged pickup. He had read a newspaper article about someone finding a car in a canal in Cape Coral. The person inside had been missing for twenty years. Maybe that would happen here. That might be interesting. At least no one would have died in this accident.

The two walked back to Aubrey's friend's house arm-in-arm. Both were thinking about the events that had led up to this moment.

Aubrey was counting herself lucky for meeting a guy like Zander. She was enjoying the night air and the walk back. Things were starting to work out. She had feelings for this midwestern boy, and she realized he had feelings for her as well.

Zander, on the other hand, wasn't feeling any of the same emotions. He knew that he had set an unknown chain of events into motion. They would have to be extra careful, but more importantly, they would need to be proactive. It made him just a bit nervous. Adventures always made him a bit nervous.

They made the four-block walk back without incident. They had seen no one, and no one had driven by on any of the adjoining streets. Aubrey had left the television on, and they climbed the steps and entered without putting on any lights. Aubrey went right to the bathroom, and Zander stepped back out onto the deck to make sure no one had been following. The deck surrounded the entire house, and by the time he made it around to the back door, Aubrey stepped out and put her arm through his. Together they looked out over the area. It was very dark. There was no moon to help shine some light on the night.

Aubrey turned and put both arms around Zander. He embraced her as well and noticed she had changed into something smooth and sheer.

"You feel extra smooth tonight," Zander said, realizing how cheesy he sounded.

"I've been saving it for a special occasion. This would be about as special as any."

She led Zander back into the house and right into the bedroom. Zander started to remove his clothes, but she would have none of it. Aubrey slowly removed his shirt and pants. He had on a pair of silky black boxer briefs. She hooked her thumbs into the elastic and pulled them down just slightly. Her forefinger was finding other places to stroke. In full arousal, Zander was concerned that there wouldn't be enough room to take them off. Aubrey didn't seem to care and continued with her interesting ritual.

Just as Zander thought he would explode, they both heard sirens.

"What's that?" Aubrey asked, pulling her hands away.

Zander fought his desire to pull her hand back into its former position.

"Sounds like a patrol car," he said, not masking the disappointment in his voice.

Aubrey was getting dressed before Zander could finish replying.

"Let's go find out what it is."

"But..."

"She stopped and looked at Zander and smiled. "We can start where we left off later. There's just too much going on for me to concentrate."

Zander wasn't sure he could agree with her. He wondered how women could just turn sex on and off on some whim. It didn't work that way for him.

Reluctantly, he put his clothes back on. "We need to be careful not to be seen, so we need to stay in the shadows."

"Lead the way, and try not to look so disappointed," Aubrey teased.

The two walked out holding hands and moved along the dark streets until they saw flashing lights coming from the patrol car. There were other sirens coming to join in as well. They sounded more like fire trucks to Zander.

As they rounded the corner, a single block from the action, Aubrey pulled back on Zander's hand.

"They're at your rental. Can you see what's happening?"

Zander dropped her hand and started moving toward his house.

"Zander, where the hell are you going? Don't do something stupid."

Zander stopped and turned around. "Go back to your place. This might have been an attempt to flush you out. I can't have you exposed."

"I want to stay with you."

Zander's voice became serious. "Do what I say. Go now."

Aubrey could see the change in Zander's demeanor instantly. She didn't say anything, but turned around and ran back the way they had come.

Zander watched to make sure she followed his direction. When he was satisfied she was indeed on her way home, he turned and walked toward the rental.

Zander had never been overly friendly with law enforcement. Maybe it was because of his dealings with the dirty deputy back in his hometown, he just didn't know. Fats had been giving him counsel about building relationships with the cops. It made some sense to Zander, especially when they bought the bar back in Frisco. He had been trying to be friendlier with deputies when they came into The Rod And Gun Club.

Zander was relieved when he saw the deputy was one of his off-duty regulars. He was standing in front of his squad car writing in some type of notebook. Zander approached him and apparently scared him. He turned around with his hand on his pistol.

"Who are you, and what's your business here?"

"Mike, it's me, Zander, from The Rod And Gun."

Mike reached for his flashlight and shined it into Zander's face.

He relaxed when he recognized Zander.

"Jees, you took me by surprise. This is a crime scene. What are you doing here?"

Zander could hear suspicion in his voice.

"Mike this is my house. Well, I mean I rent it. What's going on?"

"You better take a look. It appears you might have some enemies around here."

Zander walked past the squad car, and the first thing he saw was the Cushman. It had been drug out into the driveway and set on fire. Then he noticed the contents of his house had been literally strewn all over grounds. There couldn't be anything left inside the house. Zander figured they were looking for the money he had removed earlier. He was happy he hadn't left it there. It was a huge chip in this poker game.

The volunteer fire department put out the Cushman fire with extinguishers. Zander went over and thanked them. He knew they had a thankless job. He was sure it pissed them off having to get out of bed late at night. Then finding a small fire that could have been put out by anyone with a garden hose. Zander knew most of the guys from his job.

"Come in Monday night, and the drinks will all be on me," he said, hoping to turn the night into something positive for these guys.

A few of them slapped him on the back and said they would be happy to help him spend his money. The mood was much lighter when they packed up and went on their way.

Mike walked over and pulled Zander back over to his squad car.

"So, what's this all about?"

Zander thought about playing dumb. Aubrey had told him he did that very well without even trying. That thought made him smile, and then realized he needed help on this particular problem. He was out of his element dealing with locals. It was tough duty.

"Are you familiar with the name Corey Prescott?"

"That asshole? He's in jail. I helped put him there."

"We like to call him The Jackass. Seems to fit him better."

"Maybe so, what's this got to do with him?"

"He's out of jail. He's been around for a while."

Mike took off his hat and threw it on the hood."

"Damn it, no one tells us anything. You'd better start from the beginning."

Zander looked at his watch. "It's late. How about we meet tomorrow? I'll tell you the whole story."

"No, you tell me while we put all this stuff back into the house. If Prescott is back, I'm going to need time to lay out a strategy with the sheriff. Mostly, I need to know your involvement with this guy."

Zander agreed. Not because he wanted to work at putting the contents of his house back in place, but because he knew he needed Mike's law enforcement help. He wanted to take care of the problem with minimal violence. He didn't want anyone's death on his conscience. If he did this himself, The Jackass would have to die. He would do what it took to protect Aubrey, but he knew that once someone crossed the killing line, that someone could never go back.

Zander's story took longer than he expected, and by the time they were finished with the contents of the house and the story, dawn was upon them. Mike called one of the other officers to bring them coffee as they finished. They leaned against the hood of the patrol car drinking the coffee and not saying much. Mike broke the silence.

"I'm sorry about your Cushman. It looks like a total loss."

"It came with the house. It's not mine."

"That's a relief. You look like a real bonehead driving that thing around. All assholes and elbows, I'm thinking."

Zander had to laugh. Mike was right with that description. "I'll have to make sure my landlord gets reimbursed for the loss."

"You got insurance?" Mike asked.

"No. I think Corey Prescott will somehow stand the cost."

Mike smiled. "You say you have his money. Have you counted it?"

"Not yet. I'm going to have to figure out a way to use the money to get him back into prison. This time for a longer period of time."

"That's something I didn't just hear. You need to keep whatever plans you might have to yourself. Don't involve me until you have everything in place and there is no doubt concerning his guilt."

Zander smiled. "Afraid about a conflict of interest?"

"To be sure."

"I don't want Aubrey involved in this either."

"About Aubrey, do you know she was under suspicion as an accomplice for quite a while?"

"And?" Zander was a little peeved.

"And nothing. There was no evidence against her. Some in the department still have their doubts, but after I got to know her, I don't think she had anything to do with anything."

"Good to know. I agree wholeheartedly."

"But you aren't a very good witness, are you?" Mike asked while smiling. "Sleeping with The Jackass's woman is sure to put you in an uncomfortable position."

"Then you realize there is nothing I wouldn't do for her."

Mike nodded, "I'll see you Monday evening at The Rod And Gun. Unless your invitation for free drinks was only for the fire department."

"Of course you are invited. Mike, I need to ask you for another favor."

"What would that be?"

"I was planning to take the Cushman over to Naples and find some new wheels."

Mike started to laugh. "You were going to ride that thing all the way to Naples? That's something I would like to see."

"I guess neither of us will be treated to that vision," Zander said, and pointed to the burned up scooter.

"So, I'm thinking you need a ride?"

"Exactly."

"Well, it's Sunday and I'm off but I need some sleep. How about I pick you up right here around 1:00?"

"Okay, see you then," Zander said, and handed his empty cup to Mike. "Thanks."

Zander walked back to Aubrey's friend's house. He had a feeling that the promise Aubrey had made about continuing where they had left off had passed its expiration date.

7

Corey Prescott and his two locals had been busy. They had waited until after 2:00, before they went to the bartender's house. He didn't even know his name. He thought that maybe the guy had told him, but he never did listen very well. That was especially true when someone was kicking the shit out of him.

The three amigos went into Zander's place to look for Corey's money. When they found nothing, Corey lost his temper and began chucking items from the house onto the lawn. The other two talked him into doing it without so much noise. They had to work fast, and destroying property would just draw unneeded attention. Corey saw their point. He would have enjoyed destroying the furnishings. He decided to watch the other two do the job. He sat on the Opal's hood and smoked a cigarette. He was bored with the whole thing. He just wanted his money back. He would get it and take his pound of flesh. That was a certainty.

When his boys were almost finished, he had an idea. He found his way to the Cushman and wheeled it out into the driveway. He took out his knife and found the fuel tank hose under the seat. He put the scooter on its side and cut the hose. The gas gushed out around the scooter and pooled underneath it. Corey watched it for a time and then called out to the other two.

"Let's go. Get in the car."

The two obeyed. They always obeyed. He was paying them well.

Corey looked at the Cushman and smiled and then flipped his cigarette butt into the puddle of gas. He got back into the car, as the gas ignited with a whoosh. As they drove away, without turning on their headlights, they could see the scooter engulfed in flames. It was a good ending to a rather bad evening.

Corey decided to go back to his house on Plantation Parkway. He invited his partners to accompany him just in case there would be trouble later. They would be content to sit around, drink rum and make more plans. Mostly, they just drank the rum. By 6:00, the three were quite drunk and needed some breakfast. The Island Café opened early for the locals, and that's where they headed.

On the way, the backseat rider passed out. They tried to wake him, but he was gone. So, Corey and his other partner stumbled into the café without him. It was always a busy place, and most people minded their own business. Later in the day it would become filled with tourists.

Corey ordered coffee for the both of them. He was slurring his words, just a bit, but was heads above his partner's sobriety. Corey watched him trying to read the menu. It was obvious that he was seeing double and having a hard time focusing on any one item. Corey grabbed the menu.

"I'll order for you. You're a goddamn drunk."

"Thanks," the drunk responded, and then promptly passed out in the corner of the booth.

The waitress came back with their coffees.

"Looks like you two have had quite a night." She smiled.

"I'll have the pancakes, short stack, bacon and eggs, sunny side. Keep the coffee coming."

"Anything for your friend?"

"Does it look like he needs anything?" Corey growled.

The waitress turned around and left. She had dealt with her share of drunks, and she was skilled in that area. Corey had all he could do to keep awake. He wasn't as drunk as the other two, but he wasn't that far behind. He got to thinking that maybe coming for breakfast might not have been his best decision.

There was a group of local fisherman and airboat tour guides sitting at a round table near the entrance. They were laughing at some joke most of them had heard a hundred times.

Corey hated these locals. He was better than them. After all, he came from wealth and position. No matter that it was his family's money and social status. He would show everyone and make it on his own. Piss on everyone else.

One of the members of the round table glanced over at Corey and caught his eye. He nodded at Corey as a simple morning greeting.

"What the fuck you looking at?" Corey yelled.

The guy averted his eyes and got back into his own conversation. He had seen this guy around and wondered what he was doing in Everglade City. He wasn't about to start anything and make a scene. He decided to ignore the comment and leave the guy to his own affairs.

Corey was too drunk to think straight. Had he been sober, he would simply have nodded back. But he was drunk, and he was somebody. He was somebody who should not be trifled with. He held one hand over his left eye, so he could better see the guy who disrespected him. It didn't help much.

One of the other men at the table was looking at Corey and saying something to the rest of the group. Corey couldn't hear what he was saying, but he didn't like being the center of anyone's conversation.

"Hey, what are you saying about me," Corey slurred.

The other guy didn't have the same feelings about confrontation as the first.

"What makes you think we were talking about you?"

"I know a lot of shit. Besides, I'm smarter than everyone here."

The whole table erupted in laughter.

Corey's anger was the alcohol-fueled kind.

"Piss on all of you." Even in his state of inebriation, he realized he was badly out numbered. Maybe the prudent thing to do would be to leave it alone.

Then he made a huge mistake. The waitress came back with a pot of coffee and asked Corey if he wanted a refill. Corey didn't think. He reacted.

"What the hell did I tell you before? I said keep the coffee coming. What kind of piece-of-shit waitress are you anyway?"

The round table stopped talking, and all of its members were looking at Corey. Corey smiled, and then gave the waitress a shove to get her away from his table. She stumbled backward, and her shoe caught on the adjoining table leg. She went down, and her glass coffee pot went up in the air and crashed on the floor, leaving glass and coffee everywhere.

The eight men seated at the round table got up immediately. Two of them went over to the waitress to see if she was hurt, everyone else moved right over to the booth.

Corey realized that he had made a mistake.

No one spoke. Two of the men grabbed Corey's sleeping friend, and the rest grabbed Corey. They pushed them out of the door. Corey's partner went sprawling into the gravel. He never even woke up.

The guy who had spoken to Corey earlier moved in front of him, while the rest held him firmly. He got within two inches of Corey's face.

"That woman you just assaulted is a friend of ours. You and your friends are drunk and haven't made very good choices this morning."

Corey could only stare into his eyes. He didn't like what he saw. For the first time that morning, he was afraid.

"We aren't violent men. We believe everyone should have a second chance. Here is yours. You won't come back here, ever. If we see you here again, we'll take you for a ride in one of the airboats. It will be a one-way ride. You will never return. Do you understand?"

Corey nodded. He realized he needed to keep his mouth shut.

"You need to pay for the damages you did in the café, and you need to show some contrition for your contentious behavior."

Corey looked at him completely surprised at what he had just said.

"What? You think you're the only one that's gone to college, pretty boy? Never assume anything. Most of us are here because we want to be. It's our lifestyle, and we don't like it disturbed by arrogant pretty boys who think they're better than everyone else."

He reached into Corey's back pocket and retrieved his billfold. Corey was powerless to stop him, because he had four guys holding him upright.

"I think a hundred bucks should go a long way to covering the cost." He counted out a hundred in twenties.

"Just for the insult, we'll take it all and distribute it among the rest of the patrons for your disturbance today." He took the money and returned the billfold.

Corey had over eight hundred bucks in his wallet, and it pissed him off. He needed the money now that his stash had been stolen. He was thinking about the money, when he made another mistake.

"So, now you think you can rob me? There are a lot of witnesses here. I'm sure the cops will be interested when I report this." Corey's rate of sobriety had increased almost ten-fold.

The guy in his face paused for a second. Then he got even closer. His nose was almost touching Corey's. Corey didn't like his breath. It smelled like fried eggs.

"Maybe you didn't understand me. We can take that airboat ride now if you wish. No one in the café would ever say a thing. They don't like you. You ruined a good start to everyone's day." He paused, backed up a step and punched Corey right in the solar plexus.

That punch, and the memory of the guy's breath, made Corey throw up all over his shoes.

When he recovered, he said, "Keep the money, and please let us go."

"I thought you'd be reasonable. Please and thank you can open many doors. That includes yours." He opened the Opal's driver's door, and the others threw him into the seat. Someone else went around, picked up the guy lying face down in the parking lot, and put him into the passenger seat. The guy shut Corey's door and then leaned into the open window.

"Remember what I told you. Don't come back to this place. It would end badly for all concerned." The group turned around and went back into the café. Corey could hear applause when they opened the door. Maybe he would take the advice that was given so freely.

He reached over to start the Opal. He could smell vomit and wondered if he had hit more than just his shoes. Then, he felt something wet coming through his tee shirt. His partner in the back seat had gotten sick and threw up all over the side window. He had assumed it had been open. It wasn't. Some of splatter had found its way down the driver's seat.

Could this day get any worse? Someone would be cleaning up the car, and Corey knew it wouldn't be him. He had all he could do from dry heaving all the way back to his home even with the all windows wide open.

Corey got out of the Opal leaving his two flunkies in the car. He was taking off his clothes even before he reached the front door and walked into the house in his underwear. He went right into the bathroom and got into the shower before it even had time to get warm, underwear and all. He needed to get sober and needed the stench off him.

He didn't know how long he stood in the shower, but when he got out, he was completely sober. His head hurt, so he found an aspirin bottle and took a handful. Drinking that entire half-gallon of rum straight hadn't been the best idea. Deciding to go for breakfast had even been worse. What the hell was he thinking?

Surrounding himself with these two idiots hadn't been much better. When he needed them most, they were of no use. It seemed like his whole life had been circling the toilet bowl. For some odd reason, he equated all his troubles to his relationship with Aubrey. It was always easier to blame someone else for bad decisions.

He needed to make some changes. He needed cash if he had any hopes of making a big score and getting out of this hellhole. Corey got dressed and went out to roust the two idiots from his car. They would be spending the entire day detailing both the outside and inside of his vehicle to perfection.

He needed new wheels. This Opal was too recognizable. He would trade it in and get some financing for something new. He would worry about the payments later. Luckily his credit was still manageable. No one needed to know he was flat-ass broke. His fortune was about to change one way or another.

8

Zander reached Aubrey's house about the time Corey Prescott was puking on his shoes. He figured Aubrey would still be asleep. He opened the door as quietly as possible and kicked off his shoes before he even set foot in the house. He turned to close the door, and Aubrey came running through the house and jumped on his back. She wrapped her arms around his neck and held on for dear life.

Zander was startled, until he smelled her perfume and realized it was Aubrey. She was in the gown she was wearing, before they were so rudely interrupted. Zander started to forget about all the things he had been considering on his walk back. He wondered if he could be this lucky.

He didn't even pause, but walked into the bedroom with Aubrey still on his back. He was a big guy, and she was as light as anyone he had known. He was as gentle as possible with her.

Everything was brand new for Zander. His other relationships had been extremely physical and sometimes rough. He couldn't imagine being rough with Aubrey. He could only fathom being slow and passionate with her. It was something always in the back of his mind. He didn't know if she sensed it, but he did his best to control himself. He wanted this to be the real deal.

Aubrey retraced her former movements, and soon had Zander out of his clothes and once again in his boxer-briefs. She lightly ran her fingers up and down his rib cage. She would stop each time when she came to his shorts. Then she would move inside the elastic band an inch further each time.

Zander couldn't stand any more and took off her gown. She was so soft and smooth, that Zander just wanted to hold her close and feel his skin against hers. He picked her up, and they moved to the bed. He used his foot, kicked back the bedspread and placed her gently on the sheet. Maybe it was all the excitement of the night, but their lovemaking lasted less time than it took to remove their clothes. Zander thought it was the best thing he had ever experienced.

Aubrey promptly fell asleep on his chest with her arms around his neck. Zander didn't move. He wanted to stay like this as long as possible. He was far too excited to sleep. His mind was racing. He thought about all the things he needed to do and what he was forgetting. Mostly, he was thinking about Aubrey. She made him happy.

He almost sat straight up at that thought. For the first time since he had been a teenager, he thought he might be happy. It was a feeling very new to Zander. He had moments of pleasure, and had been happy from time to time, but there had always been something dark hanging around him. He seemed to sink back into that darkness each time he thought he had found happiness.

Had Aubrey changed all that? He thought she was most of it. She wasn't like the other women in his life. She wasn't broken.

Then it hit him. He had finally let Sara Jane go. She was no longer a force in his life. Maybe the healing had begun, and this huge burden he had been carrying around had been lifted. It was about time. He had wasted a good deal of his life chasing after something he couldn't possess. He had been irrational at best and absurd at worst.

He realized he had been smiling more and making friends with strangers. That was something he had never experienced before. He was even making friends with people in law enforcement. Who was this new person? Zander smiled, as he realized this was that thunderbolt moment that many people talked about in their lives. He was still smiling as he drifted to sleep still holding Aubrey.

~

Zander opened his eyes at 12:15. He woke up slowly and didn't realize the time. Aubrey was still asleep and had moved off his chest to her own side of the bed. He looked at her. She was nothing short of gorgeous. He needed to pinch himself to make sure this wasn't a dream. That was about the time he remembered he needed to meet Mike for his vehicle-buying trip. He looked at the alarm clock once more, and knew he had to get moving. He didn't want to keep law enforcement waiting.

He tried to move quietly out of the bed, but his movement awoke Aubrey. He kissed her on the cheek and moved toward the bathroom.

"Come back here. It's Sunday." Aubrey rested her head on her arm.

"Stop being so cute," Zander joked, "I have an appointment with law enforcement at 1:00, and I need to get moving."

"Why didn't you take care of that stuff last night?"

"It's not that. Mike is giving me a ride to Naples, so I can find that pickup I've been talking about."

Aubrey sat up. "I'm going along."

"Absolutely not. I need to do this alone. The Jackass is probably waiting for you to show your face. I'm meeting Mike at the house, and we will leave from there. I don't want anyone to see you."

"Well, then, what's the plan?"

"I'll get the pickup today and come back here this evening to pick you up. That will give you time to pack up your stuff."

"Where will we go?"

"I don't know yet. Away from here, that's for sure." Zander didn't have the heart to tell her she would be staying without him for a while. He would be returning to take care of The Jackass. He had some ideas but wanted to bounce some things past Mike on the way.

"How much should I pack up?"

"Everything that you want. You're not coming back here."

"Another surprise. I'm not sure I like the sound of this one."

"When I know more, I'll let you know. I should have most everything figured out when I get back tonight. In the meantime, stay in the house and don't let anyone see you. I don't want the possibility of you having to deal with The Jackass without me close by."

Aubrey tried to suppress a smile but couldn't. "Just don't leave me out. Remember we are to be honest with each other."

"Agreed." Zander knew he would need to keep some things from her, however. It was just the way it was.

He went into the bathroom and took care of the day's business. After his shower, his hair still wet, he emerged from the bedroom to find Aubrey had made roast beef sandwiches smothered with some kind of horseradish sauce. It opened his sinuses.

"That's got some kick," Zander said, taking another bite.

"It's kind of my specialty. I used to grow horseradish and grind it up myself," Aubrey said, proudly.

"How domestic of you. I like that in a woman."

Aubrey lowered her eyes. Zander thought he could see some redness creep into her cheeks, although it was always hard to tell with her darker skin tone.

Zander finished his sandwich and washed it down with a glass of milk.

Aubrey shuddered, "How can you drink that stuff? I never developed a taste for it."

"Unless it's chocolate milk."

"Well, there's that." She smiled.

Zander liked the banter. It was like they were a married couple. He stopped and just looked at her.

Aubrey felt his eyes on her. "What?"

"You're beautiful," was all Zander could think to say.

"Aren't you going to be late or something?" Aubrey asked, acting somewhat embarrassed.

"I should make the four-block walk by 1:00, easily."

"If you leave now."

"Okay, I'm leaving."

Zander got up, took his plate to the sink, and when he turned around, Aubrey put her arms around him and kissed him with an open mouth. Zander thought he might want to stay.

"There. Now get out of here. There will be more of that waiting for you when you get back."

It was a huge carrot. Zander would want to get his business completed and get back to Aubrey.

"See you soon," he said, and went right out the door.

"I hope so," she teased.

Zander turned back. "Remember what I told you. Stay out of sight, and get your things all packed up. When I get back, we're going to make a move to get you out of here."

"We might have time for a few other things before we go."

Zander smiled. Of course they would.

After checking to be sure no one was lurking outside the house, Zander walked to his rental. He didn't want anyone to notice where he had come from. He didn't see any strange vehicles around his house, and that made him feel better. He was just a little concerned about leaving Aubrey. He didn't know how far The Jackass's influence went in the community. He knew he could trust Mike, but he didn't know about the other deputies.

Zander climbed the steps and entered the house. Things were pretty much in place. He could organize everything later. He decided to throw a few clothes into his bag for his trip with Aubrey later. He would take it along in Mike's vehicle. He didn't want to come back here before taking Aubrey away.

A horn sounded outside. Zander looked out. It was Mike, and he was driving a jeep. Zander thought they would be making the trip in his squad car. He didn't know why. Mike was off duty, and it wouldn't be right taking a state vehicle for personal business. He would have preferred to ride in a squad car, however. He liked all the bells and whistles.

Mike honked his horn again. He had other things he wanted to do on his day off, and Zander was imposing on him. Zander bounded down the stairs two at a time and opened the jeep's passenger door.

"Nice wheels," Zander said.

"Thanks. I do quite a bit of off-road hunting, and the jeep is about the only thing that can get through this country."

"I used to do some hunting in the day," Zander said, trying to be conversational.

"What did you hunt?"

"Pheasants mostly."

Mike laughed. "You probably wouldn't like what we hunt down here."

"Gators?'

"No, that's illegal. Gators and panthers are off limits. Endangered species and all that."

"So, what do you hunt?"

"Pythons."

"What the hell?"

"See, I told you."

"You've got pythons down here?"

"Yeah and that's the problem. They aren't indigenous to Florida. People buy them as pets and when they get too big, they release them down here in the glades. Unfortunately, they have no known predators. They are the predator, so the state puts a bounty on them each year."

"I hate snakes."

"I'm with you on that. That's why we hunt them."

"Is it dangerous?"

"It can be. A big one can crush you to death. The biggest I've seen was thirty feet long. It was pretty scary. That thing could have swallowed a grown man whole."

Zander shuddered. Growing up in Iowa, he had to deal with garter snakes. They didn't hurt anyone, but Zander always thought they were creepy the way they slithered around in the grass. He used to try and kill them until a neighbor told him they ate their weight in insects and rodents everyday. Zander didn't know if that was true, but since they weren't poisonous, he would just ignore them. He didn't have to like them, though.

"I don't think I'll be joining you on any of those hunts."

Mike smiled, "It's not for the faint of heart, that's for sure."

"So where do go to find these things?" Zander asked.

"They are all over the glades. But there are a few islands we only can visit by boat, where we have the most luck. We don't tell everyone, because it's our favorite spot. If you play your cards right, maybe I'll take you there sometime, and you can see for yourself."

"In the daylight, please."

"Oh, it's way more fun at night. You can see their eyes shine in the spotlights."

"Enough."

Mike laughed.

They were halfway to Naples, when Zander ended the conversation about snakes. He looked out the window as Mike drove. He could see some alligators sunning themselves on the banks of the waterways along I-75. He wondered what would be worse, dealing with a gator or a python? This Florida was a strange place for a midwestern boy.

Zander was miles away in his thoughts, when Mike interrupted.

"I've got a buddy who has a used car dealership. He used to be on the force. I called him this morning, and he said he'd be in today. He'll give you a fair deal."

"Does he have pickups?"

"Plenty. He's got a successful business here. He works with some of the other dealerships and takes their used vehicles. It's a win/win for both of them."

"Sounds good. The easier this goes, the better."

In another ten minutes, Mike wheeled the jeep into a huge lot filled with all types of cars and trucks. Zander liked what he saw. He wandered about, while Mike went into the building to find his friend.

Zander saw a row of pickups near the back of the lot and walked toward them. This would be better than he had hoped, but the timing would be everything. He couldn't go back to Everglade City until after dark. No one could see him in his new vehicle until he got Aubrey safely away. Then he wouldn't care who saw him. The fact was he wanted certain people to know he was around and what he was driving. It would be better to wait until he had finished some personal reconnaissance, however.

9

Sara Jane booked a flight to Tampa from the Grand Caymans. She was tired of the tropical sun and the sand. Her money was safe. She had checked. There was very little to keep her in the Caribbean. She didn't know why she picked Tampa. She knew she didn't want to go to a colder climate, but she wanted to stay away from Key West and Miami. Bad experiences had a way of making her sure she would never return.

About the time Zander was wrapping up his pickup deal, she was walking to the departure area to pick up her luggage. The turnstile hadn't been activated, so she looked around for a seat. There were never enough to go around. Then she spied a kiosk with hotels listed on it. There were pictures of the hotels and grounds. One looked exquisite called the Grand Plaza Hotel Beachfront Resort. She picked up the kiosk phone, dialed the three-digit number, and ordered a suite overlooking the beach. She was told, unfortunately, that they were all booked. They did have a penthouse suite available, however. She took it and didn't even ask the price. She could afford it, and she wanted comfort and privacy to think things through. They had an airport shuttle waiting out front for their guests, and she could board it when she got her luggage. Sara Jane decided she didn't need to be riding some bus with other people. She would take a cab.

There was an empty seat near her luggage carousel, and she took it. She reached into her carry-on bag and rummaged around until she found a small zippered bag. She held it for a moment trying to decide what to do. Sara Jane De Graff was dead. She could never return. That was an easy one.

She looked at her other aliases wondering which would serve her the best. Bonnie Marco was a stupid name right from the beginning. She needed to forget that. She still had few others, that she hadn't used since she left Colorado. None of them held any meaning for her.

She decided to return to being Jayne Grafton once again. The Feds knew who she was, and she had survived that inquiry. There was no reason to complicate the matter with another new identification. She always liked the name. It was a derivative of her real name, and deep down; she wanted this baby to have a name that she wouldn't have to change in the future.

Sara Jane tucked her Jayne Grafton identification items back into the bag. She held her passports and other identifying items for a bit, and then started ripping them apart. A woman next to her looked over.

"Are you sure you want to do that?" She asked.

"You need to mind your own business," Jayne replied.

The woman took the hint.

Soon Jayne had a pile of confetti in her lap. She got up and dumped it all into the trashcan near the door. When she turned to go back to her seat, she noticed someone had already slipped into it. She walked back and picked up her bag. There was a teenager on his cell phone sitting in her seat.

"Thanks for taking my seat. Nice manners," she said, waiting for a response.

"Bite me," he answered.

It wasn't the response she was looking for. She suppressed a strong desire to haul off and slap the kid right across the mouth. She decided she didn't need the aggravation and walked over to wait at the carousel.

It wasn't long, and she heard the warning horn. The lights flashed as the carousel began to move. Jayne was watching as the bags started appearing through the opening in the wall. It always amazed her at how much all the bags looked alike. For the life of her, she couldn't see how some people found their bags at all. Most were black and about the same size as the one right next to them.

She had decided, early on, that her luggage would be brightly colored. She had a soft-side bright yellow bag she bought from Land's End. It had wheels and a retractable handle. She saw very few in that same style, and she had never seen a yellow one. It made it easy to identify, and her bag never had to go around twice. She could spot it immediately.

When her bag emerged from the hole in the wall, she waited until it came to her spot. Jayne was about ready to grab the handle, when she felt someone shove past her and pick up the bag. It was the same kid that had taken her seat.

"What the hell do you think you're doing?"

"Picking up my bag, bitch." He gave her shove with the bag, and Jayne staggered backward almost slipping of the tile floor. "Stay out of my way."

Jayne wondered if this kid was plain stupid or just had big balls. No matter. The bigger the balls, the lower they drug.

She waited until he was almost even with her, and then she reached over with both hands on his shoulders and turned him toward her. She could see some surprise in his face. Apparently, he wasn't used to having anyone stand up to him. She didn't wait for the surprise to fade. With one fluid motion, Jayne brought up her knee right into his groin as hard as she could. The kid went down moaning, dropping the bag, which Jayne picked up. He must have had big balls, because he was moaning loudly.

Jayne smiled at the kid and then leaned over and said, "Never fuck with people who are smarter than you, especially a woman."

Jayne turned around and tried to move on. A skycap stopped her.

"Is there a problem here?" he asked.

Suddenly, the woman who Jayne had told to mind her own business, came running over.

"I saw the whole thing. This woman is trying to steal this boy's bag."

"I thought I told you to mind your own business," Jayne said to the woman.

"I'm afraid I will need to see some proof that this bag is yours." The skycap was insistent.

Jayne wasn't going to make this easy for anyone. She unzipped the side of her bag and pulled out a bra.

"Unless this little asshole is a cross-dresser, what would he being doing with a bag of woman's clothes?" Jayne was livid.

"That doesn't mean a thing," the nosy woman replied.

Jayne was starting to put things together. Maybe these two were working in tandem. She had heard there was an increase in stealing other people's bags. She wondered what the market was for doing something like that.

She reached into her purse.

"Well, how about this?" She handed the baggage claim ticket to the skycap.

He examined the ticket and compared it with the strip on the handle of the bag.

He turned and handed back the ticket to Jayne.

"I'm sorry this has happened to you. We've been having an increase in this kind of thing, and we're trying to put a stop to it. Looks like you had the situation well in hand, well, in knee anyway." He smiled.

Jayne smiled back. "I hate these criminals. They are so brazen. I think they intimidate most people into not saying anything or reacting. That's how they get away with it."

"Thank you for what you did. We will be dealing with this low life. Law enforcement has been called, and he will be charged with attempted robbery. I'm sure it isn't the first time. Maybe they'll find his stash and put him away for a while."

Jayne panicked just a little. "I've got places to be. I can't stay here and make a statement."

"No problem. I am a witness. I saw the whole thing. Besides, we should have the whole thing on video." He pointed to the surveillance camera above the carousel.

"Thanks. I do need to get going."

"No. Thank you. Without your quick thinking, we would never have caught this piece of shit."

"No arguments on that label," Jayne said.

The skycap shook her hand, and then picked up the kid and took him to a side office to wait for the police.

Jayne looked for the woman but didn't see her. The terminal had thinned out considerably, mostly because no one else wanted to get involved. The woman appeared to be gone. Jayne had a nagging feeling that if she were involved; this wouldn't be over, however. She would need to be vigilant.

Jayne moved toward the exit door to find a cab. Suddenly she stopped. It was getting dark outside. Most of the people had left the area. It would be a great spot for an ambush right out those exit doors. She paused and then decided to go down a few more doors where other airlines had their baggage claims. She walked down three sets of doors and exited onto the sidewalk in front of the airport street. She saw the taxi stand close by and made her way toward it. Then she stopped. This wasn't over until she said it was over. She wouldn't be running away just yet.

She found a taxi and had the driver load her bag.

"I've got something I need to do. Start your meter. This should only take a few minutes."

"Whatever you say." The driver seemed oblivious.

Jayne moved slowly toward the automatic doors she would have normally used. She wasn't surprised, when she saw the nosy woman hiding around the corner of the doors smoking a cigarette. Jayne looked at her for a moment. She had a rough look. A drinker and smoker to be sure, but she looked like she had a hard life. She looked used up.

The woman was too busy keeping her eyes on the door to notice Jayne staring at her. She had to be thinking about how she could hurt Jayne. She screwed up her plans with her son or whoever he was, and now he was in trouble. She couldn't stay and try to help him without implicating herself, so he would have to take the rap by himself.

She had decided to grab this woman by the neck with both hands and knock her head into the concrete wall. If she lived or died, it didn't matter. She would get her pound of flesh, and then get the hell out of there before anyone knew what happened. That was the plan anyway.

Jayne had other plans. The nosy woman was clearly out of shape. That would be to Jayne's advantage. She looked around for something she could use to take her by surprise. There was a baggage cart near the curb that someone had used to load a car. Jayne grabbed it and pointed in the woman's direction. She made sure the wheels were all pointed in the right way and pushed as hard as she could.

The woman caught something out of the corner of her eye, but by that time, it was too late. The cart hit her just below her left knees and she collapsed right onto the cart. Jayne was on her instantly, but it wasn't necessary. The woman was finished before she had even started.

Jayne noticed her leg looked off kilter. It was broken, and the woman had passed out the moment her leg broke. It looked to Jayne to be a nasty break. Something she wouldn't easily overcome. She might have a limp for the rest of her life however long or short that might be.

Jayne turned around and walked back to the cab. A few people had walked past during her little baggage transfer, but no one seemed to want to get involved. Things had happened quickly, and Jane was sure her face wouldn't be recognized by anyone outside. She hadn't noticed a video camera near the door like there had been inside the terminal.

The cabby was waiting for her at the exact spot. She climbed into the back seat.

"Where to?" he asked briskly.

"Grand Plaza Hotel at St. Pete's Beach."

"Nice place." The cabby smiled. "Nice job on that woman back there. Remind me not to piss you off anytime soon."

The driver eased the cab into a space in the exiting traffic, and they were on their way.

Apparently, the cabby had been watching the entire incident in his rear view mirror. Jayne smiled and settled back for a pleasant ride.

10

The ride to the hotel had been extremely pleasant for Jayne. She realized she couldn't keep on with that kind of behavior, however. Pregnancy changed many things. She had to ratchet down her feelings of retaliation no matter how much pleasure it gave her. She needed to avoid confrontation if she planned to bring a kid into this world.

That thought brought out all kinds of emotions.

It made her sad to think about losing her way of life. But in reality, it wasn't much of a life. She needed to move on and try to forget her checkered past.

It made her afraid to think about raising a child on her own. There was so much to learn. She had never spent any time around children, and didn't know the first thing about child rearing.

It made her happy that she would no longer be alone. She had been thinking more and more about spending her life alone. She had no friends. She had burned all those bridges. She had a sister that she thought still had feelings for her, but her life was completely different from her own. Besides, she could never go back home. She had killed herself off there. It wouldn't serve anyone's best interest to resurrect Sara Jane.

She needed to stop thinking about the past and concentrate on what was best for the baby. These were all new feelings for Jayne. There weren't necessarily bad, they were just different. She had been concerned with herself and never paid much attention to the needs of others.

She thought of Zander. Had she loved him, or was he just a means to another end? She was still thinking about that, when the cab pulled up to the entrance of the hotel. After paying the tab, she gave the cabby an extra twenty. It was payment for not saying anything about what he witnessed at the airport.

The cab driver got out, took her bag from the trunk and put it next to the front door.

"If you need another ride anywhere, just give me a call." He handed her his card.

Jayne looked at the card. It appeared that the twenty worked. She shook his hand, grabbed the bag by the handle and rolled through the automatic doors.

The hotel was impressive. A bellman grabbed Jayne's suitcase the moment she walked in. The young woman at the desk was eager to help, and after Jayne told her about the reservation, she couldn't do enough to make her stay spectacular. That's what the woman said a number of times anyway. She must have thought Jayne was some kind of VIP. She wondered what this was going to cost her. It didn't matter. She could afford almost anything.

"How long will you be staying with us?" the young woman asked.

"I haven't decided. Why don't we just start with a week?"

"We can certainly do that." She began to work on the hotel computer system.

"How many keys will you need?"

"Just one."

The woman glanced up and looked at Jayne for a moment. Then she merely nodded. Jayne handed her a credit card to swipe, and the woman handed her key to the bellman.

"Take Ms. Grafton to her penthouse suite."

Jayne caught the Ms. prefix immediately. It was a safe way to treat female guests when a woman's status was unknown. Jayne wondered what she was or would become. She was a Miss. Would she ever be a Mrs.? She just didn't know. Maybe being a Ms. was the best she could do.

Her room was exquisite. It had windows that faced the beach on three sides. She could see along the shore in all directions. This was more luxurious than any hotel she had ever stayed previously. She would be enjoying it.

She gave the bellman a ten-dollar bill. He thanked her and asked if he could do anything else.

"Are there any good restaurants within walking distance?"

He went over to the guest information book and highlighted a half dozen for her that were within a few blocks. He recommended Crabby Bill's, and it was located next door. Jayne thanked him and showed him out.

She looked around her multi room suite. It was quite spacious, and she was sure it must have been over a thousand square feet. It was more room than she needed. An entire family could live comfortably in this suite.

There was fully stocked bar, but she had no taste for alcohol. There was a large refrigerator that was stocked with all kinds of mixers and soft drinks. She needed something salty, so she poured herself a glass of Bloody Mary mix without the vodka. She put in a couple of ice cubes and went out to the veranda.

It was a warm evening, and the lights all along the beach were alluring. Jayne would walk the beach in the morning and do some exploring of the area. She wouldn't need a vehicle. All the amenities were within walking distance. Besides, she needed to get some exercise and start taking better care of herself physically.

She finished her drink and decided it was getting chilly. She went back into her room and rolled her bag into the bedroom. She unpacked and put things in their place. She didn't need to live out of a suitcase, when she had drawers and closet space.

When she finished, she went back to the living room and turned on a huge flat panel television. She found the channel listings and went through the entire lineup. All those channels and there was nothing she wanted to watch.

She settled on a music channel that played solid gold oldies. It was puzzling to her. She hardly ever listened to the oldies channels on the radio. Why had she chosen it now? Maybe it reminded her of a more innocent time in her life. Had she ever been innocent? It was hard to tell. She left the music on anyway.

She wasn't hungry, but she knew she had to eat. She couldn't skip meals anymore. She was eating for two after all. Jayne ignored a desire to just call for room service and decided to give Crabby Bill's a try.

It was a happy place. Lots of tourists and locals intermingling, and everyone seemed to be enjoying themselves. Jayne ordered a large Coke and a red snapper salad. It reminded her of Key West and the last time she had been with Zander. It was a bittersweet memory. She tried to put it out of her mind, because she still hadn't reconciled what role Zander would be playing in her life and the life of the baby. It was just too complex to think about.

The food was excellent, and Jayne decided to go back to the hotel on a short walk on the beach. She bought a colorful zippered sweater that had Crabby Bill on the back. It had had all the bright Florida colors and was something she never would have worn in the past. It was time to make changes, and it wouldn't hurt to mix up her wardrobe a bit. Besides, it was warm, and the night had turned cool.

She walked by the hotel and continued north on the beach. She passed a few couples walking hand-in-hand along the shore. Newlyweds and couples on vacation she reasoned. It was a lifestyle in which she had no experience.

After fifteen minutes, she decided to turn around and head back to the hotel. The beach was soft and walking was difficult. She didn't want to walk next to the ocean where it was firmer, because she didn't want to get her shoes wet. The beach appealed to her, and she would walk it barefoot in the morning. It would be good exercise. She stopped. There she was thinking about exercise again. She never had given it a second thought before. Things we definitely changing, maybe for the better, She could hope.

The woman behind the registration desk greeted her again.

"Hello again, Ms. Grafton. I hope your stay with us has been satisfactory so far."

"It's beyond my wildest expectations." Jayne thought that it might have sounded just a little over the top, but she had meant it. "I plan to be here awhile so why don't you and the staff just call me Jayne."

"I'll make a note. Have a great evening."

Jayne took the elevator back to her room and sat in one of the overstuffed leather chairs. It was extremely comfortable. The coffee table had a number of magazines and a few current best-seller mysteries. She paged through some of the magazines, not finding anything of interest. She made a mental note to go out and find some magazines about babies and maybe a book or two on child rearing. She remembered her mother having a book written by Dr. Spock about those kinds of topics. She wondered if that book still was in print.

It was far too early for Jayne to go to bed. The oldies channel was still playing, and she was surprised at how many of the songs she still remembered. She listened to a lot of bubble gum music when she was in junior high. Her taste in music changed in high school. She was sure it was because Zander had introduced her to the Beatles. She jumped up and ran into the bedroom.

She found her yellow bag in the closet and opened it. At the bottom there was a square portfolio that had a flap tied down with a brown ribbon. She opened the file and took out her Rubber Soul album. She had kept it all these years even though no one played records any more. Most people didn't even have a turntable. She just couldn't part with it.

Jayne turned the album cover over and looked at the songs listed. She had always liked the little ballad called "Michelle" because some of the lyrics were in French, and she liked to sing along. It made her laugh out loud, because it was such typical teenage behavior. She had been just like other girls her age. At least she had been at one time.

She knew every song on the playlist, and when she got to the thirteenth track, she stopped. It was a George Harrison song called "If I Needed Someone." At that very moment she had never felt so alone.

What would she do? She couldn't hide out in this hotel forever. She had to face how she would proceed, and it had to be soon. The wheels needed to be put into motion, and there was no time like the present. Suddenly Jayne felt in control once again. It was her nature to be in command. She had an idea.

She grabbed the canvas bag she had been using as a purse and carry-on on the plane. After dumping the contents on the coffee table, she found her clutch and pulled out a small address book. It was almost 10:00, and Jayne never bothered anyone at that time. It was 9:00 in Iowa, however.

Jayne pulled out her cell phone and plugged in some numbers. She didn't want to use the hotel phone in case the conversation went south. People could trace a landline easily. It would be much harder with a burner cell.

She counted four rings, and a male voice answered.

"Hello. Would Sheila happen to be there?" Jayne tried to keep her voice light so her husband would think it was one of her friends. She didn't know if he had found out about her or if Sheila had kept her story a secret. She didn't plan on taking a chance on anything.

"Hold on." Jayne heard him call for Sheila. She could hear the television in the background.

"Hello."

"Sheila?" Jayne answered. It was good to hear her voice.

"Just a minute. Hold on, I'm going to take this in the kitchen." Sheila clicked off.

She seemed out of breath when she picked up again. "Sara Jane, is that you?"

"It's me. I needed to talk to a friendly voice, and I wanted to check in."

"Where are you?"

"Somewhere in Florida."

"Wow. You get around." Sheila was keeping the conversation light.

"You have no idea."

"I would like to. I would like to know all about you."

"I've been thinking about the same thing. I would like you to come out and visit me." Jayne said, with some hope in her voice.

Sheila was quiet.

"Sheila? Are you there?"

"Yes. Why don't you come back?"

"You know I can never do that. You're the only one who knows about what happened, and I can't have that opened up again."

"What about Zander?"

"What about him?" Jayne had an edge in her voice.

"He knows."

It was Sara Jane's turn to keep quiet.

"We've had the conversation, and he knows all about you."

"Much more than you know."

"I'm listening."

"Not on the phone. Can you come down and spend some time with me? I've got a great place to stay, and it would be a vacation for you. I'll take care of the expenses. In fact, this hotel will take care of all the arrangements and Fed Ex you the plane tickets. What airport do you use?"

"We have flown out of Sioux Falls, mostly."

"Done. I don't think they will have a direct flight, so you'll have to change planes somewhere."

"Yeah. I know. They probably will fly us to Denver and then direct flight us from there. So where in Florida?"

"You'll fly into Tampa. What will you tell Gregg and the kids?"

"I've been thinking about that ever since you said Florida. Do you remember going to visit Aunt Millie when we kids?"

"Wow. I haven't thought about her in years. Is she still alive?"

"She's doing fine. I stay in touch with her and call her a few times a year."

"You were always the good daughter," Jayne said lightly, but she meant it.

"I'll tell Gregg this call was from her, and she has some health issues and needs my help."

"What if he wants to come with you?"

Sheila laughed, but it sounded strained. "He won't. He never goes anywhere. Our life is pretty mundane. Sometimes I envy you."

Jayne thought she could detect regret in her voice.

"Don't ever say that. I would trade you in a moment if it were possible." Jayne didn't think she could ever do that, but it sounded good, and her sister needed some bolstering.

"How quickly can you be ready?" Jayne asked.

"Let's see. It's Sunday. I think I could get things organized and be ready by Wednesday."

"Okay. I'll have the tickets to you by tomorrow, Tuesday at the latest."

Jayne heard a door slam loudly through her phone.

"Oh, that's horrible news, Millie. Well sure, I'll talk to Gregg and I'll try to get there by Wednesday. Thanks for buying my ticket. If anything changes, give me a call." Sheila hung up.

Jayne didn't know how healthy it was to keep secrets in a marriage. She was glad that Sheila was keeping hers. It bothered her that she was putting her problem between Sheila and Gregg.

She couldn't dwell on it. She had arrangements to make, and there was no time to waste. Jayne went down to the concierge desk. She needed to get everything moving.

A huge weight seemed to have been lifted from her shoulders. Together, they could both find a solution for the mess she had gotten herself into.

11

Zander picked a white Ford 150 pickup. It was just a few years old and had less than forty thousand miles. It came with a rubber bed liner and a top that rolled over the bed that looked like faux leather. It covered the six-foot box. The covering could be rolled up when hauling things. It had four-wheel drive that could be selected while the vehicle was moving. Zander could remember when the drivers used to have to get out and turn the hub on each wheel to get it to work. He liked this much better. It was everything he had wanted in a pickup. The interior was black and had all the bells and whistles he needed. In fact, much more than he needed.

The drive back to Everglade City was enjoyable. He opened the windows and turned up the radio and sang along to a few of the songs. When he reached the city limits, he decided to check out his rental to make sure The Jackass hadn't returned. He was surprised to see Mike's Jeep in the driveway. He didn't see Mike. The house was dark, and he wondered what was happening. When he parked his new pickup and opened the door, he saw something in front of the jeep. He ran over and found Mike in a lump lying on the ground. Someone had beaten him pretty severely. Zander was somewhat relieved to find him still breathing, but he was in bad shape. Zander searched through the pockets of Mike's jacket and found his phone. He made another mental note to definitely get himself another phone. The 911 call was short, and Zander told the dispatcher that an officer was down.

It was less than two minutes, and Zander heard sirens. The first responders were working on Mike before Zander could hardly get out of the way. The entire police force came in squad cars or their personal vehicles. One of their own was down, and this was personal. Zander wanted to make sure Mike was going to be okay before he starting talking to anyone. His fellow officers had surrounded his gurney. The first responders were trying to get them to move back, but they were having none of it.

Mike started to come around and questions started to fly. They told him he needed to be checked out at the hospital. Mike tried to get up, but they pushed him back down.

Zander pushed his way through the throng and took Mike's hand. "Mike, what happened? What were you doing here?"

Mike moaned. "You know what happened. They were waiting for you and got me instead. Tell them." He motioned toward the rest of his police friends.

That would be the only thing coming from Mike that evening. They loaded him into the van, started the lights and sirens, and were off to the hospital.

Zander spent the better part of twenty minutes telling the story concerning Corey Prescott. No one spoke much, but Zander could feel the tension coming from the police officers. He thought that perhaps The Jackass wouldn't be showing his face around Everglade City if he wanted to live very much longer. That would be good news for Aubrey. Then he remembered that he needed to get her away from here. He already spent too much time, and he was worried for her safety.

He didn't mention his plans to relocate Aubrey. He didn't know if there was a mole in the police department, and he didn't need to draw any more attention to Aubrey.

He told the officer on duty that he would come to the station and file a report the next day. Most of the other off-duty folks left for the hospital to make sure Mike was going to be all right. Someone had to tell his family. Zander was glad it didn't have to be him.

He made quick work of getting to Aubrey's house. The lights were on and things looked normal. He ran up the steps and burst into the room. Aubrey was sitting on the couch surrounded by the things she had packed to take wherever Zander decided. There wasn't nearly as much as Zander had suspected. He liked that in a woman.

Aubrey had been dozing, while she waited for Zander. She scared awake when the door slammed shut.

"What?" She jumped off the couch.

"It's just me," Zander said, sorry that he had frightened her.

"You scared the shit out of me."

"Your eyes are still brown," Zander tried to joke.

Aubrey walked over to Zander. He thought she would slug him. Instead, she put her arms around him and hugged him tightly.

"You are late. I was worried about you."

Zander hugged her back and told her an amended version of what had happened to Mike. He could feel her body stiffen.

"Are we in danger?" she asked.

"Not at the moment. The cops are pissed. He won't be around here for quite some time, I'm thinking. But we're not taking any chances. We're still moving you out tonight."

"I'm ready."

"I can see that. Let me get you loaded and then we'll be on the road."

"Where are we going?"

"I booked you a cottage on Sanibel Island."

"That sounds nice. We should have a nice little vacation there."

"Well, for a few days anyway. I'll need to come back here to take care of some unfinished business."

Aubrey didn't like what she was hearing.

"Let's just get out of here and never come back. Everything can just settle back to the way it was without us around."

"Things don't settle. They get settled." Zander liked to use the quote he remembered from the TV show *Gunsmoke*.

Aubrey could only shrug her shoulders. She liked this guy, but she didn't always understand him.

They were on their way in fifteen minutes. Aubrey had left the keys on the table and pulled the locked door shut. She wouldn't be returning here. She would call her friend and thank her for the use of the house in the morning. Time to move on. The last thing Zander loaded into the pickup were the water bottles filled with money. He would be leaving them with Aubrey on Sanibel.

They had been traveling for almost forty-five minutes, when Aubrey mentioned that she was hungry. With everything that had happened, Zander had forgotten all about dinner. He was somewhat familiar with the Fort Myers area because of the time he and Herbie had spent there. He decided to take Aubrey to the Parrot Key. He was sure she would like it as much as he had. He needed to make a quick stop at the Wal-Mart just off Tamiami. He had promised Aubrey he would get another phone. He didn't need much, and the burners they sold there would meet his needs.

When they walked into Parrot Key, there was someone playing guitar in the corner. Zander and Aubrey elected to sit at the bar, because it just suited the both of them. After an order of calamari, they ordered a grouper sandwich, which came with fries. They split everything evenly, and it was all they needed. Zander would have liked to stay and have a few more beers, while listing to the music, but it was time to move on.

When they came to the tollbooth on the causeway that would take them to the island, Zander paid the six-dollar toll.

"That's ridiculous. Six bucks to drive onto the island?" Aubrey was incensed.

Zander thought about it for a moment. Perhaps she was right, but then he abruptly changed his mind.

"It might help keep off the riff-raff like The Jackass."

"Maybe, but I think he would drive through and not pay anything."

"They've got cameras so they would get his license. He would have to pay one way or another."

Aubrey decided not to tell Zander how when she was young, her friends would cover up the numbers with all kinds of things so they wouldn't have to pay any tolls in Miami. She wasn't proud of it, but she was young and foolish back then. She tried to be a good citizen these days.

Soon they were traveling on Periwinkle. When they reached Tarpon Bay Road, Zander turned left and traveled until he ran out of road. He turned right onto West Gulf Drive and continued north until he passed Rabbit Road. The sign said it was the last turn before continuing on to Captiva. Aubrey wondered where they were heading. It looked like they were in a residential area with no outlet at the end of the road.

A few blocks further, Zander slowed down and turned into a dimly lit little area with a number of cottages. The name on the sign said: Mitchell's Sand Castle Resort.

Zander checked in at the office, while Aubrey stayed in the pickup. She thought the resort looked nice enough from what she could see in the darkness. She would make a better determination the following day.

Zander returned with the key, and he drove to a cottage right next to the beach.

"Nice spot," Aubrey said.

"Only the best for you."

Aubrey socked him in the arm. She seemed to like that move a lot. She took the key from him and went to unlock the door. It left Zander to move her things inside on his own. She was excited to see the cabin, and that made him happy.

Zander chose the resort simply because it was off the beaten path. Most of the daily tourists would never even know about this place. It had everything she would need. There was a pool, and bicycles were available for use by the guests. She wouldn't have a vehicle, but everything she needed was within easy biking distance. It would give her things to do, while he was busy planning the demise of The Jackass.

Zander moved Aubrey's things into the cottage and put all her clothing into the master bedroom. It was a nice two-bedroom with old world charm. Zander felt like he might have been in northern Minnesota at a fishing cabin on some little lake. It felt good.

He put his backpack into the master with Aubrey's things. She was busy organizing things.

Zander went back out into the kitchen/living room area. They needed to do some grocery shopping in the morning, but right now they needed some wine.

"Aubrey, while you're busy organizing, I need to scout us some wine."

She came back out of the bedroom. "Good idea. Is there a liquor store around here?"

"I saw that little market on Tarpon Bay that looked promising. I'll go check it out."

"Bring me a surprise to go with the wine."

"I'm not sure they sell French ticklers in a place like that."

She was ready to sock his arm again, when he made a quick exit.

Baileys General Store had everything that anyone could want or need on the island. Their wine selection was superior. Zander picked out a variety of reds. He knew that Aubrey preferred reds. He did as well. When he finished, he had twelve bottles in his cart. He wondered if they gave case discounts.

Then he wandered around looking for a surprise for Aubrey. He hated when people said things like that. He always preferred when people said what they wanted. He settled on a bag of chips. He thought the salty taste would go with wine, but what did he know.

When he returned to the cottage, Aubrey had begun making the cabin her own. It felt comfortable for Zander. He opened a bottle of Merlot and found the place had a great supply of wine glasses. He over poured two glasses.

"Lets go take a moonlight walk on the beach," he said.

"What a romantic idea. Too bad you didn't buy some chocolate and roses instead of those chips."

Zander looked over at her and could see she was teasing him.

"Not my best move, huh?"

"You could have brought sauerkraut for all I care."

"I'll keep that in mind for next time." Zander was feeling a bit playful, now that the stress of being at Everglade City was behind them.

They took their wine and walked the path to the beach. It was a radiant evening with a full moon. Zander had taken a small flashlight but didn't need it. The moonlight was all they needed.

There were a few beach chairs at the edge of the beach, and they ended there after they tired of strolling the beach. The ocean waves gently rolled in, and the moonlight glistened and sparkled on each wave.

Neither said much. It wasn't necessary. The wine was excellent.

The evening was spectacular. The company was perfect.

If this were happiness, Zander would take a boatload of it. He was wondering how anything could get better, when Aubrey came over and sat on his lap. Suddenly, they couldn't get each other's clothes off fast enough.

12

Zander woke to sounds coming from the kitchen. He got up and walked out to see what was happening. Aubrey was standing by the sink looking out the window. She had on just her bikini underwear with no top. Zander was aroused, again.

He grabbed her from behind just as she was pouring the last of the water into the coffee pot's reservoir. She almost dropped the glass pot but caught herself and slid it under the basket of fresh grounds.

"You need to make some noise when you approach someone from behind," she said, turning around.

"Where's the fun in that?" Zander asked.

Zander cupped both breasts with his hands. It was almost more than he could stand.

"We've got some time before the coffee is ready."

He wasn't disappointed. Aubrey led him back into the bedroom and lost her bikini bottoms on the way.

When they were finished, Aubrey bounced out of bed and went to the shower. Zander could hear her humming some tune he didn't recognize. He put his hands behind his head and contemplated staying here forever. It was a nice thought but unrealistic, as he well knew.

When she emerged from the bathroom, she was dressed for the day. Zander was disappointed to see she had on a pair of shorts and tank top. She looked quite fabulous, but Zander preferred her naked.

She went over and gave Zander a peck on the cheek.

"Get up. We've got things to do today, she said, as she headed for the kitchen."

Reluctantly, Zander got out of bed and made his way to the bathroom. He would spend the day with Aubrey. Then, he knew, he had to get back to Everglade City and survey the situation. Besides, he promised he would be back to work Tuesday evening at The Rod And Gun Club. At least he would have one more night with her, before he had to leave.

When he made it to the kitchen, Aubrey had the coffee poured and was sitting at the table.

"What's the plan today?" she asked.

"Whatever you want. It's your day today."

"Well, sit down and drink your coffee. I want to take a walk on the beach, and then go for breakfast somewhere."

"Sounds good. Maybe you could get my new cell phone programmed."

She laughed. "You are so helpless."

"Guilty." He knew she was right. He hated technology. But he knew he needed to get with the program or at least be on the periphery.

He handed over the blister pack containing the phone. Aubrey found a knife and cut out the phone carefully so she didn't damage the phone or the charger.

"What numbers do you want stored in here?" Aubrey asked.

"Well, yours for sure. How about The Rod And Gun?"

Aubrey entered the two numbers. "Any others?"

Zander reached into his billfold and pulled out a list of numbers and handed them over to her. The list included Fats, Herbie, The Glass Onion, and his answering service. There were two numbers crossed out as well. They belonged to Sara Jane and her sister, Sheila.

"What are these two numbers you crossed out?"

"Part of my forgettable past that I want erased."

"Fair enough." Zander had told Aubrey most of his story, and she had told him not to worry so much about the past.

Zander was working hard on that aspect of his life. He found it was easier when he was around Aubrey.

They went for a lengthy walk on the beach, and both were amazed at the piles of seashells on the beach. People were bent over in the "Sanibel Stoop" picking them up by the bag loads. Zander had read about the tradition of shelling on Sanibel. It was considered the second best island in the world for shelling. He had forgotten the first.

Zander asked at the desk for a good café for breakfast. The receptionist gave them a few choices and they settled on The Over-Easy Café just across the street from Bailey's Market. After breakfast, they could get the groceries Aubrey would need for the rest of the week. Zander hoped he wouldn't be gone that long, but they needed to be prepared.

After grocery shopping, they returned to the resort. When everything was put away, Zander thought there might be time for a bit of bedtime delight. He was to be disappointed. Aubrey wanted to explore the island.

"I need to know what there is to do when you leave me tomorrow." Zander was surprised. He hadn't told her he would be leaving in the morning. Aubrey had just reasoned it out. It was another reason he liked this woman. He liked people who were perceptive. She was better with that skill than anyone else he had ever met.

"So, do you want to explore on bikes?" Zander asked.

"That will be my means of transportation when you leave. I want to see what's out there so I can explore it later."

"Okay. Let's go." He led her out to the pickup, and they were on their way.

Aubrey had taken a map of the island from the office and was deciding where she wanted to start.

"Let's go up to Captiva and work our way down."

Zander just nodded in agreement. This was her show. He was along for the ride and hoping for a different kind of ride later. He smiled at the thought. Aubrey had her head in the map and took no notice.

The tour of the islands took them a little over three hours. Aubrey was interested in everything. Zander noticed the traffic on Periwinkle was extremely heavy and slow. He found a back road involving West Gulf Drive and Middle Gulf Drive that led him right to the Causeway.

It would be the road he would use to enter and exit the island in the future.

Zander's big find was the restaurant called Doc Ford's. It was named after the main character in Randy Wayne White's novels. Zander had discovered him and read most of his work. It was close enough to the cottage that Aubrey could easily bike there in less than ten minutes. They decided to have a late lunch, or maybe an early dinner, and pulled into the parking lot. Parked right in front of the restaurant was the pickup that Doc Ford used in the books. Zander explained the background to Aubrey, and she seemed to share his excitement.

When they walked into Doc Fords, they were greeted with stacks of books before they even got to the host stand. Of course, they were all by Randy Wayne White. Aubrey loved to read, and she was totally enthralled with the display.

"Why don't you pick one out?" Zander offered.

"Which should I read first?"

"I don't think it matters. He catches you up in every one I've read."

"What's his first book?"

"Sanibel Flats."

"I'll take that one first."

Zander thought it was a good idea. Once you read that book, everything else fell into place.

They decided to sit at the bar, order drinks and whatever else they thought sounded good. Zander loved this place. It would be somewhere he could spend a lot of time.

The waitress suggested one of their signature dishes. It was a panko-covered fish sandwich that came with black beans and rice. Couple that with one of their rum drinks, and it would be all they needed until dinner.

While they were waiting, Zander was admiring the wooded boats hanging from the ceiling. There were banks of televisions within the vision of every patron. This was truly a guy's bar. When he glanced at Aubrey, he could see she was studying the back of the book and then looking over toward the other side of the bar.

"What's up Aubrey?"

"Look over there. I think that's the author sitting at the bar."

Zander looked at the picture on the back cover of the book and then back to the guy at the bar."

"Sure looks a lot like him. He probably owns this bar, so it would be pretty natural for him to spend time here," Zander said.

"You like his writing. Why don't you go over and talk to him."

"We shouldn't bother him. I'm sure he just wants to spend some time without having people fawn all over him. I won't be one of those star-struck tourists."

"It's too late for that. I can already see you are star-struck. I'm going over to get his autograph."

Before Zander could stop her, Aubrey was off her barstool and walking right over to where he sat. Zander felt his ears getting red. This was embarrassing, but it was also a bit exciting. Aubrey had no qualms about doing what she decided.

Zander watched as Aubrey spoke to Mr. White. She was quite animated and he was listening intently. Finally, he took her book and signed the inside front cover. Aubrey shook his hand and returned to her stool. She smiled at Zander, as she sat down.

"He's a nice guy."

"How would you know? It looked like you did most of the talking." He winked at her. Zander knew what a prize he had.

Suddenly, he felt a hand on his shoulder. It was Randy Wayne White looking right at him. Zander was speechless.

"Aubrey tells me you are a huge fan."

Zander nodded in the affirmative.

"Well, that's what sells my books. I want you to have one of the latest Doc Ford mysteries on me."

Zander couldn't believe it. He finally found his voice.

"Thank you so very much. Would you sign it for me?"

"Already have. You two have a great evening."

He went back to his spot at the bar.

Zander just watched him return. Aubrey elbowed him in the ribs.

"Focus. Your tongue is hanging out. You aren't that attentive with me, even when I'm naked."

"Maybe I would be if you wrote books." Zander was back to being his usual smart-ass self.

The food came and about partway through the meal, Randy White got up to leave. He waved at the couple and walked out the door. What a great day it had been.

When they finished, Zander called for the check. The waitress told him that Randy had picked up the tab and wanted them to know he appreciated their business.

When they got back to their cottage, Aubrey decided to spend some time in the pool. Zander watched her change into her skimpy two-piece swimsuit. He couldn't help but stare. It wasn't just her physical attributes, although they were outstanding, she was truly beautiful on the inside as well. He had never met anyone like her.

He watched her walk to the pool, decided to open some wine and join her at the chairs on the pool's apron. The sign said there was no glass allowed, so Zander poured the wine into plastic cups.

He placed Aubrey's wine on the edge of the pool, and she swam over and took a sip.

"Thanks so much. The water is a bit chilly and this warms me up."

"You warm me up," Zander said, and she smiled.

"Would you be a dear, and hand me one of those towels," she said, indicating the stack of pool towels on a cart nearby.

Zander handed her three towels. He thought she might need to wrap up in the cooler afternoon sun.

Aubrey joined him at the pool chair next to him. There were still a few people on the other side of the pool area, but they were picking things up and appeared ready to leave. Aubrey and Zander soon had the pool to themselves.

"I don't know if I can handle seeing you go tomorrow," she said, sliding her hand down his leg."

"No one will be sorrier than me." Zander meant it.

"Then let's make use of the time we have." She stood and pulled him along toward the cottage.

She was covered from head to toe with the three towels Zander had provided. Zander had what was underneath etched in his memory, however. When they reached the front door. Aubrey dropped the towels and headed into the bathroom. Zander heard the shower start and poured himself another glass of wine. He had to be careful. Too much wine always gave him a whiskey dick, and he wanted to be able to perform for Aubrey. He didn't know when he would return, so tonight had to be special. He wanted Aubrey to miss him as much as he would miss her.

Aubrey joined him on the small deck just outside the door. She had poured herself another glass of wine in a regular wine glass.

"Have you ever noticed how much better wine tastes in a wine glass?" she asked.

"I think it has something to do with the shape of the glass and the airflow."

"Is that right?"

"I have no idea, but it sounds plausible."

Aubrey sat on Zander's lap and hooked her free arm around his shoulders. Neither said anything, but looked out across the ocean and watched the sun sink below the horizon.

"Did you see the green flash?" Zander asked.

"What's that?"

"Don't really know, but everyone comes out at sunset to look for some kind of flash of green just as the sun sinks into the ocean. I guess it must be some kind of local phenomenon."

Aubrey looked out and didn't respond. Zander saw that her face was absolutely radiant.

She stood up and pulled Zander by his shirt.

"I guess it's time to share our own phenomenon." She pulled him right into the bedroom, was out of her robe and taking his clothes off, while they walked.

Zander decided if he died at that moment, his life would never have gotten any better anyway.

13

Sheila hung up the phone. She walked into the living room where her husband, Gregg, was watching television. She prided herself in being as truthful as possible, especially with her husband. It was time to tell him everything.

She hadn't lied to Sara Jane about Gregg not wanting to go anywhere, but if Sheila would ask him, he would do most anything she wanted. They had always had a great marriage, and she wasn't about to jeopardize it by keeping Sara Jane's secrets. Zander was right. Sara Jane was a user, but she still was her sister. Sheila would do what she could to help.

"That's quite a story," Gregg said.

"It's one that only gets repeated here, right?"

Gregg just looked at her, and Sheila knew it was something she should never have verbalized. Gregg would never give up family secrets. She felt bad.

"I'm sorry. I shouldn't have said that. I'm just so worked up over all this. Just when I think Sara Jane is out of my life once and for all, bam, she's back. It's like a horror movie." Sheila didn't know if she meant it, but it sounded pretty good as an explanation.

Gregg pulled her onto the couch and put his arm around her.

"She's your sister. She's dead to most people but still very much alive in your life. Whatever you decide, I'll support you." Gregg said, simply.

"You're the best." Sheila replied, and gave him a peck on the cheek.

"I know." It was all he would need to say.

~

Sheila's flight from Sioux Falls went well. Traveling in January was always risky weather-wise. She flew to Denver and changed planes. It was a direct flight from there.

When she walked to the baggage claim in the Tampa airport, she saw a man in a suit holding a large sign with her name on it. Sara Jane had sent a chauffer to pick her up. At first Sheila was pissed. She assumed Sara Jane would be there to greet her. Then, she thought that maybe it would be nice to travel in style for a change. Besides, she didn't know what Sara Jane had gotten herself into this time. Maybe she just couldn't be seen in public.

Sheila went over to the man wearing the hat and suit and made her introduction. He tossed the sign in the garbage can and went to wait with her for her luggage. Sheila tried to pull it off the turnstile as it came around, but the chauffeur would have none of it. He pulled off her case, and soon they were on their way out of the airport lot.

Sheila enjoyed the forty-five minute ride. There was a bar stocked with almost anything she might have wanted to drink. Her tastes went more toward the light beer venue, and she noticed a small cooler filled with a number of different beers. She passed. It was too early for her.

They pulled into the hotel, and the driver stopped in front of the lobby's front door. He bounced out and retrieved Sheila's suitcase. Sheila fumbled for her purse to offer him a tip. He put up his hand.

"All expenses have been paid. There is no need for anything on your part," the chauffeur said, and wheeled the suitcase into the lobby in front of the registration desk. He tipped his hat and went back out the doors.

The young woman at the desk looked over and smiled.

"I'm thinking you must be Sheila."

Sheila nodded. She wasn't used to being the center of attention, and she didn't know how to react.

The young woman rang a bell, and the bellman emerged from another room.

"Please show her to Jayne Grafton's room and take her luggage." She handed a key card for the room to Sheila. "Have a nice stay."

Before Sheila could respond, the bellman was wheeling her case to the elevator. Sheila had all she could do to keep up.

When the elevator doors opened, the bellman took the lead to show her the way. There was no need. Apparently, the desk had called the room and there was Sara Jane, standing in front of the penthouse, waiting for her.

Sheila ran around the bellman and straight into Sara Jane's arms. They hugged each other for what seemed to be an eternity. Oblivious to them, the bellman wheeled the suitcase in front of the door and made a quick exit. He didn't want to break up whatever this greeting was all about. The woman in the penthouse had taken care of him very well over the past few days, and he wasn't about to anger her with his hand out at what appeared to be a very sensitive meeting.

When the hug began to wane, Sheila pulled away.

"My God, Sara Jane, I never thought I'd ever see you again."

"Sara Jane is dead. Only Jayne Grafton remains." Jayne replied, and looked down.

"So I've heard. I don't know if I can play that game."

"Just pretend that over the years, I've decided to go by Jayne for convenience sake. People do that all the time. You don't have to use my last name."

"So, De Graff isn't good enough for you anymore?"

"I don't know, seems to me that you've changed your last name as well."

"That's different. It's my married name."

"And what makes you think you know anything about what's happened to me all these years? Maybe that was my married name as well."

"I've talked to Zander. I think I have a pretty good idea what you've been up to since you left us."

Jayne walked over and looked out the window. Sheila sat on a bar stool waiting for a reply. It was quiet for an uncomfortably long time.

Jayne turned around.

"I guess it was inevitable that we would have to clear the air before we could get past what has happened."

"I'm angry with you," Sheila said, simply.

"I know, and I don't blame you in the least. Everything was my fault. I was so young and made a huge mistake back then. Sheila, if you could find it in your heart to accept my apology, I would be grateful. I don't expect that you'll ever forgive me."

"Oh, don't be stupid. I forgave you a long time ago. The apology is nice though." She smiled.

Jayne turned back to the window trying to mask the tears in her eyes. They weren't lost on Sheila, however. It made her soften somewhat. She walked over and put her arm around Jayne, and together they looked out over the beach.

Breaking the silence, Sheila said, "Nice place you've got here."

Jayne turned and put both arms around her sister. It was a long time coming, and for the first time in many years, Jayne no longer felt alone.

"I can't wait to show you around. This whole area is fabulous."

"There will be time for that. Right now let's get some lunch. I'm starving."

"Do you want room service, or do you want to go out?"

"Let's go out. I need to move around after that flight. Then, after lunch, lets get some sun. I'm tired of the gloomy Iowa winter already."

Sheila realized that Jayne had something she wanted to share with her. It was going to take some time, so she wanted her to feel comfortable. Later, she could share whatever it was that made her reach out.

They decided to have lunch in the hotel and then take a stroll on the beach. Sheila didn't want to walk very far. She wanted to spend some time at the pool and get some color before she had to go back to Iowa.

They went back to the penthouse, and Sheila unpacked her things into her bedroom. It was nice having her own bed and bathroom for a change. When she finished, she tried on her swimming suit. It still fit. She was a bit heavier than Jayne and attributed that to having kids. She still looked pretty good she thought. At least, that's what Gregg always told her.

When she walked back out of her room, Jayne had changed into her suit as well. She had a beach cover-up over top.

"I don't have a cover-up," Sheila said, a bit disappointed.

"It's not mandatory. The area is pretty casual. If it bothers you, there's a white robe in your room. You could wear that to the pool."

"Thanks, it would make me feel a little less conspicuous."

"Still sporting that Dutch puritanical guilt, I see."

"It's a hard habit to break."

"You shouldn't be so hard on yourself. You still look fabulous in that swimsuit."

"Thanks, Jayne. You don't look so bad yourself. Especially being so much older than me. Of course, I've had a couple of kids. What's your excuse?"

Jayne got suddenly quiet. It didn't go unnoticed by Sheila. She got up and took out a beer of the cooler.

"You want one?" Sheila asked Jayne.

"Not right now. Take that beer, and let's go get some sun while it's still up."

They found a few beach lounges around the apron of the pool. They both shed their cover-ups and were enjoying the warmth of the sun.

"I can't believe I'm sitting around a pool in January. It's below zero back home."

"One of the reasons I'll never go back to the Midwest," Jayne replied.

Sheila decided to leave the comment alone. There were many other reasons she couldn't go back.

She finished her beer and looked over at Jayne who had turned over onto her stomach. Sheila thought she still looked beautiful. As a child, she had always been somewhat resentful of her looks and slim figure. Sheila had always had a courser figure. Her mother always told her she was just bigger boned. Jayne could eat anything she wanted. Sheila had to constantly keep a vigil over what she put into her body. It just never felt fair to her.

She had always wanted to be Jayne. Now she was grateful to have been spared that wish. Sheila was happy with her life. It had taken some time, and she never understood what she had, until she saw what Jayne didn't.

Sheila was about to follow Jane's lead and turn over, when a pool staffer came over with another beer. It was in a can because glass wasn't allowed. Sheila felt stupid handing the empty bottle to her.

"Sorry about the bottle. I guess I wasn't thinking. I didn't order this beer, however."

"Don't worry. It happens all the time. This is from the two guys at the pool bar." She pointed at the two men. "They also want to buy her a drink." She pointed at Jayne who looked to be dozing.

Jayne spoke up. "Tell them to mind their own business." She turned over. "She's married, and I have no interest."

"Jayne. You don't have to treat people so badly for trying to be friendly." Sheila was embarrassed.

"You know the reason they want to buy us drinks. Try not to be so naive. This isn't Iowa."

Sheila turned to the pool girl. "Tell them thank you but we were just leaving." She handed back the beer. "You'd better give this back to them as well."

The waitress went back to the two guys and was explaining to them what the women had told her, as they watched both Jayne and Sheila. One of the guys just waved them off like he didn't care. The other guy placed his palms up in a questioning gesture.

Jayne gave them the finger.

Sheila took Jayne by the hand and led her inside to the bank of elevators. She punched the button and turned to Jayne.

"Could you try to be a little kinder and gentler while I'm here. I hate the embarrassment."

The elevator opened, and they rode back to the room in silence. Sheila opened the door with her card, and once inside, closed the door.

"I left my cover-up, and you left your robe at the pool. I'm going back to get them," Jayne said.

Sheila grabbed her arm and forcefully pushed into the couch. All that farm work over the years had made her strong and much tougher than Jayne.

"What the hell is wrong with you?" Sheila knew the time had come for some truth.

Jayne paused and looked up at Sheila who was hovering over her.

"There's nothing wrong with me. A few of my past transgressions still seem to be haunting me."

"Transgressions? What's that supposed to mean?"

"Bad decisions. I've made my share. More than most."

"It's not like you to live in the past. You always had a knack of getting the most out of your present problems. Used to drive mom and dad nuts as I recall. You were always pushing their rules."

"They were unreasonable. We lived like the Amish."

Sheila started to laugh. Don't confuse the conservative Dutch with the Amish. They are nothing alike."

"In my mind they are. I could never be a part of that life."

"You took care of that little factoid quite a long time ago." Sheila wasn't one to let things go.

"I suppose you're right."

"Of course I am. Now, maybe it's time for us to talk. I want to know why you seem so angry and why you wanted me to fly down here."

"I don't know why I'm angry. I've always prided myself in being control of my emotions. It just seems like lately every little thing pisses me off. Then I get pissed off at myself for getting pissed off in the first place."

"Is that why you called me down here?"

"Who knows? Maybe. It's just that I've been feeling so alone lately, and I needed to know there was still someone out there that remembered me. I have a need to connect for some odd reason."

Sheila sat down next to Jayne on the couch. She took her hand and looked into her eyes.

"How long have you been pregnant?"

Jayne's eyes widened. "How did you know?"

"You've been leaving little signs all over the place. You aren't drinking anything. Your food choices have been heavy on salt. You are short tempered. You're wearing a full swimsuit instead of a two-piece. With a body like yours, it's a dead giveaway to me. The biggest clue for me was that you wanted to connect with family again. Maybe it's because you are having family thoughts yourself."

"Fine. You caught me. Now what? What the hell am I going to do? I've never been a parent. I never thought that I even liked kids."

"It appears you've decided to keep the baby. That was your first decision and the hardest for you. I think I can help with the rest. Is there a father in the picture?"

Jayne shook her head. Then looked at Sheila.

Sheila could read everything in her eyes right then and there.

"My God, Jayne. Not Zander."

Jayne could only nod her head. It would be the end of the conversation.

14

Sheila needed to think things through. She excused herself and went back down to the pool to pick up the swim cover-ups, and hopefully, apologize to the two guys at the pool bar. The tops were where they had left them, but the two guys were gone. Maybe it was just as well. Sheila didn't know what she would have said to excuse Jayne's behavior, anyway.

She decided to take a stroll on the beach to try and make some sense out of what her sister had done. She had asked her what she had been thinking; having sex with Zander, but Jayne was finished talking about it. In truth, she hadn't even begun, and if she wanted Sheila's help, she would have to do much more with explanations.

She remembered her phone conversation with Jayne. She had brought up their trips to see Aunt Millie when they had been kids. Sheila wondered why? When people brought up things that seemed to come out of the blue, it was no coincidence.

Sheila walked a bit farther down the beach and saw a little tiki bar close to another hotel. She decided to go over and order a beer. They had Corona on tap and she ordered a sixteen-ounce glass. Beer always made her pee, but she didn't care. She might stay at the bar for a while. She found a small table that looked out over the gulf. It was peaceful here. Maybe she could talk Gregg into coming back here someday. She sipped her beer and glanced over at the horseshoe-shaped bar. There were two guys sitting together, talking loudly. The sun was in Sheila's eyes, and at first she couldn't see their faces. She put her hand over her eyebrows to block the sun, and then realized it was the same two guys that were at the pool. They appeared to be quite drunk.

Sheila knew what she had to do, but she didn't think it would do much good in their condition. She decided to ignore them and turned her back to the bar. It was warm, and the beer tasted pretty good. She watched as the beachcombers walked by with their heads down, looking for seashells. It was a great way to spend the end of an afternoon. Then a thought popped into her head. She needed to call Aunt Millie. Somehow she knew that her aunt would be playing a crucial role in Jayne's future.

Sheila found the cell phone in her bag. She went through her contacts and found Aunt Millie's number. It was a landline; she didn't have a cell phone.

Aunt Amelia was her mother's younger sister. Sheila's mother told her that she had run away from home when she was sixteen, but she had always stayed in contact with her. Somehow she ended up in northern Florida. That's where the story ended. Sheila always thought there was more to it, but her mother wasn't sharing anything else.

When they were little girls, they took the train to see Aunt Millie a few times. Sheila and Jayne had always enjoyed those trips. Millie couldn't seem to do enough for them.

The last time they had visited, Millie and her mother had gotten into a terrible fight. They would never see Millie again. Her mother had cut off all ties with her sister. Neither of her daughters understood why but kept it to themselves. Their mother would never talk about it again.

When Sheila's parents died, she ran across her aunt's phone number and address hidden away on a card in the family Bible. She had remembered the city her aunt had lived in was called Lake City but the card listed her address in a community called Perry. It was a mystery, and Sheila needed to get to the bottom of it all. She had contacted her aunt by phone, and they reconnected. She had always asked about Sara Jane, and Sheila didn't have the heart to tell her the truth. She just said they had lost contact with her. In retrospect, it wasn't a lie at all.

Sheila had the same feeling when talking to Aunt Millie as she did with her mother; something was being kept secret. All families had their secrets, but this one was a real mystery. Try as she might, Sheila never could uncover what it might be.

Sheila looked at her phone again and thought about what calling her aunt might mean. She decided to throw caution to the wind. Jayne would need someone to rely on during her pregnancy. Whatever happened after that would be between Aunt Millie and Jayne. Sheila knew she wouldn't be of much help to Jayne when she returned to Iowa.

She dialed the number. She had no idea if it still was current. It rang for an uncomfortably long time. Sheila was about ready to end the call when someone answered.

"Hello?" The voice was robust and in charge.

"Hello, Aunt Millie?"

There was some silence and then an even stronger response. "Sheila De Graff, is that you?" Millie never called her by her married last name.

"Yep, it's me."

"It's so good to hear your voice, girl." Then her voice changed. "Is something wrong?"

Sheila thought for a moment. There was something wrong, but she didn't want to share it over the phone.

"No, not really. I just wanted to call and see how things were with you."

"Well, I'm an old lady. Just sit around and check on the lumber business. Boring stuff. How about you? How are things back in Hospers, Iowa?"

"They were good when I left. I'm in Florida."

"What? Where?"

"I'm staying in a hotel on St. Pete's Beach."

"That's not that far from Perry. You need to come for a visit. I won't hear 'no' coming from you, either."

"That's why I called. I want to come and see you."

"Then make it happen."

"There's just one little wrinkle. I'm not alone."

"Did you get that husband of yours off his dead ass? Bring him along." Millie paused. "You aren't with another man are you?"

"Well, of course not. But I'm not here with Gregg."

"Whoever it is, I'm sure they will be welcome."

"Aunt Millie, it's Sara Jane."

"My God. You found her."

"I did. But she goes by the name Jayne Grafton now. She says Sara Jane is dead."

"Or, so we all thought," Millie said.

The comment took Sheila by surprise. Millie knew more than she had been letting on. Had her mother been communicating with her aunt in secret?

"I was wondering if we could come for a visit. Jayne could use a friendly face."

"When can you come?"

"You say. We're just hanging out here at the beach."

"Give me another day to tie up some loose ends. Then you two come and stay for as long as you like."

Sheila thanked her, and Millie gave her the address. She told her it was just outside of Perry but easy to find. Sheila told her they would meet her the day after next, but it wouldn't be until after lunch. As she hung up, she hoped the offer to stay as long as they liked applied to just Jayne, because she would be leaving just as soon as things could be worked out.

Sheila stuck the phone into her purse and finished the last of her beer. She stood and fished a few dollars from her clutch to leave for the server. Just as she turned, the same two drunks were standing right in front of her. Sheila jumped back.

"Sorry, but you frightened me."

"Kind of like that woman you were with earlier. She scared us." The guy talking was slurring badly.

"Well, about that, I wanted to apologize for that. You were just trying to be friendly, and she turned on you. That wasn't right, but you need to understand that she has had a rough time of it lately."

"Apology accepted. Now come back with us to the bar, and let us buy you that drink."

"Thank you, but I'm out of time and have to get going. Maybe some other time if you are still around."

"No time like the present." They grabbed Sheila by the arm and began pulling her toward the bar. Sheila was starting to think they might have other ideas, and it scared her.

"I don't want to seem ungrateful, but I need to go," she said and looked around to see if there was anyone to help her. It looked like the bartender was off doing some errand. The other guy pushed her from behind, and Sheila lost her balance and fell to her knees.

"Get up. We are about to accept a real apology from you up in the room." He grabbed her by the breasts and pulled her up.

"Looks like you've got enough up there for both of us." The guy, who pushed her, grabbed her from behind and ran his hands from her breasts to her pelvis.

Sheila was strong and had never feared for her safety in the past, but she was no match for two guys. Maybe Jayne had been right in trying to avoid these two. They weren't the nice guys she had thought they were.

Just when she was ready to scream for help, she was jarred off her feet and the guy holding her let go. She heard another crash behind her, and as she turned to see what happened, she saw a bar stool come down on her attacker's head. He wouldn't be moving for quite awhile.

Sheila felt some movement beside her and saw the other attacker moving toward his friend. She stuck out her foot, and he stumbled. She saw the bar stool come down first on his back, when he turned over in pain, the back of the stool hit him on the head. He wouldn't be moving for quite awhile, either.

Assuming it was the bartender who had returned, Sheila got back to her feet. It wasn't him at all. It was Jayne. Sheila was speechless.

"Pick up your purse, and let's go. We don't need to stay around and answer questions."

Sheila did as she was told. Her head was spinning, and she followed along without speaking. She was always in control, and what had happened was totally foreign to her. She didn't know how to react. Luckily for her, Jayne knew.

When they reached the room, Jayne opened the door, and hugged Sheila tightly.

"What the hell were you thinking?" she asked, when she let her go.

"I was trying to apologize to them for earlier. I guess I misread their true intentions."

"You're not in Iowa anymore. You need to be more careful. People will chew you up and spit you out." Jayne was suddenly tired and fell into a chair.

"Well, I'm glad you were looking out for me."

"It wasn't by chance. I had been searching everywhere. I was afraid you might try to do something stupid. You are just lucky I heard the commotion when I was walking by."

"I think they were planning to rape me."

"Believe it."

"I don't know how I could have lived with that." Sheila shuddered at the thought.

"Live with it? You would have been lucky to survive at all. Sometimes I am just astounded by your naiveté."

The comment angered Sheila.

"And yet, you're the one pregnant."

Jayne looked away, and Sheila was sorry she said it.

"I'm sorry. I shouldn't have said that. Maybe I'm just too shaken up to make much sense of anything."

Jayne nodded. "There's a bit of truth in every statement we make. You weren't wrong."

Sheila seized the moment to change the subject.

"You're going to have to rent a car tomorrow."

Jayne was interested.

"Are we sightseeing?"

"I think I want it to be a surprise."

"In that case, maybe you should rent the car." Jayne did a good job of pretending to be serious. She had Sheila convinced.

"Okay, I'll tell you because I can't afford to spend that kind of money just to drive somewhere."

Jayne laughed. "So what's the big surprise?"

"When you called me, you asked about visiting Aunt Millie when we were kids. Do you remember?"

"Sure. They were good memories."

"I've made contact with her. She wants us to come for a visit."

"A visit?"

"Well, she wants us to stay as long as we like. So, I think you'd better check out of the hotel after tomorrow. I told her we'd be there sometime after lunch the day after tomorrow."

"You found her after all these years? Where is she?"

"She lives in Perry. I have her address."

Jayne was nodding her head. "That's right I remember that name. I think I was ten years old the last time I saw her."

"Does she know my story?"

"I don't know. Who knows? Everything was always such a big secret between mom and her, so it's hard to say. She knows you're with me, and I might have said we just lost contact with you in the past."

"So, you've been keeping in touch with her all these years?"

"Once or twice a year. I always tried to call her around Christmas. You know, family and all that."

Jayne sat back in the chair, while Sheila went to the cooler looking for a beer to help calm her nerves.

"Family," she thought.

15

Zander woke up with Aubrey sleeping soundlessly next to him. He looked at the clock and saw it was 6:00. He was never an early riser, but he knew he had a lot to do. It made him too excited to sleep. He decided to lie with Aubrey until 7:00 and then get his day moving. He thought about waking her up for some morning sex but decided against it. Making love was important with Aubrey. Having casual sex, just for the sake of it, no longer held much importance for him.

He looked at her. She was beautiful even after a night of sound sleep. It was hard to fathom. He was sure he never looked good after waking up, and yet, here she was, more beautiful than the night before.

Zander decided he was just getting stupid with all this love stuff. He got up and went into the bathroom to shower and shave. He still wasn't comfortable taking care of his other bodily function around her. He would take care of that elsewhere.

When he returned to the bedroom, Aubrey was stirring. He gave her a kiss on her cheek.

"Where's the fire?" she asked.

"Sorry, I need to leave. I've got to start putting things in motion. I want to stop at the hospital and find out how Mike is doing."

"How long before I see you again?" Aubrey asked.

Zander patted his pocket. "I don't know, but I'll call."

"If you don't, you'll have hell to pay. Shall I make breakfast before you go?"

"I'll just grab some fruit on the way out."

"Just remember to eat. You need to keep your strength up for me." She winked at Zander.

He messed up her hair. Zander was surprised that she looked even better than she did a few minutes before. He had all he could to keep from jumping back into bed with her.

He grabbed a large banana on the way out and consumed the entire thing before he made it to his pickup. He called his boss at the Rod And Gun Club before he left the parking spot. He found out that Mike had checked himself out of the hospital and had taken his family to visit some relatives while he convalesced. He had dropped off a something for Zander in a sealed envelope. Zander decided to go to The Rod And Gun before he did anything else.

Traffic coming onto Sanibel was brutal, but leaving the island was a breeze. Soon, he was over the causeway and traveling Summerlin Road. Tamiami was busy with people getting to work so he jumped up to I-75 by taking Alico Road.

Zander had a hard time thinking about anything but the woman he had just left. He had to take care of the Corey problem soon. When he put that back into perspective, he was at the city limits. Time had slipped away. It always did when he thought about Aubrey.

When he arrived at The Rod and Gun, the boss was just getting out of his vehicle. They opened for lunch and dinner, so the place was still closed. Zander parked next to his boss.

"Well, look who decided to show his face."

"Sorry. I've had a lot on my plate," Zander said.

"So I hear." He reached into his coat pocket and pulled out a business envelope and handed it to Zander. "This was left for you by Mike. He wanted you to look at it right away."

"Thanks. I'll do that," Zander said, taking the letter. "I wanted to tell you about Aubrey."

"Don't tell me anything other than you are handling this problem."

Zander smiled. "That's the plan."

"Good. See you this evening." He went into the restaurant.

It wasn't a question. Zander needed to report for work that very evening. It was just as well. Zander knew he needed some kind of plan to take care of The Jackass problem. He was still trying to figure that part out.

He sat back in the pickup and opened the envelope. It was written just the way Mike talked.

Zander,

I'm doing okay. I've got some sick leave, so I thought I'd spend some time with relatives. I'm not up to facing Corey until I feel better. Just to be on the safe side, I haven't told anyone where we're going. I don't know how long this guy's fingers are, and I don't need him trying to do something to my family to get at me. I hope you understand that I can't really get involved in this. The guys at the department are plenty pissed enough for everybody. I think if he shows his face anytime soon, he won't have much of it left. But we both know that he's smarter than that.

So, I guess it falls on you. I don't know what you are planning, and it's better that way. Something you asked me about when we talked last stuck in my head. You wanted to know about my hunting trips. I think we talked about pythons and alligators.

It might be something to think about.

If you need any assistance, there are some guys who meet for breakfast at the Island Cafe every morning. They might be of some help if you are interested. I told them you might be in to see them, so they are expecting you. They had an issue with Corey previously and seem eager to help.

Be careful. Once you're out in the glades, it's a whole other life. People follow their own set rules. Most have no rules at all.

Thanks in advance. You should destroy this letter.

Mike

Zander reread everything and then tore it up into tiny pieces. There was a garbage container just outside the door of the restaurant. After Zander deposited the letter fragments, he decided to head over to the Island Café to check in with Mike's friends.

There were six guys sitting at a round table, and everyone stared at Zander when he walked into the café. It was definitely a local's place. Zander recognized a few of the faces from the restaurant.

Finally one of the guys spoke.

"You wouldn't happen to be Zander?"

Zander nodded.

"Mike told us about you. I'm glad you caught us. We were about ready to break up for the day. You can only stand so much bullshit from this crowd."

Zander laughed and walked over. Everyone shook hands and introduced himself. Zander wouldn't remember their names. He was bad with names, but he would know their faces.

"How can we help?" a guy named Ed asked.

"I'm not quite sure yet. I might need someone with a boat," Zander said.

"A few of us do the airboat tours but if you need stealth, then that's not the answer."

"I'm sure I'll need to be as quiet as possible."

"I've got a skiff that should work. It can go right through two feet of water and it can be pushed with a pole if necessary," one of the guys offered.

"That sounds good. I just need to figure out where this guy is hiding out. I think any plan would need to start with his location."

"We meet here every morning, so if you need us, we're usually here between 7:00 and 9:00," Ed offered.

"That's good to know. I don't want to involve any of you unnecessarily, so meeting here is a good solution," Zander said.

"We know lots of locals. We'll put out the word and we're looking for this character," Ed said.

"I like to call him The Jackass," Zander said.

The entire table liked the idea. Zander felt like he could fit in with these small town boys quite easily. Zander agreed to meet for breakfast every morning to check for any new information these guys might stumble upon. He hoped it wouldn't take very long. He didn't want to be away from Aubrey any longer than necessary.

Zander decided to go back to his rental and assess any damages The Jackass and his boys might have caused. After an hour of rearranging, Zander could see some scratches on the appliances. That, and the Cushman, seemed to be the extent of the damage. He called the owner, explained what happened and offered to pay to replace everything.

The owner was more understanding than Zander expected. Apparently he had been very happy with having someone taking care of the house for him. There was an awkward moment when he stumbled around, before telling Zander that he planned to put the property up for sale. He apologized if he was causing Zander any problems. Zander told him he was planning to leave anyway just as soon as he took care of a few loose ends.

Zander offered cash to settle the damages, and the owner was more than happy to accept. He told Zander he was sorry for his troubles, and that Everglade City was usually a quiet and safe place to live.

Zander wondered if trouble just followed him around. Maybe he was the problem. It certainly seemed like he had his share of troubles. This latest chapter was part of his share, but by default. It seemed like most of his conflicts were because he was trying to help someone else. None of the discord was his doing. Zander needed to think that whole thing through when he had more time. Right now, he had to find Corey Prescott, and then decide what to do about him.

His shift started at 4:00, so he decided to ride up to the marina in Chokoloskee and check on The Jackass's boat. He would ask around to see if anyone had seen him lately.

The marina wasn't busy, and the owner was behind the counter when Zander walked into the building.

"Can I help you?" The owner didn't look up from his paperwork.

"I was wondering if Corey Prescott has used his boat in the last few days?"

The owner stopped what he was doing and looked up. "Who wants to know?"

"The guy whose house he just destroyed, and the guy whose law enforcement friend got beaten pretty badly by this asshole's flunkies." Zander was more forceful than he had intended, but he was beginning to lose patience.

The owner smiled. "You must be Zander." He held out his hand,

and Zander took it. "Mike stopped in and told me you might be coming around."

"That sounds like Mike," Zander said, trying to continue the conversation.

"I have no love for Corey Prescott for some of the same reasons you just mentioned. He also owes me a crap-load of money for storing and working on his boat."

Zander thought of The Jackass's money he had hidden. Maybe, if things worked out, Zander would be paying off Corey Prescott's debts.

"Has he been around lately?" Zander asked again. This time he was less forceful.

"No. His boat hasn't moved in a week, and I haven't seen him anywhere."

"Do you know any of the other guys he hangs with?"

"I try to stay away from people like that. They are a rough crowd. Probably have an area in the glades where they base. They're all drug runners if you ask me. Users too. Got no use for them."

"Sounds about right. Could you let me know if he shows up for his boat?"

"Better than that, I'll put his rig in dry storage. It would take an hour or so, minimal, for us to get it ready. Plenty of time for me to call you, and you can do whatever it is you're going to do."

Zander gave the owner his phone number and went down to the dock to look at Corey's boat. He wanted to make sure he knew it from top to bottom. He climbed aboard and searched every part of the boat looking for weapons or anything else of interest.

Satisfied, he jumped back onto the dock and walked back to the marina office. He didn't see the guy in the lawn chair, in front of the motel, sucking on a cigarette. Before Zander got into his pickup, the guy had pulled out a cell phone and was dialing a number. He was certain Corey Prescott would be pleased. Pleased enough to keep him in whiskey money for the next month or so.

16

Corey Prescott was holed away in a little run-down shack between Everglade City and Marco Island. Corey thought it looked like a chicken coop. It smelled like it too. It was just south of Highway 41 and buried in the trees back about a mile. If you didn't know it was there, you would never have noticed it at all. It was one of those places that even the Seminoles abandoned. But he had to lay low, and this was as good as anything. Maybe it was just better than nothing. No matter. He would take care of this Zander prick and get his money back. He would find and deal with Aubrey later. There would be plenty of time for that.

Corey kept a low profile during the day and tried to do his reconnaissance by cover of darkness. He had to be careful. He never went out past 11:00. That would draw attention, and he didn't need the cops stopping him. He knew he would be toast if they found him.

He traded his Opal for a used black Jeep Wrangler. He figured it wouldn't draw much attention, because there were a lot of them in the glades. It was more about the function than anything else. It would go through almost anything. He financed it through the used car dealer where he bought it. If he got his money back, he would pay off the loan. If he didn't, the dealer would be shit-out-of-luck. He didn't care. He would make one more drug buy and leave Florida forever. He hadn't thought about where he would go, but it would be someplace outside of the U.S. That's why he needed his money. He couldn't purchase the amount of drugs he needed without the capital. He knew he could triple his money with just one more deal.

Corey spent most of his time during the day cleaning his arsenal of weapons. He didn't possess the usual assault weapons that many of the drug runners used. His collection consisted of five shotguns, a few high caliber rifles, and two 45-caliber handguns. He knew that these weapons wouldn't draw much attention in the Everglades. Everyone hunted and had similar weapons. He didn't need any unnecessary attention, and these guns would serve the purpose if he got into a firefight.

He could take the weapons apart and put them together by rote if necessary. It was a good skill to possess when all of your business was handled in the dark.

The phone call came while he was in the middle of his gun cleaning. The old guy on the other end was explaining about seeing some big tall guy on his boat. Corey was incensed. What was Zander doing on his boat? He knew there was nothing there to incriminate him, but he didn't like people invading his space. That would be especially true of this Zander prick. He pushed back the desire to go out and pump a few shotgun shells into his head. He knew he would need to find the money before he could kill him.

His two-man crew was at their day job. They would check in when they got off work. Corey decided they would stake out The Rod And Gun Club that night. If they found anything, they would call him and he would join them later. There was no sense showing his face unless the target was located. Corey's biggest fear was that this guy and Aubrey had left. That would make it almost impossible to his money back. It was driving him crazy, and it was all he could do to stay back in the chicken coop to wait it out.

A little after five, his boys checked in. They were loyal, and Corey liked that. They were also very stupid, and he had to remind them constantly that he needed Zander alive until they could locate the money. The boys just wanted to kill him and throw his body deep into the glades. Corey felt like he was more of a babysitter to these two. No matter, they would do what he said, because they were a little afraid of him. It was a trait he fostered to keep them in line.

When they drove into the little hideout, Corey was ready for them.

"I want you both to drive separately to Everglade City. One of you needs to stakeout the north end of The Rod And Gun Club, and the other the south end. I don't care which."

"We'll need our guns," the one called Johnnie, said.

Corey had taken their weapons after their last debacle at the Island Café. He didn't need them running around half-cocked.

"Don't be stupid. If the police are still on the prowl, that's all they would need to get back at me."

Neither said anything. But Corey could see they weren't happy about going into Everglade City unarmed. He tried to defuse the situation.

"If you find this Zander guy, you call me and I'll bring all the weapons we'll need."

That seemed to placate them for the moment.

"Just remember, we need him alive. I've got to get my money back, and that won't happen if we are trying to talk to a corpse."

They both nodded in agreement. Corey was pleased, but knew he would need to keep his eye on both of them. They were too unpredictable.

"Johnnie, you go into town and check to see if he's working tonight. Then pick up some food for us. We'll decide how to proceed after you find out the information."

"What kind of food?" Johnnie asked.

"I don't care. Just something."

"Okay. I'll get pizza."

"Fine, just get a move on. We'll be waiting. Don't take forever, either."

Johnnie was out of the door and into his beat-up pickup. He fishtailed out of the little dirt path leading to Route 41, leaving a cloud of dust.

Corey watched the dust settle and shook his head. How he ever hooked up with these two birdbrains was beyond his scope of understanding. He was smarter than that.

It was close to an hour before Corey heard Johnnie's pickup roaring through the trees coming right at them. The pickup had a sound that was hard to miss. The exhaust pipes came up behind the cab instead of the usual exhaust out the rear end. There were two glasspacks that tried to serve as mufflers just before the chrome pipes exited above the cab. They weren't of much use. The thing was loud. Much louder than Corey would have liked. He hated anything that would draw attention.

Johnnie didn't seem to mind, however. He had a need for speed, and the more noise the better. The dust was flying again, and Corey stepped back inside the tiny building and shut the door. He didn't need to breath in that shit. He would need to put his foot down hard if they were to survive what was coming next.

When the truck slid to a halt, Corey charged out of his door and grabbed Johnnie by the shirt through his open window before he could even open the door.

"Listen you somnabitch, I've told you before that we don't want to draw attention to ourselves."

Johnnie shook his head in agreement.

"Then what the hell do you call this?" Corey was livid.

"Hey, there's nobody around here for miles."

Corey slapped Johnnie's face twice. "Do I have your attention?"

Johnnie said nothing and looked at his shoes. He reached over and handed Corey the pizza box. Corey grabbed it and went back inside leaving Johnnie to follow if he wanted to be fed.

The other guy they called Ferd had remained inside. He seemed just a little smarter than Johnnie. Corey threw the pizza on the table, and Ferd opened the lid and grabbed a slice. He had two pieces crammed into his mouth before the other two even sat down.

Corey took a piece of pizza just to make sure he would get something before the other two annihilated everything. He wondered if they would stop at the pizza or consume the box as well.

"You two are assholes," Corey said, "You don't even share an once of brains between ya'."

They both stopped eating and just looked at Corey. He couldn't take it any longer. He tossed the slice of pizza back into the box. He had lost his appetite. He needed to go for a walk and clear his head.

When he returned, it was dark, and Johnnie and Ferd were sitting on the step waiting for him. Corey was feeling better.

"It's time to go. Remember what I told you. We need him alive, and don't do anything stupid to draw attention."

They both got up and went over to their vehicles. Corey watched them move up the lane. Maybe there was hope for them after all.

While Corey had been on his walk, Johnnie rummaged around in back of the cabin and found his rifle. It was 30.06 that he used for hunting gaters. It was his gun, and he didn't understand why Corey thought he had a right to take it from him. He placed the rifle behind his seat in the pickup so Corey wouldn't notice it.

Ferd wasn't sure it was a good idea.

"What will Corey do if he finds out that you took a gun with you?"

"Just keep your mouth shut. Besides, it's my gun. I don't need him to tell me when I can have it."

Ferd decided to play dumb. It was easy for him.

When they drove onto Highway 41, Johnnie reached around and put his gun on the gun rack in the rear window. He was proud to display his firearm.

Ferd led the way into Everglade City. He took the north "y" off the main drag and parked about a block from The Rod And Gun Club. That left the south end for Johnnie. They parked so they could see each other's vehicle. Ferd flashed his lights twice. Johnnie responded in kind. Now all they had to do was wait.

Johnnie had a pint of Black Velvet under his seat and took it out and took a huge pull from the bottle. He coughed once and replaced the lid. Ferd was trying to be more vigilant and had nothing to drink. It would be a long night.

~

Mike's good friend, Artie, was off duty that evening, and Mike had asked him to try and keep an eye on Zander when he could. Artie decided to sit at the bar at The Rod And Gun that evening, and he was in his car without his uniform when he went by Johnnie's pickup. He noticed the uncased gun in the back window. Something wasn't right. Why was the guy just sitting there? He decided to drive around and check things out. It wasn't long before he noticed another guy in a pickup sitting north of the restaurant. He drove to the front door of

The Rod And Gun and went inside.

"Hey Zander. I need to use the phone," Artie said.

Zander reached under the bar, brought up the rotary phone and placed it on the bar for Artie.

"Thanks." Artie dialed a number and then took out a notebook from his front pants pocket. He read off some numbers into the phone and hung up.

Zander was about to take the phone and put it back when Artie stopped him. "I still need that. Someone will get back to me."

"What can I get you in the meantime?" Zander asked.

"I'll take a draw. Make it something light." Zander turned and grimaced. He hated light beer. He always thought that if people wanted to drink water, they should just order water. It tasted better and was so much cheaper. Since there was no accounting for taste, he went over and ran a Miller Lite into a glass.

The phone rang, and Artie picked it up. Zander could see him become quite animated. He tried not to listen to other people's conversations. Tonight was no different.

When he returned with the beer, Artie hung the phone.

"Looks like we've got a little problem outside." Artie smiled.

"What's that?" Zander asked, and then placed the beer in front of Artie.

"Let's see, what did Mike say you called him? Jackass, I think. Is that right?"

Zander didn't like the sound of it.

"Looks like one of his buddies is waiting for you outside in his truck with a gun. The other one is just a block the other way. Can't tell if he's armed or not."

"So what do we do?" Zander asked, with just a bit of concern.

"You do nothing. Someone will take care of it. We just wait here." Artie said.

Zander couldn't help feeling nervous. Anytime someone mentioned a gun, his level of concern always spiked.

Artie was almost finished with his beer, when the phone rang again. This time Zander tried to listen to the conversation. Unfortunately, there wasn't one. All Artie did was listen to someone on the other end of the line.

When he hung up, Artie turned to Zander.

"It was Corey Prescott's friends as suspected. The one called Johnnie Prudhoe had an unsheathed firearm in his truck. He's now in custody. The other guy is called Ferd Allen. He was just sitting in his truck and didn't have any guns. We couldn't hold him."

"So what will happen now?" Zander asked.

"Well, you need to watch your ass. They were definitely looking for you."

"What will happen to this guy with the gun?"

"It's just a misdemeanor, and we will charge him. Maybe keep him the rest of the night. I can't see Corey coming in to bail him out, can you?"

"No, I guess not."

"You need to watch for the other one they call Ferd."

"I'm more concerned about that Johnnie character when you let him go."

"Oh, you shouldn't worry about him for a while. We've got a little hunting camp in the woods not far from here. There's a trailer on the premises that makes a great place to sweat people. We've done it before, and we'll do it again. Nobody will miss this guy for quite some time, anyway."

"How will I be able to thank you?" Zander asked.

"Oh, we'll think of something. Don't you worry," Artie said, and smiled broadly. "Besides, this is payback for what they did to Mike."

"This isn't going to set very well with The Jackass." Zander said.

"I'm sure of that," Artie agreed.

"I think I like it."

~*

Ferd saw everything happen just before they came for him. After the cops searched his truck and told him to get moving, he drove into a motel lot and parked. He pulled out his phone and dialed Corey.

"They got Johnnie," he said before Corey could even say hello.

"What the hell are you talking about?"

"They arrested Johnnie. Took him away to the jail."

"What's the charge?"

"I don't know. I wasn't there. I just seen it. Maybe it was his gun in the back window." After he mentioned the gun, Ferd was sorry he brought it up.

"Jesus H. What did I tell you? Do you even listen when I talk?"

"It wasn't me. They stopped me too but let me go, because I didn't have anything they could use against me."

Corey stopped talking. The cops were onto him. Whatever it was he would be doing, he'd have to do it quickly. He knew Johnnie would talk just to save his ass. He would need to care of him when the option presented itself. Right now, he had to make plans, and it started with getting Ferd back to the cabin.

"Get back here as fast as you can without breaking any laws," Corey said, and hung up.

Ferd agreed. He always did. When he drove into the camp, Corey was waiting. He waved him over to the cabin. When Ferd got out of his pickup, Corey pulled out one of his shotguns and fired at Ferd's head. The shot hit him almost entirely in the neck. At that close range, it separated his head from the rest of his body. Corey put down his shotgun and walked over. He dragged the body behind the chicken coop and then retrieved the head. He felt just a little sad. He had always liked Ferd better than Johnnie. Ferd had always been more compliant.

17

The drive to Perry from St. Pete's Beach took almost three-and-a-half hours. It was a pleasant drive, because it was away from most of the tourists. Sheila drove the rental car. It was some foreign silver model that looked just like every other rental. Could cars get any more boring? Sheila wondered if Jayne noticed the same things, or was she was concentrating on what would come next now that she was pregnant?

They had some trouble finding their aunt's address. After riding through town, they stopped at a convenience store, and Sheila went in and asked the clerk. The clerk looked at her in disbelief.

"You passed it about two miles before you came into the city limits. I would be careful if I were you, the woman is reclusive. Doesn't take kindly to strangers showing up on her doorstep."

"Thank you. I'll keep that in mind." Sheila decided to buy two bottles of water as a small gesture of thanks.

When she got back into the car, she handed a bottle of water to Jayne.

"It sounds like Aunt Millie has quite a reputation around here."

"Does that even surprise you?"

"I suppose not." Sheila headed back the way they came.

She watched the speedometer, and when it approached two miles, she started looking for her aunt's driveway. Jayne spotted it first.

"Look to your left. That must be it."

Sheila saw a huge black gate hung between two stone pillars. The drive was concrete, but they couldn't see much beyond the gate. The entire property was lined with huge pine trees, and nothing was visible from the road. Sheila drove up to the gate and noticed there was a box with a button. Apparently they had to communicate with someone in order to gain access.

She pushed the button and waited. After a few minutes, she pushed the button again. There was a squeal and then a voice squawked loudly from the speaker.

"State your business."

It was hard to recognize a voice through the squawk box, and Sheila couldn't be sure it was her aunt.

"We're here to visit out aunt. Her name is Amelia DePont but she goes by Millie."

"Damn it, is that you Sheila?"

"Yes it is, and Sara Jane is with me."

Jayne leaned over and spoke.

"Its just Jayne now. That's the name I go by."

"Well, come on up to the house. I hate talking on this thing."

There was a buzzing sound, and the gate began to move to the left on its rollers. When it had opened up enough for them to pass through, Sheila put the car in gear and drove through. The gate closed behind her.

It was a flawless landscape with trees canopied over the road leading through the grounds. Everything was manicured to perfection along the half-mile track to the house. There was another gate that led to the carriage house and driveway, but it was already opened.

Sheila drove through and parked the car in front of the huge-double door main entrance. She popped the trunk and opened her door. Jayne followed suit, and by the time both had reached the trunk, a Hispanic man came from the carriage house and grabbed their bags.

"Ms. Amelia is expecting you. I'll take care of your luggage and your vehicle. Are the keys in the car?"

Sheila assured him they were.

"Go on in. You don't have to knock. Ms. Amelia is in the solarium awaiting your arrival. My name is Hector but Miss Amelia calls me

Hernando."

Jayne screwed up her face; finding the name change distasteful.

Hector noticed and laughed warmly.

"I don't mind. She says it reminds her of a musical. She sings Hernando's Hideaway to me sometimes. I like that."

"Thank you very much, Hector." Jayne was having none of that nonsense.

Sheila thought it was cute, and she liked Hector/Hernando.

Hector put the luggage on the drive, got into the car and drove it into one of the vacant stalls in the carriage house. The sisters climbed the stairs to the front door.

The house was enormous. It looked like one of those southern mansions with the columns out front. The front doors were at least ten feet tall, and the doorknobs were in the middle of each door. There was a huge doorknocker on each door as well. The two had all they could do not to try them out, but Hector had told them to go right inside. They didn't want to anger Aunt Millie by not following her directions.

The inside was even more palatial than the outside had appeared. Just beyond the doors was a huge atrium that went up three stories. A huge crystal chandelier hung in the center, and a circular staircase wrapped around the sides of the room. Neither had ever seen anything like it. Jayne knew this property made Martin Van Vugt's home at Cripple Creek look shabby by comparison. Too bad he would never see this place. It would be difficult from his location at the bottom of the mineshaft, where she had helped dump his body.

"Have you ever seen anything like this?" Sheila asked.

Jayne could only shake her head.

A strong voice came from somewhere deeper in the house.

"Stop whispering and come here. I want to see you both."

It was Millie. She was in charge as both had remembered her when they had visited as girls. They hadn't visited this area, however. They could remember a small house in a town somewhere. They had both been too young to remember much else.

They walked through a few rooms, and then they saw the sunroom. Sheila couldn't believe her eyes. The room was bigger than her entire house back in Hospers. There were flowers, plants, and even trees growing all around. There were colorful birds chirping and flying from tree to tree. Apparently, their entrance had disturbed the natural order of things.

"Oh, don't mind them. They'll get used to you soon enough." Millie moved to her nieces, grabbed them both around the shoulders and pulled them close.

Sheila couldn't fathom how strong she seemed. Jayne dropped her arms around her stomach to protect herself from an unnecessary amount of pressure to her stomach.

Millie noticed and withdrew her bear hug without drawing attention to it. It wasn't unnoticed by Jayne and she wondered how much Aunt Millie knew about her condition. She was angry with Sheila for saying anything, but after she thought about it, she knew that it had to come out sooner or later. Maybe it would be easier this way.

"You two are a sight for sore eyes. Come over and sit with me. We need to catch up."

The three went over to a conversation pit with overstuffed chairs. The two sisters sat on one side, and Millie sat across from them.

"Have you eaten anything? I've got a kitchen full of anything you might like."

"We stopped for lunch on the way." Sheila said.

"How many servants do you have around here, anyway," Jayne said, aggressively.

Millie looked at her and then laughed heartily. "I don't have servants. Oh my, no. I don't believe in that sort of thing. I have a cook that makes me breakfast and lunch. She makes dinner and keeps it warm in the oven for me until I'm ready for it in the evening. I think you've met Hernando. He's my handyman and whatever else I need him to do. He'll take good care of your car. You'll find your luggage in your rooms by the way. He did that as well."

"His name is Hector. Why do you call him Hernando? It's demeaning." Jayne said, a bit too edgy to suit Sheila.

"Jayne. Stop it. We're guests here." Sheila was fuming.

Millie laughed heartily. "Oh, stop making me laugh, you two. Not everything is as it seems. These people are my friends."

"My cook takes care of the kitchen and does some light housework. She lives in town in a house I bought for her and her son. Her husband is no longer in the picture after years of using her as a punching bag. I took care of him as well."

"The Hernando thing is a little joke between us. I pay him well. He makes more money working for me than anywhere else he could find around here. Hector even lives above the carriage house with his wife and two children. They are the family I never had. We spend all the holidays together."

"What about us?" Jayne asked, but she had softened her tone a bit.

Millie stopped and looked at Jayne for a long time. Something in her eyes mirrored sadness. Jayne and Sheila both noticed it.

"How long have you been dead?" Millie said, changing the subject.

The comment took Jayne by surprise. "I don't know how to answer that."

"I should think not. It was devastating when we heard the news of your accident. Sheila was the one who held out hope. I thought she was just avoiding the truth, but she has some sort of empathy that most of us don't understand."

"My life was in a constant state of turmoil. I just couldn't afford to involve anyone in the family, and I could never return to Hospers."

"You forgot about the most important thing in this life. Family. When things are the most trying, family can help."

"Yet, you have strangers as your family. Why didn't you have children?" Jayne asked.

Millie paused and looked out of the solarium windows.

"I did. But that's another story for another time. First, I want to know about you and your sister."

"You know about me, Aunt Millie. I call you once or twice a year," Sheila said.

"Humph. That's not enough to wet one's whistle. A phone call on Christmas Eve doesn't tell me much at all, and I'm quite sure it doesn't do much for you either."

Sheila nodded.

"I want to know everything. I want to know about my sister's last days on this earth."

"Why did you two have a falling out? I remember coming to visit you a few times on the train when we were young. Once, when I asked mom when we were going out to visit you again, she just started crying. She would never talk about you after that."

Jayne had always been curious about her mother's behavior. Her mother was strong-willed, however, and when she decided not to talk about something, that was the end of it.

"That's another part of my story. I'll share it with you when I'm ready." Millie was firm.

"You're just as stubborn as she was," Jayne said.

Millie laughed again. "Well, duh. We were sisters after all. I see a lot of those same traits in you two. Especially in you, Jayne."

Jayne noticed that Sheila wasn't saying much. She wondered why that was. She had as many questions about Aunt Millie as Jayne did.

"What's your take on all this?" Jayne asked Sheila.

Sheila shrugged her shoulders. Millie could see she was uncomfortable and stepped in.

"Just remember, we've been in communication all these years that you've been dead. It might point to the fact that she knows much more than she has ever shared with you."

Jayne just looked at Sheila. Sheila looked away.

"I hope you haven't been keeping things from me," Jayne said, accusingly.

"You've got a lot nerve saying something like that to me. I still don't know much about your life after you faked your death. Don't think for a moment that I owe you any explanations."

Jayne knew she was right. She had no expectation of anything after what she had done.

"I'm sorry, Sheila. You're right. Just like always. You were always the best of us, and I owe you an apology."

Sheila jumped up, threw her arms around Jayne and just hugged her. Jayne had no idea what to do, so she hugged her back.

Millie smiled. "Where are my manners? Can I get you something to drink?"

"How about a glass of Chardonnay?" Sheila asked, not letting go of Jayne.

"Of course. How about you, ah, Jayne?" Millie caught herself before she said Sara Jane.

"Just some iced tea for me," Jayne said.

"Sweet tea is all I have. You're in the South you know."

"That would be fine."

Millie left for the kitchen, and the two let go of each other.

"There seems to be quite a bit a mystery around her," Jayne said, lightly.

"For sure." Sheila knew more than she was saying.

Millie came back into the sunroom with two glasses of wine and a glass of sweet tea.

After a few sips, Millie put her glass on the table.

"How's the tea, dear?"

"Sweet," Jayne said.

"It's our Southern tradition. I know it's not for everyone's taste. Especially you Northerners."

"I've been trying to consume less sugar lately," Jayne said.

"So, I was wondering, how long have you known that you were pregnant?"

Jayne acted as if she were startled. She looked over at Sheila. Sheila was in the middle of a sip of wine and almost did a spit-take.

"How would you know I'm pregnant?" Jayne asked.

"I've been around a long time. There isn't much that escapes me. I figure that's why you're here. You need some help with this situation. Am I right?"

Of course she was right. Jayne's head was spinning, and she thought she might get sick. This whole thing was getting more complex by the minute.

"I'm keeping the baby."

"Of course you are. Have you told the father yet?"

"He's not in the picture, and I want it to stay that way."

"We'll see," was all Millie would say on the matter.

18

Corey Prescott drove the few miles back into Everglade City. He had to act fast. Johnnie was in custody, and he knew he would be talking soon, if he hadn't already done so.

He drove through town on his way to Chokoloskee. He figured the cops would probably go out to the chicken coop before they checked the marina. That was his hope anyway. Time was of the essence.

~

Zander walked over and looked into Johnnie's pickup. Nothing unusual caught his eye. The police had taken the rifle he had displayed in the back window. What a dumb shit. At least the other guy they called Ferd was a little smarter. He didn't have a gun.

Zander stopped and pulled out his phone. If Ferd had gone back and talked to the jackass, it would make sense that he would be heading to the marina. He had to warn the owner. His number wasn't programmed into his phone, but his card was in his billfold.

Zander dialed the number. The phone rang a few times, and a voice answered.

"The marina is closed for the evening."

"This is Zander. I believe that Corey Prescott is headed your way. You need to take your family, and get away from there. Now."

The owner didn't argue. He knew all about Corey Prescott, and he wasn't about to hang around.

"I'll be in the motel down the street. What are your plans?"

"I'll be there as soon as I can. I want to try to intercept him."

"His boat is in dry storage, so that's going to piss him off. You'd better be careful."

"I won't be alone. I'll have a guy from the airboat rides with me, but I have to find him. It might take me a little time."

"Prescott's nuts. Don't wait too long."

The line went dead. Zander decided to return to The Rod And Gun and call Ed from that phone. When he walked in, the owner told him someone was waiting for him in the bar. He was hoping he would see Ed when he walked in, but he was disappointed.

What he saw was a gigantic Native American. Zander figured he was a Seminole. The remaining natives, the Caloosa, were built smaller like the Mayans. However, some historians thought they were related.

Zander walked over and sat next to the big man.

"I was told you were looking for me."

"Depends. Name?" the big man answered.

"They call me Zander."

He stuck out his hand. "Name is Holata. Mike said need help."

Zander didn't believe in coincidences. This big man was sent for a reason.

"I was just about to call Ed. You know him? He runs an airboat."

Holata nodded. "Good man. Work for him some. Add local color."

Zander dialed Ed's number and waited. Ed answered on the second ring.

"Hello."

"It's Zander. I think we might have a situation where I could use your help."

"I can be ready in five."

"Meet me at the marina in Chokoloskee."

"Do I need my boat?"

"I think we might. I won't know until we get there."

"It's hooked to my pickup, so it won't be a problem."

"Ed, I have a big guy here named Holata. He said Mike asked him to help."

"A good man to have along."

"Thanks. See you at the marina."

Zander turned to Holata. "You come highly recommended."

Holata grunted, but Zander could see the corners of his mouth turn up. He could tell this man was not used to showing much emotion.

"When we leave?"

"Now, if it works out for you."

Holata nodded. They both got up and on the way out, Zander explained to his boss that he would need the night off.

"Just don't tell me about it. The less I know, the better off for everyone."

Zander smiled at his boss. He was a good guy and wanted the best for Aubrey. He knew all about Corey Prescott, and there was no love lost on the guy.

Zander and Holata got into Zander's pickup and set off for the marina. Zander tried to make conversation, but it was like pulling teeth. Holata wasn't much of a conversationalist.

"Holata. That's a name I haven't heard before. What does it mean?" Zander asked.

Holata looked out the window. Zander didn't think he would answer.

After a few minutes, he said, "Seminole. Means alligator."

Perfect, Zander thought.

~

Corey drove into the marina and noticed the office was dark. It was late, and he expected it to be closed. He drove right over to the docks where his boat had been parked. It wasn't there. He cursed under his breath. What had they done with it? He walked around the storage building and saw his boat had been dry-docked on the second level. He supposed it was because he hadn't paid his bill. He would deal with this asshole later when everything died down.

He walked over to the old man's apartment. He had been his eye for quite some time. Of course, Corey had made sure he had what he needed. The old guy was a rummy, and as long as he had his booze, he was somewhat reliable.

The old man was sitting on his porch with a tumbler of whiskey in front of him. Corey could smell it as he walked up the path.

"I wondered when you would show up." The old guy grinned. Corey could see by the porch light that the few teeth in his mouth were black. He was more repulsive than Corey had remembered.

"What's with my boat?"

"Don't really know. After that big feller checked it out, they put it in storage. Seems to be related somehow, don't you think?"

"No shit."

"I'm thinking you need to get out of here. I might have the answer for you."

"I'm listening."

"It's going to cost you."

Corey realized the guy was being cagey. "It usually does."

"I think it would be worth a couple cases of whiskey."

"I wouldn't argue, if I like what I hear." Corey had no intention of paying him anything.

"There are a couple of rentals docked over there." He pointed toward the docks.

"Keys in them?"

"Of course not. But I just might have some that fit."

"Hand them over."

"Not so fast. Let's see the green before we do business."

"Okay. How much will it take?"

"A couple hundred ought to do just fine."

Corey reached for his billfold and looked into it.

"Damn it, it's too dark out here, let's go inside where I can see something."

Corey didn't want to take care of business out in the open where someone might be a witness.

The old man was quite drunk, and he slipped while trying to get up. Corey reached out and helped steady him. They both staggered through the door.

"Let's see the keys," Corey said.

The old guy went to a cupboard and pulled out a set of keys.

"How did you get those?"

"You don't live around a marina for very long before you find out that the keys of a brand fit most of the ignitions. When they salvage boats, I just take the keys. They don't need them anyway," he slurred.

"Can I see them?" Corey asked.

"Money first."

Corey placed his billfold on the table in front of them. "Take what you want."

The old guy licked his lips and reached for the billfold, dropping the keys on the table next to it. Corey made no move for the keys. Instead he reached behind his back and brought out a pistol. The old man was too busy salivating over the possibility of a huge payday to notice Corey picking up a throw pillow from the couch. He didn't want a lot of noise coming from his .45.

The billfold was open and the old man removed a stack of bills. He wasn't drunk enough not to notice that all he had in his hand was a fistful of singles.

"Hey there isn't…"

It was all he could say before Corey shot him in the head through the pillow. He was standing less than two feet away. The bullet went through-and-through. It blew out the back of his head and most of his brains onto the kitchen floor.

But the possible mess that he could have caused Corey had been neutralized. Eventually there would be no witnesses. It would take some time, but he would deal with Johnnie later.

Corey walked down to the docks and found a cruiser. It was something he could use on the open sea, unlike his skiff. Corey had a bit of luck. There were two navigation areas on the boat. One was in the cabin so the captain could be protected from the elements in inclement weather. The other was above the cabin on a tripod. The captain could navigate from the crow's nest and be able to see for greater distances. It also helped to see above the swells in the ocean during rough seas.

Corey found a key that fit and checked the fuel level. He crossed his fingers. He wanted the fuel tanks to be full. He could hardly believe his luck. Things like this just didn't happen to him.

He jumped back onto the dock, and he untied the three lines holding the boat from their cleats. He jumped back into the boat and pushed off. He drifted away from the dock a few yards before he started the engine. It roared to life, and he pushed the throttle forward to almost full. He would ignore the no wake signs. It was dark and he couldn't see them. He also didn't care; he needed to get away fast. There would be no running lights until he was away from there and deep into the glades.

~

Zander drove faster than he would have liked. Holata didn't seem to mind and said nothing. When they reached the little motel, Zander drove past, heading for the marina. He knew the owner had gone there to hide from The Jackass, but he wanted to see if he could beat Corey to the punch.

The lights were on in the office. Zander went over and stepped inside. The owner was there on the phone; he looked over at Zander with wide eyes and then relaxed when he recognized him. He hung up the phone.

"I was just about to call you."

"Did he get his boat? Am I too late?"

"Well, he didn't get his boat, but you are too late. He stole one of mine. What's worse, it's a cruiser. He could go all the way to Cuba if he wanted."

"Damn it." Zander didn't know how to proceed.

The owner smiled. "All is not lost." He reached underneath the counter and brought out what looked like a large phone. "All my rentals have GPS trackers on them." As long as you're within fifty miles of the craft, you can follow."

He handed the electronic device to Zander. There was a screen with what looked like the area's terrain and something was blipping on and off.

"That's the boat."

"Awesome," was all Zander could think to say.

"Do you need one of my boats to follow him?"

"I've got someone coming to do that. He's got his own boat. He knows the area and has no love for Corey Prescott. You wouldn't want me out there in one of your boats anyway. I don't know enough about the ocean to do anyone any good."

"Is it just the two of you? Do you need me to go along?"

"No. You've got a family and a business to worry about. We are going to be accompanied by a Seminole by the name of Holata. Do you know him?"

"Do I know him? Everybody knows about Holata. He's a legend around here. You will be in good hands. You won't need me with him on board."

Zander saw headlights coming into the marina. It was Ed pulling his skiff. He pulled next to the boat livery area and made ready to launch. Holata helped him without being asked. Zander could tell that these two had a relationship. That would be helpful in this pursuit.

When the boat was in the water, the three climbed aboard. The owner handed over the ropes.

"This is a small boat. It will be quicker than his, but you'll need to get to him before he gets out in the ocean or you'll never stop him."

"That's the plan," Ed said.

"Just bring my boat back intact. That's all I ask," the owner said.

Zander nodded, "We'll give it a try."

"And by saying my boat, that's all you should bring back."

The three understood his meaning.

19

Jayne and Sheila talked with Aunt Millie far into the evening. Once they got past the uncomfortable questions about her pregnancy, Jayne found the conversations to be quite stimulating. Sheila had been talking non-stop about family back in Iowa. Jayne hadn't heard some of the family stories and found them interesting. She couldn't help but feel she had missed a good portion of her life.

Jayne decided that it was time to tell all. She started from the time they blew up half of Hospers up until her phone call to Sheila from St. Pete's Beach. It was a long story, and she tried not to leave anything out. She even told them both about getting rid of Martin's body and Fabiano losing his life in her car explosion. What she didn't tell them was that she had orchestrated both of those situations. They both had questionable opinions of her, and she didn't need to add anything to the table.

Sheila seemed somewhat shocked at the turn Jayne's life had taken over the years. Aunt Millie appeared to just take it in stride. That surprised Jayne. She had supposed Millie would have more of a puritanical viewpoint of life, since she was from a more conservative generation.

It was getting late and Millie said so.

"I want to show you around tomorrow. We'll have a big day, so let's stop for now and get some sleep. Breakfast is at 8:00 tomorrow morning. Don't be late."

Aunt Millie got up and walked toward the solarium door.

"What about you? Jayne asked. "We haven't heard anything about your life."

Millie turned toward Jayne. "When I'm ready, I'll tell you everything. For right now, look around. You can see which direction my life has taken. How I got to this point will be the story for another time. You both need to go to bed."

Aunt Millie left the room. Sheila and Jayne looked at each other.

"I guess we should go to bed." Sheila smiled.

"She's a bossy old bag."

"You see anything familiar?" Sheila asked.

Jayne didn't know how to respond to the comment, so she shrugged it off.

"Let's go check our rooms," Jayne said, changing the subject.

The two sisters climbed the staircase they had passed near the entrance. They felt like they were in the movie, "Gone With The Wind."

"Where's Rhett Butler when you need him?" Jayne asked.

"You burned that bridge, I believe," Sheila said.

Jayne didn't respond. Of course Sheila was right. She had burned so much. Now there was a chance for a fresh start. Hopefully she wouldn't screw it up. There would be someone else to think about beside herself. It would be a new experience for Jayne.

The bedrooms were gigantic. Each was as big as Jayne's entire suite on St. Pete's Beach. They were set up almost identically but with different furnishings. Jayne decided to let Sheila choose the one she liked better. She decided on the blue room and left the yellow room for Jayne.

The yellow suited her. It was bright and lifted her mood. How long she would be able to stay here was yet to be determined. They said goodnight, and just before Jayne closed the door to her room, Sheila came back and hugged her tightly.

Once again, it took Jayne completely by surprise.

"I'm so sorry for the life you had to live. But it's going to be better now," Sheila said.

Jayne hugged her back. She hadn't ever considered that her life had been some horrible experience. It was just something she had endured and always supposed that others had similar experiences. Apparently, Sheila didn't think so and felt her sister's life would be better now. Jayne hoped she was right.

The morning brought typical Florida sunshine. Jayne's eastern window flooded the entire room with light. She stayed in bed as long as she could. Millie had said breakfast was at 8:00, and Jayne knew she meant it. It wouldn't be a good start to a relationship by being late.

Both Jayne and Sheila were ready for the day a little before the 8:00 deadline. Sheila went to Jayne's room and knocked on the door.

Jayne answered in a cute sundress. It was low cut and showed off Jayne's expanding breast line. Sheila felt underdressed in her shorts and tank top.

"Cute dress," Sheila said, and touched the fabric.

"It's the only thing I can squeeze into anymore." Jayne replied.

"It will get worse. We need to go shopping and get you some maternity clothes."

"I could use a little help in that area. This is all new to me, and I don't know what to expect."

Sheila laughed. "You are in for some big surprises."

Jayne couldn't help but smile as well. It was sister talk. That was something she had been lacking in her life. Now it was the younger sister schooling the old. Jayne liked the irony.

Breakfast was simple. Each plate had a huge pancake on it. On the center of the table were all types of fruits to put on top. There were also three kinds of syrups with fruit bases to match whichever fruits selected. There was coffee, orange juice or milk to drink.

It was enough to satisfy a woman eating for two.

Before they were even finished eating, Millie began sharing her plans for the day.

"Here's what's happening today. After breakfast, I'll show you the house, and then we'll walk the grounds. I think you'll be pleasantly surprised. After that, I'll let you decide what it is you would like to do. We can lounge around the pool, or I can take you to the paper mill and show you our timber acres."

"I think the first thing we should do is go shopping. Jayne is going to need some clothes that actually fit," Sheila said.

"Oh, that sounds like fun. I've always wanted to do that. I know just the place. It's a little boutique in Perry that specializes in maternity clothing." Millie seemed excited. "If you let me help pick out some things, it will be on me."

"I can't let you do that," Jayne said.

"Nonsense. What else do I have to spend my money on, if not my nieces?"

Millie's cook was clearing the dishes, and when they spoke there was a lull in the conversation, she took the opportunity to speak.

"You'd better do as Millie says. She generally gets her way." The cook laughed and made a quick exit to the kitchen.

"Remind me to fire her later," Millie said, but neither sister took her seriously.

Well, the days-a-wasting. Where shall we start?" Sheila asked.

The first thing was the tour of the entire house. Up to this point, they had seen just a few rooms. The house was even bigger than they had imagined. There were six bedrooms and eight baths. There was an Olympic-sized pool with a pool house on the deep-end side. It wasn't a cabana, but rather an actual house with a bar where the patio might have been.

"My God, I could live in the pool house and still have more room than an entire family would need," Jayne said, in awe.

Both, Jayne and Sheila, were rethinking the idea of spending the day at the pool. Millie could see it in their faces.

"Come on girls. There will be plenty of time for this later."

The grounds were even more impressive. Millie told them the estate was two miles square and contained a small lake at one time.

"What happened to it?" Sheila asked.

"My husband drained it and filled it with earth. He planted trees and built a park out of it."

"Why would he do something like that?"

"The gators. He hated gators, and it was a freshwater lake. Those critters loved it here. So, he said they had to go. We lost too many hunting dogs. One day they were here, and the next day they just disappeared. Those gators ate well for a while."

Jayne shuddered. "Seems like Florida would be a bad place to live if you couldn't stand alligators."

"That's what I told him. But he said there was just too much money in the trees. He put up with the gators when he had to. He got rid of them when he could."

"How much money?" Jayne asked.

"Billions, I think. Of course, this business went back generations, and most of the money was made before William found his way. It was my William who made some sense in the lumber industry. The family had always stripped the countryside of the pines, and when they were gone, they would just buy more acres with trees and do the same thing. William decided to invest in reforestation. It was a new concept here in Florida. He still made money, but he gave back to the land. I was always proud of him for that."

"That's the first I've heard you talk of your husband," Jayne said.

"Lost him a number of years ago. It's still a little raw for me. A hit-and-run driver got him one evening when he was coming home from one of the mills. They never found the guy. He was just too young to be taken like that."

"So, who runs the business now?" Sheila asked.

"You're looking at her. I had to learn fast. William had me take care of the estate, and he took care of the business. Now I have to do both."

"How is that even possible?"

"You just hire good people with your best interests at heart. It helps if you pay them better than anyone else. That's been my secret. People are loyal if you treat them right and pay them well."

"Martin could have taken a page out of your playbook." Jayne hadn't realized that she had spoken out loud.

"I seriously question whether anything would work in that type of business for very long." Millie responded.

Jayne couldn't argue, and they moved on.

The park was fascinating, and beyond that, there was a small stream that bubbled and snaked around the back of the estate. They saw all kinds of birds and assorted wildlife.

"Doesn't that stream draw alligators?" Sheila asked.

"It would usually, but the entire two miles is surrounded by an eighteen foot fence. This entire area is a preserve, mostly a bird sanctuary. We've got all the birds native to Florida here. We have other animals as well, but we try to keep the predators out. The fence serves that purpose quite well."

"Snakes?"

"Some. None of the poisonous varieties and no pythons."

"This is unbelievable. I wish my husband could see it."

"You need to bring him along sometime, dear. I would love to meet him and show it off. This was my job for many years. I planned this entire two miles, and other than draining the lake, all the ideas were mine."

"I am more than impressed," Jayne said, meaning every word.

Jayne sat on a little bench at the edge of the park area where they had walked and rubbed her ankles.

"Your feet look like they are starting to swell. Maybe all this walking isn't so good for you in your condition." Millie was concerned.

"I'll be okay. I just need to rest here a bit."

"Does anyone besides us get to appreciate all this?" Sheila swung her arm around in a semi-circle.

"Oh sure. I open it up for special occasions and fundraisers. The school kids come in busses to count and label the birds every year for science projects. I've had a number of weddings out here. And one funeral." She stopped talking for a few minutes. "This place is for people to enjoy. William is still enjoying it. His ashes were spread over the preserve. Our wish had always been for the public to be a part of all this, and I'll keep it going as long as I'm alive."

"With all your resources, I can't believe you weren't able to find that hit-and-run driver."

"I think I said, they never found him. I never mentioned anything about me. Come on, we've got some shopping to do before we waste the rest of the day out here in the sun."

Sheila and Jayne just looked at each other. The more they tried to peel away the onion that was Aunt Millie, the more layers they found. They were ready for her story, but she wouldn't share it until she was good and ready.

Sheila remained quiet on the way back to the house. She didn't know everything about her aunt, but she knew more than anyone in this group was aware.

20

Perry was a nice community of around seven thousand and covered about nine miles. Shopping would satisfy most of the residents, and what they couldn't find in town, they could find in Tallahassee or Gainesville. Perry was almost dead center between those two larger communities.

Millie drove them to a small strip mall just north of the business district. The little boutique was just a storefront but filled to overflowing with all kinds of cute clothes for pregnant women.

Sheila was in her glory finding things for Jayne that she thought would look stunning on her. Aunt Millie joined in and either gave her approval or disdain.

The clerk obviously knew Millie and joined in the fun, while making her own suggestions. They spent two hours picking and choosing all the right garments. It was a new experience for both Jayne and Aunt Millie. Sheila was an old hand at it. However, she never had been able to shop for things with someone with such deep pockets. It almost made her want to be pregnant again. Luckily, she was able to forget that thought.

~

Jayne's time was mostly spent in the fitting room. She would emerge with either thumbs up or thumbs down from her two companions.

It was during this clothing marathon, that one of those coincidences happens, which no one really believes is a coincidence at all.

Gail had sent Herbie to Perry's Piggly Wiggly to stock up on items they couldn't get at the market in Cedar Key. The Piggly Wiggly was across the street from the maternity shop. Herbie had finished with his long list of items. He decided to stock up on some beer and wine at the little liquor store across the street. As it turned out, the Grog Shop was located in the same strip mall where the women were shopping.

Herbie found an open space and parked the car right in front of the maternity shop. He reached over to turn off the engine and glanced up looking straight into the window of the shop. The sun was to his back and it was shinning right into the store. Jayne had come out of the fitting room at about the exact same time. Herbie's jaw dropped open. He couldn't move but sat transfixed at the scene that was playing out in front of him.

Jayne twirled around and then pulled the top tight around her waist trying to see if her baby bump was showing. Herbie could see there was a thickness around her waist that hadn't been there when he met her in Key West. His mind was spinning, not comprehending what he was witnessing. He looked at the sign on the front of the store and then at the woman in front of him.

"My God. Sara Jane is pregnant," Herbie said, out loud, to nobody.

He started the car and backed out. He was sure she hadn't seen him, and he wanted to keep it that way. He would find another liquor store. It was difficult for Herbie to keep his mind on his driving.

He would need to talk to Gail, and he knew he would also have to tell Fats. Why did this shit always happen to him? Things were going along so well up until now, and now he was being drawn unwillingly into another Zander drama.

He hoped Zander would call him soon. He needed to find out if Zander knew anything about Sara Jane's condition. He had no doubt it was Zander's, but he needed to be subtle. It would be just like her not to tell him anything about it. Herbie wrestled with the whole idea all the way back to Cedar Key.

When he got to their house, Herbie forgot all about taking in the groceries. He burst into the kitchen where Gail was putting away some dishes.

"Sara Jane is pregnant."

Gail just looked at him.

"Gail, it has got to be Zander's, and I don't know what to do."

Gail went over and led Herbie to a chair next to the table.

"Why don't you start by telling me what you are talking about?"

Herbie told her the short story. Gail listened intently and sat back in her chair when he finished.

"Did you get my groceries?" Gail asked.

Herbie nodded.

"Good, go out and get them, and I'll think about this while you put everything away." She smiled at Herbie.

Herbie knew she was trying to get him to calm down. He smiled back and went out to the car and brought everything in. Together they put everything away.

When they were finished, Gail turned to Herbie. "What do you think you should do about this?"

Herbie wanted her to tell him what to do. He didn't like making these kinds of decisions. He wasn't good at it.

"Well, I think I need to find out if Zander knows anything. If he doesn't, then it would be up to me to let him know," Herbie said, hoping it was the right answer.

It wasn't.

"You will do no such thing. If you go fishing, Zander will know something is up. He'll see right through you. The very worst thing you could do is to tell him what you saw. It 's not for you to say. This is between Zander and that woman." Gail didn't like to even use her name.

"What am I supposed to do then?"

"Keep your mouth shut, and pretend you saw nothing or..."

"Or what?"

"If you want to get this off your shoulders, you could call Fats and dump the whole thing on him. It wouldn't be the nicest thing to do, but it would take the pressure off you. I think Fats could handle this easier anyway. He doesn't have the same amount of guilt that you seem to carry around."

Gail knew she was being hard on Herbie, but she knew he anguished over these kinds of decisions. He needed some harsh reality, or he would be dragging this around for far too long.

Herbie sat still for a long time. He was running things through his mind, and it was taking longer than he would have liked. He realized Gail was right.

"I need to call Fats. I hate to put this on him, but you're right. You usually are, and I thank you for the consult."

Herbie took out his phone, but Gail went over and grabbed it from his hand. "There will be plenty of time for that. Right now there's something else we need to take care of." She led him into their bedroom. Herbie forgot about Zander's problems for a while.

~

After the maternity shopping, the trio decided to stop for something to eat. Millie drove down some back road and found a little roadhouse with a number of cars around it.

Sheila was concerned. "Is this place safe?"

Millie laughed. "It better be. I own the building. The guy that runs it used to work for us at the mill."

"You're in the bar business?" Jayne asked.

"Of course not. I don't own the business, just the building. This is more of a local eatery than a bar. They've got the best food around. The guy's wife is the cook, and they've made a nice little living here."

The three entered and noticed the day's specials were written on a white board just inside the entrance. There were three things listed.

"Look closely. That is the extent of the menu. So choose something you want, because that's all there is."

Sheila and Jayne paused to look. Millie charged through the second door, and the sisters could hear voices calling out her name. Sheila looked at Jayne.

"It's a local place all right. Sounds like everyone knows her name."

"Cheers," Jayne said, and held up an invisible glass of beer.

The three items looked like typical food you could find at anywhere in the country. There was pan-fried chicken, a meat loaf dinner and a hot beef sandwich.

When they followed Millie into the roadhouse, she was already sitting at a table. There was a man and woman at the table next to her, and they were visiting about something. Jayne could see a room off the sitting area filled with arcade games. They were silent, but she could see this was a family place. Jayne liked that idea. It was something she had never considered before, and it puzzled her.

Millie proudly introduced her nieces. The woman and the man worked for Millie. She was a receptionist at the mill, and he drove a logging truck. It was evident that they were quite fond of Millie.

Millie ordered the meatloaf and a Yuengling beer. Jayne and Sheila decided on the chicken. Sheila decided on iced tea and Jayne had water. Neither had ever heard of Yuengling, so Millie schooled them.

"You never heard of it, because I don't think they sell past the Ohio River. It's America's oldest brewery, and it's located in Pottsville, Pennsylvania."

"Wait a minute. I was told that Shell's beer in Minnesota was the oldest brewery."

"I believe it is the oldest brewery west of the Mississippi River, but Yuengling has it beat by a number of years."

Jayne was impressed by Aunt Millie's confidence. Apparently being in charge of things had that effect. Jayne always believed she had the most confidence of her family. She had more than Sheila or her parents, but she didn't quite measure up to Millie.

Lunch was an enjoyable experience. It lasted almost two hours. People constantly came over to their table to pay their respects to Millie, and she couldn't help but introduce her nieces in her masterful way.

It was quiet in the car on the way home. They were all tired. It had been a busy day. They decided they all needed some pool time, and Jayne was anxious to try out her new swimsuit. It would be something different for her. She had worn nothing but bikinis since she had been in high school, but she had never been pregnant before. It was time to cover up that baby bump.

When the three emerged from the house and took places around the pool, Jayne was surprised at how glamorous her aunt looked in her swimsuit. It was a two-piece but conservatively cut.

Jayne knew that she was younger than her mother, but they had never discussed how many years. Jayne thought that maybe she was somewhere in her fifties. She didn't look like she had even seen forty. She had a great body and not an ounce of extra weight anywhere. Jayne thought it must have been because she never had any children. It made her concerned with how her own body would react.

"You look wonderful, Aunt Millie," Sheila said, always the one to give the compliment. Jayne might think the same thing, but it was difficult for her to share any of her feelings. Years of being with Martin had taught her never to share what she was thinking. It never turned out well when she did.

But Martin was gone. She needed to make changes in her life if she planned to raise a child. She might as well start now.

"I hope I can look as good as you do, after I have this baby," Jayne said.

"Thank you. We will make that a priority around here."

Jayne stopped and looked at her.

"Well, you'll stay here with me. Unless you have someplace better to be."

"That's a very generous offer, but being a burden isn't something I had planned."

"Burden? Are you touched? Having you and a baby here will help me experience what has been missing in my life all these years. I don't want to hear another word about it."

Sheila smiled broadly. It was something she had been hoping to hear. Jayne needed help, and she wanted Jayne back in her life. If she were living here, both of those concerns would be handled.

Jayne knew she had enough money to handle being on her own, but she had this urge to be part of something else. She wanted to be part of a family once more. It would be good to raise a child in a loving and nurturing atmosphere like this one.

Then she thought of Zander. She didn't know what she would do about that one obstacle. She was thinking about options, when Millie asked her a question.

"Do you know what you're having?"

"Having?"

"Well, is it a boy or a girl?" Millie asked.

Her tone made Jayne feel like she was a little short on the gray matter.

"I don't know. I haven't been to the doctor yet."

Millie sat up. "Are you crazy? You need to be checked out and then have regular visits." She walked into the house.

"My bet is that you'll be seeing the doctor quite soon," Sheila said, good-naturedly.

"I won't take that bet."

It wasn't long before Millie came back out.

"Tomorrow at 10:00. I'll be taking you. I think you'll like this doctor. She's new and quite personable."

"She?"

"Yes, as in female."

"I've never heard of a female doctor let alone gone to visit one."

"We've got to get you two out more."

They all settled back into their beach chairs. The sun was bright and warm, and soon, they were getting hot. Sheila was the first to jump into the pool followed by Aunt Millie. After some coaxing, Jayne followed.

The water was extremely warm. "It feels like bath water," Jayne said.

"I keep it at 88 degrees. No sense getting cold. In the summer we don't have to heat it all. The sun does the job. It just gets a little too cool during the winter nights."

The sisters had forgotten that it was winter in almost all of the rest of the country. Sheila knew she would be headed back to the snow and cold all too soon. The thought brought everything back to her reality.

When Jayne got out of the pool, Millie and Sheila followed suit and went into the pool house pretending to look for drinks. Sheila called out to Jayne and asked her if she wanted anything. Jayne was almost in never-never land and waved her off.

The two were in the pool house planning Sheila's exit strategy.

21

Ed and Holata were taking time picking their way through the mangroves. Zander expressed his concerns that they were going too slow, and The Jackass might get away. Ed tried to calm him down.

"He can't go any faster than us. If he tries, he'll ground that big boat. Then we'll have him."

"But if he gets to the gulf, we'll never catch him."

"He'll never get there. Trust me on that." He pointed at Holata sitting in the bow of the boat crossed-legged.

Ed had a spotlight that Zander seemed content to light up the mangroves from time to time. Holata spoke.

"No more light."

Zander looked at Ed.

"You'd better listen to him," Ed said.

Zander followed direction. He checked his handheld GPS and saw that Corey's boat had turned to the left. He showed the screen to Ed. Ed nodded.

"Which way, Holata?" Ed asked.

Holata pointed to the right. Ed turned the boat starboard.

"But…" Zander tried to say something.

Ed held up his finger and pointed to Holata.

Zander decided to stay quiet. He was squinting, trying to see openings in the mangroves in the dark but neither Ed nor Holata seemed to have the same impediment. Maybe it was time to trust his boat mates.

Zander stayed quiet but kept the GPS handy, so he wouldn't lose sight of Corey's boat. There was no moon, and Zander couldn't believe how dark the night had become. There was a small stern light and the usual red/green light off the bow. How Ed could navigate without light puzzled Zander. He thought that Holata might have some kind of native sixth sense. He could see that Ed never questioned Holata's directives. These two were as comfortable with each other as an old pair of shoes. They smelled about the same. Zander smiled to himself. When you spent so much time on the water, you started to take on all its smells. It was hard for a midwestern boy to get used to all the new smells. Zander thought it might be similar for these two coming to Iowa and smelling the cattle and hog lots. It was what you got used to, he supposed.

Zander could hear sounds coming from the small mangrove islands as they passed them.

"What's with all the sounds coming from the trees?" Zander asked Ed.

"Night sounds. Everything is on the hunt. The glades are mostly nocturnal except for the birds. They get the hell out of the way at night so they don't become some other critter's meal."

"What am I hearing?"

"Gators mostly. There are snakes out there, but you never hear them coming. Quite a few mammals, including a few panthers, but they're endangered. Every year there are a few less of them. Haven't seen one for over a year. The last one I did see was squashed on the road. It looked like some truck hit it. Sad, really."

Zander didn't know if he thought it was so sad. He didn't think he would like it very much, coming face-to-face with a panther. He looked down at his GPS and noticed that Corey's stolen boat was no longer moving. He was about to point out that fact to Ed when Holata spoke.

"Stop boat."

Ed stopped the boat. Zander had no idea how Holata knew things in advance without the help of any electronics whatsoever. He had heard stories about the Native Americans as a kid growing up but never had the luxury of having any experience with them. There was something mystical about their culture, and Zander wanted to learn more about it. Maybe, after all this was over, he could learn more.

"It looks like Corey has found an island," Ed said, cutting the engine.

"What do you think he's doing?" Zander asked.

"Let's find out." Ed went to the back of the boat and messed around with what looked like battery cables.

Zander could see that an electric trolling motor had been mounted next to the boat's motor. Ed came back up and started steering the boat quietly into what looked like a small river.

"We need to be quiet now. No talking. We want to come in on stealth mode," Ed whispered.

Zander nodded in agreement. Holata said nothing but appeared to be looking at the sky and the stars.

Ed reached into his console and brought out a pair of binoculars. He handed them to Zander.

Ed whispered into his ear, "Night vision. Push the button on the top when you want to see something."

Zander decided to try them out. He had heard of these things but never had the opportunity to use a pair. He put the contraption to his eyes and pushed the button. Everything turned a light green. It took his eyes a few seconds to adjust, and then he was amazed at what he saw. There was movement all around him. He saw an alligator slither into the dark water in front of their boat. There were birds roosting in the mangroves not moving or making a sound. They passed right by three or four brown pelicans. It looked like they had their heads tucked under their wings.

Zander could not believe what he was seeing. He had been out in the everglades during the day on an airboat but never got to see anything like this. He almost forgot why they were out here in the first place.

Ed stopped the boat and moved Zander and his binoculars toward the bow. Off to the right, Zander could see light coming through the trees. Ed pulled the boat into a small passage in a group of mangroves and tied up to some overhanging branches. They would be almost invisible in this position.

Ed took the night scope from Zander's hands and looked out

toward the light. He said nothing. Zander looked at Holata. He was peering toward the light as well.

"What do you see?" Zander whispered.

"Can't be sure. Looks like he's setting up for a meeting of some kind."

Holata turned toward them. In a very low voice said," Drug runners." He turned around and continued his vigil.

"Are we safe here?" Zander asked.

"No one will try to come through this way. There's way too much stuff in the water to navigate, especially with a bigger boat. We should be safe for the time being. We just don't want to be out here when it's light."

"Can't we just go in and take him right now? He's alone and there are three of us."

"Absolutely not. If he's got a drug deal going down, we need to wait until it's over and those people are gone. They can come in with all kinds of firepower, and you just never know their strength. I avoid them like the plague. That's why I'm still alive."

Zander got the message. He was still confused, however. He didn't think Corey had much money since Zander had found his cache. He wondered how he would pull off a drug buy without the necessary cash. Then he had a thought, maybe these guys would take care of the Corey Prescott problem. It would be nice to witness something like that. Zander smiled to himself. They would wait as long as it took. These two guys were patient, and Zander was learning quite a bit from both.

Ed went to one of the coolers on the deck and took out three bottles of water. He passed two over to Zander who in turn gave one to Holata.

"I'd rather have a cup of coffee," Zander said, feeling exhaustion coming on.

"Can't do it. Can't have any smells coming from the boat. Coffee wafts all over the glades. It has a distinctive smell. It might give us away." Ed reached back into the cooler and took out some granola bars and passed them out.

"I suppose sausage and eggs are out as well," Zander whispered.

Holata shook his head in what appeared to be disgust. Zander thought he could see the corners of his mouth turn up, however. He thought it should be one of his goals to try and make this man laugh out loud. Maybe he would try, when they were finished with The Jackass.

There had been a bit of breeze, when they had been following the stolen boat. Now that they were tied up, the air was stifling. It was hard for Zander to breathe, and even worse, the mosquitoes had found them. Zander had never seen so many, and they seemed like they were totally attracted to him. Once he had gone on a fishing trip with his father to northern Minnesota, and they had encountered something similar. The resort owner called them the Minnesota state bird. They didn't even come close to these Everglade monsters.

"Ed, do you have any mosquito repellent?" Zander asked.

"Can't do it. It's got a scent, and you can smell it for miles."

Ed reached under the steering column and brought up some sheer material.

"Here, put this over your head and arms. It's mosquito netting."

Zander followed direction. The netting came to his waist and covered just about all of his exposed skin. He wondered how he looked with it over his head. It wasn't any kind of fashion show out here, but he felt foolish anyway.

"How come they're bothering me and not you?" Zander asked, indicating Holata as well.

"Well, you're fresh meat. They aren't used to you farm boys. It's like a new dish to them."

Zander just looked at Ed.

Ed laughed. "Seriously, we're used to them. I guess you build up an immunity over time."

Zander sat on the rim of the boat and thought the less he moved, the better it might be for him. They were buzzing around his ears, but at least they wouldn't be biting through the netting. The night was dragging on. Zander wanted it to be over.

He had been dozing while trying to sit up. It was quite a trick, but he managed to at least pass the time a little quicker. Suddenly, he was jolted awake to the sound of a boat engine. It was loud, and it appeared no one on board cared if anyone heard them.

The lights went off on the little island, and the boat engine stopped. It seemed quieter than it had been all night. Ed had the field glasses and was trying to make out the scene across the water.

"Can't see too well through all the mangroves, but it looks like there are at least five of them on the boat," Ed said.

"Can you see Corey?" Zander asked.

"No. He's not in the open. He must be hiding."

"Why would he do that? Isn't this his drug deal? I would think he would be down there trying to get the deal done."

Holata never turned around but pointed to the right edge of the clearing.

"Look in trees."

Ed moved the field glasses over and found the spot.

"There he is. He's got himself a stand in those pines."

"It is trap," Holata said.

It made sense. If Corey didn't have the cash and wanted the drugs, he would have to take it from them.

Ed let a little breath escape. "He's got an arsenal up there with him. This is going to be a blood bath."

"Do you think he can take all five of them?" Zander asked.

"Maybe," Ed said, not taking his eyes from the field glasses. "He's got shotguns and rifles. It looks like they have handguns. Their long guns are stored away someplace. They're not expecting trouble."

"Wait. Watch." Holata said. He appeared to be enjoying the whole scenario.

They didn't have to wait long. After the boat was beached, the three heard what sounded like some sort of birdcall, and then a few seconds later the call was answered. It must have been the cue to unload the goods.

One of the men started walking toward the little grass shack in the clearing, while the others unloaded the drugs. Ed was watching and filling in the details to the other two. Zander didn't think Holata needed the play-by-play. For some unexplained reason, Zander thought he could have told them everything that was happening.

The boat was unloaded, and the single guy was becoming

animated. He called for some of his men to join him. They all had their pistols out. Two of the men stayed with the boat. Ed wondered out loud what Corey's move would be.

"Needs the boatmen out first," Holata replied.

Zander realized he was right. If Corey wanted the drugs, he needed to be sure they would stay where they were and not be loaded back into the boat when the shooting started. The whole thing was playing out like some movie script. Zander was thankful he was in the audience and not one of the actors in this scene.

A shot rang out, and one of the men at the boat went down. Everyone froze. There was just enough time for Corey to take out the other man before everyone took cover.

"He must have a night scope on that rifle," Ed said.

"Shooting pretty good," Holata said.

They heard a number of shots from various places on the ground. It appeared the three remaining men were shooting blindly in the direction of the shots. Corey had hunkered down.

Ed was watching and saw Corey move to another tree fifty yards from where he had made his first shots. They heard one lone shot ring out and someone screamed on the ground.

"He's got a walkway up there. He might have a chance to take all these guys out. He might be smarter than I had given him credit for. Looks like he got one of them in the shoulder. He won't be much good."

"Men already dead. Just don't know it," Holata said.

Ed looked at Zander. "You know he can predict things. I don't know how he does it, but I've never known him to be wrong."

"After what I've seen tonight, I have no reason to doubt you in the least," Zander said.

Ed focused back on the trees. Corey had moved back to his original spot. He quietly climbed down from his perch and used the trees on the edge of the clearing as cover.

"He's got a shotgun. I don't see the rifle. He's moving in for the kill. It should be a real surprise to these three. They're still looking where the other shots came from."

Zander saw the muzzle of the shotgun light up at least five times. Then it was quiet.

"Everyone's down," Ed said, and lowered the field glasses. "It looks like he's reloading."

They heard three more shots, and then after a minute or two, heard two more.

"Making sure no one survives," Holata said.

"Now what?" Zander wondered.

"Won't stay here. Find other place to hole up for night. Away from here." Holata was quite sure of himself. So was Zander.

"He'll try to clean everything up fast. Just watch," Ed said, back on the night vision binoculars.

Ed gave play-by-play commentary concerning Corey's actions. He put all his weapons into the drug boat. Zander figured it wouldn't be as hot as the boat Corey had stolen earlier that night. He pulled the bodies together in the center of the clearing and poured something over them from a five-gallon can."

"Burn bodies. Drug deal gone bad." Holata said.

Suddenly the area lit up with a fireball.

"The idiot is using gas. He could have offed himself right there. Where would the fun be in that for us?" Ed asked.

Corey was running to the boat. He reached it, pushed off and fired up the engine. Soon he was backing out of the little cove carefully. He turned around, and as quickly as he dared, made his way deeper into the everglades.

"What should we do, Holata?" Ed asked.

"Bring boat back to marina. Can't be involved in this."

"Good idea. We owe the owner that much," Ed agreed.

"Wait. We need to follow him. He can't get away. You've seen how dangerous he is. We've got to take care of him." Zander was furious.

Holata got up and put his hand on Zander's shoulder.

"Holata knows where he's going. Been following him for long time. He no leave until middle of night tomorrow. We be waiting then."

After what he had seen that evening, he wasn't about to argue with the big native. He still didn't like it.

"You go visit woman tomorrow. Be back at 7:00 and we find The Jackass." Holata smiled broadly.

How the hell he knew about Aubrey was beyond Zander's comprehension. He just decided to do what he was told.

22

At 10:00, both Millie and Jayne were in the waiting room at the doctor's office. Sheila had elected to stay back at the house and get a little more pool time. Jayne didn't blame her. She knew how doctor's offices played out. They would be expected to be there at the appointed time, but then they would have to wait. It was a pattern everyone in the country had learned to expect.

At precisely 10:00, the nurse asked the pair to follow her to an exam room. Jayne knew that meant they would wait there for however long it would take to see the doctor.

Much to her surprise, the doctor was in the room waiting for them. Jayne looked over at her aunt. How much clout did this woman possess? She was more than impressive.

"Well, it's good to see you Millie. I couldn't believe you actually set up an appointment. It's been a long time coming," the doctor said.

"You know I'm as healthy as a horse, Wilma. No, this appointment is for my niece. She's in the family way." Millie said.

"Hello, my name is Carol. Happy to meet you," the doctor said to Jayne, introducing herself.

Jayne looked confused.

"She always calls me Wilma. She thinks I look like Wilma Flintstone from that cartoon show."

Jayne grinned. "You kinda do. I'm Jayne by the way."

"Well, Jayne, how can I be of service?"

"Aunt Millie thinks I need to have some doctor tell me I'm good to go."

"She's pretty good at telling people what to do, not so good at doing it herself."

"Yap, yap yap. Just do what we pay you to do." Millie said.

"Okay. Here's the deal. I'll do a work-up on Jayne here, but you'll be having your physical first. We need to make sure you're up to having a little one running around your estate," Carol said.

Millie was about to protest when Jayne spoke up.

"I think that would be an excellent idea, and there is no time like the present. I'll just step out so you have a little privacy." Jayne began to stand.

The doctor stopped her.

"There's no need for that. I've got a room all set up for Millie. I'll have a nurse come in and do your history. We'll need as much information as possible. That includes any family history that might be important with this pregnancy."

Millie and Carol left the examination room and found another across the hall.

"So, what's all this cloak-and-dagger stuff?" Carol asked.

"I needed to talk to you in private. There are things you need to know about Jayne, that I don't want her to hear just yet."

"Well, that's fine. You can tell me all about it while we're doing your physical. Put this on." Carol threw a gown at Millie.

"Damn. You're one tough character."

"I've dealt with you before. There always has to be a quid pro quo or it just turns out to be whatever Millie wants."

Millie knew she was defeated.

The visit to the doctor's office lasted a bit over an hour for both Millie and Jayne. There didn't seem to be any issues, and the doctor said she would phone with the results of the blood work on them both. For Jayne, an appointment was made for the following week. Millie told Carol that she didn't care if she ever saw her again. Carol said that was fine with her as well. Jayne could see that these two had been giving each other a hard time for a long time. It was all in good fun.

After a stop at Millie's roadhouse for lunch, the two headed for home. When they drove into the carriage house drive, Jayne noticed the rental car was gone.

"That's strange," Jayne said.

"What's that dear?"

"The car is gone. I wonder where Sheila went to?"

"She left for home today on an 11:00 flight. She had to get back home."

"Why wouldn't she tell me that?"

"I don't think she likes goodbyes, especially goodbyes to you. She thinks it's bad luck. So, maybe if she doesn't say goodbye, she'll be able to see you again. You won't turn up dead again."

Jayne looked at her aunt. There was something she wasn't telling her. Maybe it was time to hear her story.

"You know all about my story. Isn't it time I heard about yours?"

"I doubt if I know everything about you. I'm sure there are things you are not sharing, but you are right. It's time you heard from me. Let's grab something to drink and go out to the cabana. I don't want to be disturbed when I explain, and I only want to do this once."

Millie grabbed a pitcher of sweet tea, and Jayne found the glasses. Together they went out to the cabana and went inside the small house. Millie closed the door, while Jayne poured the iced tea.

"Where do you want me to start?" Millie asked.

"How about starting from the last time we visited you when we were little girls?"

Millie nodded and sat back. She took a few minutes to get things straight in her head.

"I think we need to start much earlier than that. You'll need to hear what happened to me at an earlier age. It might help to answer some questions you may have about yourself."

Jayne was puzzled but decided to let her aunt continue uninterrupted.

"When I was sixteen, your mother and father were married. Your father had come home on leave. It was a typical midwestern wedding with all the pomp and circumstance. It was nice. Your parents never took a real honeymoon, because your father had to report to Tyndall Air Force Base near Panama City. I think he was assigned to their radar control division or something like that. I never understood all that military stuff."

"I knew all that," Jayne said, hoping she would get on with her story.

"Patience, my dear. This is where the story goes off its tracks for a bit. The next year, when I was ready to go into the 11th grade, I went to a field party one summer night. I had quite a bit to drink, and I passed out. In today's world, I would imagine they would have called it rape, but back then it was my fault. I never knew who made me pregnant. It could have been any number of guys."

Jayne's eyes widened. Millie saw her reaction.

"Oh, it gets way worse than that. By the time school would have started, I was almost three months pregnant. That wasn't acceptable, by anyone's standards, back in that day."

"So what did you do?" Jayne asked.

"Nothing. It was all done for me. My parents sent me away to live with my sister and her husband in Florida. I stayed with them, until I had the baby. Then after a year, your father got relocated to another base. They invited me to go with them, but I couldn't see any future in staying with them. I needed to go off on my own, and I would never go back home again. My parents had swept me out of the door with very little regard for my future or me. I was bitter and hated them. In fact, I never talked to them again. They both died without ever knowing where I had gone. I swore your mom to secrecy on that issue."

"My God, I never knew anything about that."

"We're pretty good at keeping secrets in our family, aren't we?"

Jayne nodded, thinking of her own secrets.

"But when we came to visit you, you weren't in Panama City. I forget the name of the town," Jayne said.

"It was Lake City. I had a little two-bedroom apartment there. After drifting around a bit, I found a waitressing job at a local café there. I had no skills, no education, and life was pretty tough. Your mom came to visit and took you girls along twice. She helped me out with some cash when she could."

"Then we stopped coming to see you." Jayne reminded her.

Millie paused and looked out the window.

"Your mother and I had a falling out of sorts. It was a sad day for me. I never got to talk to her again." Millie stopped talking and took a large drink of her sweet tea.

"Mom wouldn't ever talk about you. We tried to ask about you, and she would pretend she didn't even hear us."

"I know, if it hadn't been for Sheila, I wouldn't have known what happened to the family over the years."

"Sheila called you?"

"At least twice a year. It gave me some comfort to know about the family. It was about that time that I met William. I called him Willie. William seemed too stuffy a name for a man like him. He was a few years older than me. He was good looking and full of confidence. I liked him right away. He liked me as well.

He would come into the café everyday for lunch. At that time, he was driving a logging truck for his father, but he was being groomed to take over the entire business. I didn't know anything about all that. I just thought he was worth a second look. We were dating, when you came to visit the last time."

"I don't remember any man with you. Is that why you and my mother fought?" Jayne asked.

"I suppose that was part of it. She always thought I would come back to Iowa. If I met someone down this way, the chances of that would be zero."

"What happened with you and Willie?" Jayne asked.

"He kept me a secret from his family. He knew they would never accept me as I was. Willie made me quit the café and get my G.E.D. After that I enrolled part-time at the University of Florida in Gainesville. Willie took care of all of my expenses. We would meet on the weekends."

Jayne smiled. "You were a kept woman."

There was a twinkle in Millie's eyes. "I suppose I was. But I was okay with it. I was truly in love with him. He was the first man that ever treated me with respect."

"Why did you go part-time to the university?"

"Remember the times. I had a high school equivalency. They wanted to see if I could cut the mustard before they accepted me. It was just fine with me. I wanted to start slow to make sure I could handle college."

"And did you?"

"I certainly did. The first semester I took six hours of general education requirements, and the second semester I took twelve hours."

"Let me guess, you aced everything," Jayne said.

"You got it. It turned out I was made for college. After the first year, they took me off provisional and allowed me full-time status. I went to summer school and took an average of twenty hours per semester. I was able to graduate in three years. Willie pushed me to go to graduate school, and I finished my master's during the fourth year."

"What was your major?"

"Business and finance. It turns out that I had a gift for it. Willie was pleased, and when I finished my master's degree, he took me home to meet his parents."

"And they loved you?"

"Of course they did. What was there not to love?" Millie asked, liking the joke.

"So, what did you do with all this knowledge that was bought and paid for by your benefactor?" Jayne wanted to know the answer.

"Somehow, I got a job in the bank in Perry. I'm sure the family had something to do with it. Willie's dad was on the board of directors, I found out later. I worked there for a year and got to know Willie's family. After the requisite year, we got engaged and married that same summer. I stayed working in the bank and became a vice president. I enjoyed the work, and met a lot of great people. I would have stayed until I retired, but Willie's dad decided to retire and let him run the business. Willie decided he needed me in the business office to keep an eye on the bottom line."

"How did that go over with his other siblings?" Jayne asked.

"I thought I told you, he was an only child. By this time, I had won over his parents, and I think they liked me more than their William. They were quite happy seeing me getting involved in the business."

"I guess timing is everything," Jayne said, "if you had tried to push your relationship with Willie, it never would have worked."

"I've thought about that quite a bit. Patience had never been my virtue. I was always unsettled, but William taught me to relax and let things happen as they will."

"Easier said than done, in my case at least."

Jayne was running the story through her mind. She could relate to some of the things her aunt was sharing with her.

"Nothing about my life has been easy. Don't let this rosy little story, I'm telling you, cloud the reality of it all. Things never are as bad in retrospect. You seem to forget all those things that almost did you in. It's human nature to try and remember all the good things. It's in the middle of the night, when you wake from a bad dream, that they all come rushing back."

The statement puzzled Jayne. Her aunt's life seemed almost idyllic. She wondered what she wasn't telling her.

"You said your husband got killed by a hit-and-run driver?" Sheila asked.

"Yes. It was almost too much for me. It was over ten years ago, and I remember it like it was yesterday. I went into depression, and I was skidding close to the edge."

"What brought you back?" Jayne wondered out loud.

"William's foreman, and a few of the employees, came to see one day about a month after Willie's death. I had been active in the financials but the day-to-day workings of the business had always been Willie's. I had been taking care of the estate but didn't get involved with much else. The foreman told me they were floundering. They needed direction. They all wanted me to take control and get things rolling again. It took me by surprise and served to shake me out of feeling sorry for myself. These people relied on the company for their livelihood, and if I didn't get off my big fat ass, they would all have to suffer. Either that, or I would need to sell the business. I couldn't even fathom that idea. I'm sure Willie and his parents would have come back to haunt me if I even considered such an idea."

"Did they ever find your husband's killer?" Jayne wanted to know.

"Law enforcement was never able to find the guy."

Jayne saw that there was something she wasn't saying. "Did you know who it was?"

"That was part of my discussion with the foreman. I told my employees that I would take over the business, but I needed them to find the man who killed my Willie. The foreman said they would do their best. It wasn't long before he came to me with a name. The guy was a drunk and probably drunk when he ran into Willie. Someone had noticed his vehicle had been worked on, and the front end didn't match the rest of the car.

If you wait long enough, people generally hang themselves. It was that patience quality I was talking about before. Unfortunately, at that time, I didn't possess anything close to patience."

"What did you do?" Jayne asked.

"I knew I wouldn't have the patience to turn it over to the police, so I decided to handle it myself. I followed him around at night. I found his patterns and his favorite haunts. Most everyone have habits they follow pretty much all of the time. I waited one night, about six months later, and watched him walk out of his favorite bar. He was walking, I assume, to keep his vehicle out of the public eye and also because he was too drunk to drive most nights."

Jayne assumed she knew what was coming next, but she wanted her aunt to tell her everything.

"I followed him for a few blocks. When he tried to cross the street, I ran him over. I wasn't going that fast, so he didn't die like I had hoped. What I didn't know was while I was following Willie's killer, the foreman was following me. He drove up along side of my car and got out before I could open the door. He frightened me at first. I didn't know where his loyalties started or ended."

Jayne was entirely engrossed in Aunt Millie's story. Her life hadn't been a whole different than her own.

"I forgot to tell you. The foreman's name was Hector." Millie could see the understanding light up in Jayne's eyes. "That's right, it was Hernando. He told me to go home, and he would handle everything. I tried to object, but he would have none of it. Needless to say, I was extremely disappointed. I wanted to see him die. I had already decided I would bury his body back of the little lake on the estate. As it turned out, I would have been angry to have to share that area with Willie's ashes, so everything worked out for the best, I suppose."

"Other than you didn't get your pound of flesh," Jayne said.

"Exactly. I was ready to fire Hector, and I called him into the office the next day. He fully expected to be fired, but he wanted me to know that my presence at the company was too important to be jeopardized by a murder investigation. There were too many people that relied on me. When he got up to leave, I made him sit down. It was the first time I cried since my Willie had died. I couldn't believe that someone like Hector would have that much respect, for me and the company, to try and protect my backside."

"So, you brought him into the compound, then?"

"Yes. We shared a secret. I made Hector tell me what happened. I figured that if I didn't get the satisfaction of killing the guy, at least I could get some gratification from the details. That's when I started calling him Hernando."

Jayne looked puzzled.

"You know, that song, "Hernando's Hideaway?" It seemed to fit because Hector drove him to one of our reforestation projects. He told me that section of trees would need no additional fertilizer."

"So he killed him. How?"

"With a shovel. He hit him over the head with it and then pushed the blade down until he severed the head. Hector is a strong man. The description was enough for me, and I was able to go on with my life. Of course, I was worried about how it would affect Hector. Killing a man is never as easy as it sounds."

Jayne knew that was true. She decided not to share it, however.

"So, now you know my story. Now you and your sister know the truth about Amelia DePont." Millie looked out the window.

Jayne thought for a moment.

"You never had any other children?"

Millie looked at her. "Just the one. I was too torn up inside to ever have any more. Willie knew that when he married me, and we decided to lose ourselves in the business and estate. We donated to many children's causes instead."

Jayne turned and looked right at Millie.

"You haven't told me what happened to that child you had when you lived with my parents."

Jayne could see sadness creep into Millie's eyes. She kept looking at her until finally, she spoke in a throaty voice.

"I'm looking at her."

23

Zander drove back to Sanibel as dawn was approaching. He needed to get gas and decided to stop at a Shell station on the corner of Gladiolus Drive and Summerlin Road. He went into the building, handed the clerk a hundred dollar bill and went out to fill his truck. If you didn't use a credit card in Florida, you had to prepay for your gas. The big bill would be enough, and he would go back for his change.

Just as he was ready to put the nozzle back into the pump, he could feel someone coming up on him on his right. He reached for his boot as if he was scratching an itch on his ankle. He pocketed the stun gun, so it couldn't be seen.

When he turned around, he could see it was a woman. She was dressed poorly and looked like she had a love affair with some pretty strong chemicals. Zander decided not to put the pump nozzle back, but stood looking at the woman, waiting for her to explain why she was in his space.

"Hey, mister. My husband and I are in a bind. We need to get formula for our baby, but we're broke. We had car trouble, and it took all our money. I was wondering if you might be able to help us?" The woman smiled, and Zander could see she was missing quite a few teeth.

"I'd be glad to help. There's a Wal-Mart down the street. I'll take you there and buy whatever you need," Zander said, playing along.

"Oh, that won't work. He needs a special formula that they don't sell there," the woman said, hoping Zander would take the bait.

There would be no fish caught on this expedition, however.

"Why don't you go panhandle somewhere else? I'm not buying your bullshit. I see a help wanted sign in the window over there. Why don't you go and get a real job?"

"You don't have to be such an asshole about it."

"If you've got a child on formula, then I just graduated high school." Zander was enjoying the repartee.

Suddenly, a man lurking behind the other set of pumps, came striding over and pulled the woman out of the way. He pulled his shirt aside and showed Zander a pistol hidden in his waistband.

"If you don't want any of this, you'd better give me your wallet, and you'd better do it now."

Zander was beginning to tire of the annoyance.

"How about I give you some of this." Zander raised the gas nozzle and pulled back on the lever. He figured he had run about 75 cents worth all over the pistol packer.

The guy sputtered and coughed, as the gasoline ran down his face and soaked his clothing. He pulled out the gun and aimed at Zander.

"I'm going to shoot you. You miserable sonofabitch."

Zander quietly hung the nozzle back into the pump and turned to face him.

"I'd be real careful if I were you. The muzzle flash from that gun will pretty much set you and everything else on fire."

Zander could see the confusion flash into his face. The woman was already running toward the street. Zander reached into his pocket and pulled out "old sparky."

"Maybe you'd like me to do the honors." Zander hit the switch. The guy's eyes got wide, as he watched the sparks arc from pole to pole.

He backed up into the steel pole that kept people from running into the gas pumps. He fell to one knee and dropped his pistol. He was about to pick it up, when Zander stepped forward and hit the stun gun once more.

The panhandler took off for the street, following the woman who had fled a few moments before. Zander picked up the gun and threw it into the pickup. He went back into the convenience store for his change.

The cashier was smiling. He had been watching the whole thing.

"Here's your change, dude. That was awesome. These two have been working the area for a while."

"Tell the Fort Myers Police Department." Zander said.

"We do, but these two seem to know when to leave and get out of the area. When the shit storm dies down, they show back up."

"Call them, and tell them to look for a guy who smells like a gas tank."

"Already have. What's even better, they left their car here. They never did that before. I hope the cops get here before they get back."

"Where's this car?" Zander asked.

The clerk pointed to a rust-bucket not far from Zander's pickup. Zander said nothing and went out to the vehicle. He took his switchblade from his boot while replacing the stun gun in the other. He plunged his knife into the front two tires. Two would be enough to keep the car where the cops could find it. Then, Zander decided that if two tires were good, four tires would be better. Before he drove off, the car was sitting on all four rims.

He drove past the front door of the store, and the clerk gave him thumbs up. Zander apparently had made his day.

He had wasted more time than he had planned. He wanted to get to Aubrey's cabin before she woke up. He wanted to spend most of the day in bed with her.

As he crossed the causeway, he reached over to the passenger's seat where he had placed the pistol. He put it in his left hand. As he crossed the second bridge, Zander made a terrific hook shot over the pickup. The gun splashed into the ocean and disappeared. He enjoyed getting rid of firearms. Pistols were for killing people. The NRA was always preaching about gun rights, but Zander couldn't fathom how pistols fit into any hunting trip. Hunters wouldn't own a pistol.

He drove into the parking spot next to the cabin, bounced up the stairs and knocked on the door. There was no answer. Zander wondered if Aubrey was still sleeping. He knocked louder. There was a voice behind him.

"You don't have to knock the door down."

Zander turned around. Aubrey threw her arms around him, and she hugged him tightly. She was dressed in some kind of spandex, and she had just come from a run on the beach.

"You're getting up early I see," Zander said.

"I'm into a routine, and here you come and spoil it." She smiled.

"Sorry. I had today with nothing to do, so I thought I'd just waste it with you."

"That's what I am to you? Wasted days and wasted nights?"

"The nights aren't wasted," Zander said, playing along.

"Well, I'm glad to see you, anyway. I've got to shower, and then let's go to breakfast at the Over Easy."

"I've got to shower too," Zander said.

"I'll be quick," Aubrey said. Disappointment crept into Zander's face.

"Oh you big jerk. Come on in, and join me."

Zander was undressed before he even made the bathroom. He was running the shower, as Aubrey took off her running gear.

The shower was small, and it would be crowded with both of them in it, which was just the way Zander liked it. Going out for breakfast had destroyed his vision of them spending the entire day in bed, so he had to make up for it somewhere. The shower was as good a place as any.

Aubrey had some sweet smelling bath gel that made more suds than a bubble bath. They were both covered in a matter of seconds. Zander found it strangely provocative.

Zander's 6'7" height was no match for Aubrey in a shower. He picked her up by placing his arms under her seductive little butt and hoisted her up. Her back was against the shower wall, and they both hoped it would hold their combined weight.

When they finished, they both tried to wash all the soap off their bodies without much luck. They toweled off, and the bubbles spread across the bathroom floor.

Zander had experienced his share of sex over the years, but nothing matched his experience with Aubrey. It wasn't just sex, it was much more. He was sharing himself with someone. He didn't want to think about the word love. Somehow, he thought it would jinx the whole thing.

Aubrey looked fabulous in her sheer robe and a large towel wrapped around her head.

"It's going to take me a half day to get the bathroom back to being presentable." Aubrey tried to sound perturbed.

"What else do you have to do, anyway? Sit on the beach and read romance novels?"

"Oh, you know I hate that shit. After breakfast, I'll show you what I've been doing."

Zander could see that his hopes of being bedridden were dashed again. He decided to get dressed in the bedroom and let Aubrey have the bathroom. She could do whatever it took to get ready to be presentable in public. He was always happy that men didn't have the same stringent standards that women put on themselves.

Zander went out to the enclosed porch and looked out over the ocean. The seas were a bit angry. Maybe a storm was brewing in the middle of the gulf someplace. He hoped it wouldn't affect his plans for the evening in the Everglades.

Aubrey emerged dressed in a pair of white shorts that allowed everyone to see the bottoms of her cute little butt cheeks. She had on a little black low-cut sleeveless shell top. Zander could see her navel as she walked into the porch.

"How the hell am I supposed to go anywhere with you dressed like that?" Zander asked.

"Oh, keep it in your pants."

"And that would be the problem," Zander said.

"Just whack it on the doorknob a few times before we leave. I could always find a stick and take care of that for you, when things come up." Aubrey was enjoying this more than Zander would have liked.

"You make it hard for a guy," Zander said, fully aware of the double entendre.

"There will be plenty of time for this later." Aubrey was enjoying being the tease.

Zander stood and embraced her. "Maybe not as much as you think. I've got to be back by 7:00 this evening. Things are going down fast, and if we are planning to take care of The Jackass. It will need to be tonight."

Aubrey pulled away. "I don't like this one bit."

"Well, you're not the only one. I feel like I've lost control over the whole situation, and I'm just along for the ride. I'm not comfortable with it at all."

Aubrey looked at him. She liked the fact that this wasn't to be Zander's responsibility. She knew Corey, and she also knew how dangerous a man he really was.

"So, you're not the only one involved in this. Tell me who else is involved."

"Well, the Ed guy with the airboat and some Native American named Holata. I can't get a read on him. He seems to have some kind of sixth sense. He doesn't talk much. Ed seems to put a lot of stock in him.

Aubrey tried to hide a smile, but Zander caught a bit of it.

"You are in good hands," she said, and turned away hiding a bigger smile. "Let's go to breakfast."

They left the cabin and walked toward the pickup. Just as Zander was about to open his door, he noticed Aubrey walking toward the street.

"Hey, where are you going? Our ride is here." He pointed to the pickup.

"This is what I did here while you were gone playing cops and robbers. I do everything by bicycle, so that's what you will do also. Pick out a bike and let's go. You got money?"

Zander wasn't at all excited about spending much time on a bike. He hadn't ridden a bicycle, since he was a kid. After spending some time trying to pick out something that would be close to fitting him, they took off.

Zander knew he looked dopey trying to find his rhythm on the two-wheeled beast. That was one of the reasons he didn't continue to ride bicycles after he grew in high school. He always felt awkward, and his friends reminded him of the fact constantly.

He had raised the seat as far as he could, and he peddled with his knees out to the sides hoping to avoid hitting them on the handlebar. Whoever said that you never forget how to ride a bike didn't have Zander in mind. He was wobbling all over, and if they met anyone on the bike path, he would stop and pull over, much to Aubrey's disapproval.

"Buck it up, mister. If we don't get cracking we'll miss breakfast."

"Just remember, this was your idea. I'm not liking anything about it."

"Stop being a big baby, and ride the thing like you own it."

Zander listened to Aubrey. By the time they reached Tarpon Bay Road, he had things well in hand. At least he didn't have to stop for other riders any longer. He pushed hard and reached the Over Easy Café a few minutes before Aubrey. His speedy arrival was due because of Aubrey's constant barrage of criticism.

Breakfast was good, and Zander had found a local paper called the Sun-Times. He looked at all the local happenings and the pictures of people who found rare shells. He showed a few to Aubrey.

"Have you found any like this?"

She looked at the pictures. "I found an Alphabet Cone, but I've never even seen that Junonia character."

"Looks like you have some work to do," Zander said, and resumed looking at the paper.

"Are you finished with breakfast?" Aubrey appeared restless.

"What's the hurry? Let me enjoy the last of my coffee."

"If we don't stop wasting time, you won't be able to see everything I've been doing."

Zander didn't care but decided not to convey that message to Aubrey.

"Okay, I'm all yours. Let's move," Zander said, hoping the quicker they did what she wanted, the quicker he would get what he wanted.

He would be wrong.

They rode all the way to Captiva and had an early lunch at The Mucky Duck. On the way back, they rode through the Ding Darling National Park. Zander was interested because he remembered Ding Darling used to have his political cartoons printed in the *Des Moines Register*. They were hard to miss because they were on the front page. He hadn't realized the guy had been into preservation of wildlife and natural resources. He wasn't ready to move on, but Aubrey had already explored the area and wanted to show him more.

The next stop was the Shell Museum. It was where Aubrey got her idea for her own collection. It was interesting, even to Zander. When they left the museum, Zander checked his watch.

"I think we should head back. I've got to be back to the marina before 7:00."

Aubrey was disappointed. She had just begun to show him the island. There was so much more to see.

"Well, you've got to eat before you go. Let's go to the Timbers. They open at 4:00 for happy hour. They've got some of the best oysters on the island. We should be right on time."

"I suppose there would be enough time for a drink and some appetizers."

"They've got three kinds of baked oysters, and we will try all three."

Zander groaned. "Just what I need, an aphrodisiac, right before I have to leave you."

"You need all the help you can get. Maybe it have some residual effect for the next time." Aubrey pedaled off.

Zander could do nothing but follow. His plans for the day had turned to nothing. Surprisingly, he wasn't all that disappointed. Being with Aubrey was enough. It made him smile as he wobbled off.

24

Jayne's head was spinning. It wasn't often she was so blindsided. She tried to think back to try and remember any clues that she might have missed. She couldn't think of anything. Her family had always been tight-lipped. But they hadn't been her family at all. For all intents and purpose, she was just an adopted child. It took her some time to wrap her head around that fact.

Millie watched her, trying to let her process what she had just revealed. She could tell that it took Jayne by total surprise.

Jayne looked at her aunt. "I've got a lot of questions."

Millie nodded, knowing full well it would take a great deal of time to work through all this new information.

"Did you give me the Sara Jane name?"

"No. That was your mother." Millie stopped.

"She wasn't my mother," Jayne said. There was a nasty sound to her voice.

"Of course she was your mother. I gave birth to you, but it was my sister who raised and loved you. If you're to be angry at anyone, you should be angry with me."

"Oh, I am. Make no mistake about that."

"I don't blame you. However, I did what I thought would be the best for you. I was in no position to raise a child on my own. I hardly had enough strength to keep myself going."

"You were just angry because of what happened to you. I would be a reminder of that every day. You didn't want me."

"No, that's not true. Oh, I was angry at first, but I came to realize that I had to take responsibility for my own actions as well. Don't get me wrong, what those boys did to me was terrible. They should have had to pay for it. But the times were different back then. I had no business being at that field party. I shouldn't have been drinking all that alcohol. So, in many ways, I was as much to blame as anyone. Who would I blame anyway? It wasn't a spin the bottle game, now was it? Once I got past all that stuff, I had to decide what to do about you."

"It was pretty easy palming me off to your sister."

"Jayne, it was the hardest thing I had ever done. It still is the thing that haunts me most everyday. It is the greatest regret in my entire life."

Jayne looked at her aunt. She could see she was being honest with her. It didn't change what she was feeling at the moment, however.

"I need to think about all of this," Jayne said, more to herself.

"Take a walk in the garden," Millie said, getting up to leave the room.

"One question. Were you ever planning to tell me all this, or was this just some accident as well?"

"Why do you think you are here in the first place? Sheila and I have been communicating constantly lately, and I couldn't tell you anything until my sister was gone. It wouldn't have been fair to her."

"Fair to her? What about me?"

"Go take your walk." Millie left the room.

Jayne huffed out the front door and turned right toward the garden path. She had a lot to consider.

Millie watched from the window in her bedroom. The whole scene was about what she had expected. She had a rueful smile. It might have been too much information all at one time, but she was confident that Jayne was strong and would make the best decision. What that might be, even eluded Millie at the moment.

Jayne walked on the path toward the bench. Her mind was racing with everything she had just learned. How could she have been so blind? She was usually more intuitive. In fact, she prided herself in it. She had escaped many tight spots, because she could read into almost every situation. She had always felt there was something missing in her family life, but it had been too elusive.

She got to the bench and fell on it. Her head hurt. She wasn't paying any attention to the alluring aesthetics of the garden. She was in a bind, and she knew it. She wanted to be angry, but she also knew that her options were very limited. Her pragmatic side kicked in. She needed Millie's resources. She had also needed Martin Van Vugt, until she didn't. She could play that same game with her aunt. It wouldn't have to be forever. She would persevere.

Something was tugging at her chest, however. She didn't know what it was. She had never experienced anything like it before. Some may have called it a conscience, but Jayne didn't have one.

Millie watched from her window. She thought she noticed a calmness creep over Jayne, as she sat on the bench. Maybe a decision had been made. It was hard to tell from this distance. Millie watched her for a few more minutes and decided to take some of the situation in her own hands.

She walked over to the phone and dialed Sheila's number. She waited while it rang a few times. Sheila answered.

"Aunt Millie, is everything okay?" She sounded nervous. "How are you and Jayne getting along?"

"It remains to be seen. I told her the whole story a few minutes ago. She is in the garden weighing her options right now."

"So, she didn't take the news very well?"

"About like I expected. It's a lot to take in all at once."

"She'll come around once she figures everything out. She's a survivor, and I would think she knows her options are pretty scarce."

"I hope her decision employs more than just her lack of options."

"You'll have to work on that yourself. She needs family, and I can't be there for her. You are all she's got."

"I'll give it my best. By the way, you mentioned that boy she used to like back when she was a girl. What was his name again?"

Sheila's warning siren went off in her head.

"Why? What are you thinking?"

"He's the father, I believe you told me. I should know as much about Jayne as I can. I've missed so much, and I just want to be totally immersed in her life from here on out."

Sheila wasn't buying it.

"That's something you should talk to Jayne about."

"I tried, but she's not willing to give me anything." Millie knew it was a lie, but she wanted to have all the options at her disposal.

Sheila was quiet for a moment.

"His name is Sander Van Zee but he goes by Zander. Jayne hurt him really bad, and I don't think he wants anything to do with her anymore."

"Does he know he's going to be a father?"

"I doubt it very much."

"Don't you think he should be told? He has a stake in this whether he likes it or not." Millie knew it sounded a bit hypocritical coming from her mouth. "Don't say anything. I know I'm the last one that should be talking about this topic, but there should be other options available if this doesn't go like we planned."

"Okay. I'll give you the number to his answering service, but you have to promise that you won't call it unless you have no other choice."

"Done." Millie took down the number. "Doesn't he have a telephone?"

Sheila laughed. "I can see you've never met Zander. He's rather headstrong. Not at all unlike you and your daughter. He doesn't believe in cell phones, and he doesn't stay in one place long enough to even consider a landline. I don't think he would have one anyway."

"Good God. What kind of child can come from all this family history?"

"Remember what I told you. Don't involve him unless there is no other choice. If it comes to that, call me first," Sheila said.

"Of course." Millie said, but she already knew her decision wouldn't involve Sheila.

Millie watched Jayne from the window and saw that she was making her way back to the house.

"I've got to go. Jayne is returning to the house."

"Okay. Let me know what happens."

Millie hung up the phone and walked to the kitchen. She told the cook to make some coffee and bring it to the pool house. She moved to the pool area and placed some chairs facing each other. They weren't lounge chairs. This conversation would need them both sitting upright and looking at each other.

Jayne reached the house and looked around for Millie.

"Aunt Millie? Where are you?" Her tone was softer now.

The cook stuck her head out of the kitchen door.

"She's at the pool house. I'm making you coffee. Would you like something to eat with it?"

"That would be nice. How about a ham sandwich with pickles and mustard? Oh, and maybe some horseradish, if you have it."

The cook smiled and ducked back into the kitchen. Millie had already told her Jayne was pregnant, so the sandwich request was no surprise. She had wanted to ask her if she wanted some chocolate ice cream on it as well. But it wasn't her place to make jokes, so she kept her mouth shut.

Jayne made her way to the pool area. She saw Millie reading some novel she had purchased when they were in town together.

Millie saw Jayne and motioned to join her. She placed a bookmark in her book and dropped it on the table. Jayne quickened her pace.

"I want to apologize for my behavior."

"Nonsense. You received a pretty large blow back there. I don't know how I would have reacted. It probably would have been much worse. Let's not speak of it again."

"But I do want to talk to you about us."

"Well, of course you do. I'll be right here for you, and I will answer truthfully about anything you ask me." Millie knew that was a lie, but it sounded good at the moment.

Jayne seemed to relax, and she took the chair across from Millie. Her mind was still spinning, and she didn't know where to start.

"What's on your mind, dear?" Millie was showing all kinds of patience, because she knew that's what Jayne needed at the moment. There would be time for the hard sell later.

"I don't know where to start."

"I understand. There will be time for that later."

Jayne looked up.

"Does that mean you still want me to stay around? The way I reacted, I expected you would want me to leave."

Millie looked at her for an uncomfortably long time.

"You are my daughter. I didn't do right by you for so many years. I think it's high time to do the right thing now. I don't want you or the baby to leave, ever. This is your home now."

Jayne smiled, fell to her knees and buried her head in Millie's lap. Millie stroked her blonde hair. It was something she had missed for so many years.

"I'm so sorry for the pain that I've given you," Millie said.

"I've been thinking about that for the last hour, and I realized that my childhood was a good one. Your sister loved me, and she was the only mother I knew. I'm sorry that I wasn't as good a daughter to her as I could have been."

"I think it was very difficult for her to share you with me. She always thought I would swoop in someday and just take you away."

"That's why you two were estranged, I assume."

"That's exactly right. When she thought you were dead, she contacted me again. She thought she had failed as your mother. I don't think she was ever the same again. She even asked for my forgiveness."

"Did you give it to her?"

"I had no business wanting her to apologize to me. She was everything to you that I wasn't."

"I hurt her badly, didn't I?"

"You were young and impetuous. There was a lot of blame to go around in our family, so I guess we all had a stake in it. Like mother like daughter, I'm told."

Jayne lifted her head and threw her arms around Millie.

"If you still want me, I want to stay with you."

"Of course I want you. It will take some time to get to know each other, but I think you'll find that in the end we are kindred spirits." Millie looked out over the pool.

"Thank you. We will raise this child together and make her the best person ever." Jayne looked past Millie at the pool house.

Perhaps they both should have had their fingers crossed behind their backs, while they were playing out their little dramas. Apples and trees they say.

25

Neither, Zander nor Aubrey, had noticed the guy on the motorcycle. It was a nice day, and there were quite a few of them on the island, so this one didn't stand out. Aubrey was intent on showing Zander what she had been doing, and Zander was once again thinking with his little head and not concentrating on much else. It didn't leave much time for keeping an eye on the surroundings. Besides, neither were worried that Corey would be able to find Aubrey.

The man on the cycle was one of Corey's friends. His name was Ignacio. Ignacio had been in business with Corey until he got sent to prison. Then he went from restaurant to restaurant pretending to be a waiter. In reality, he was just there to steal the information off the patrons' credit cards. He would then sell the information to someone, who would use it to steal the identity, and gain cash or goods from businesses half a continent away. He was good at it, but from time to time, Ignacio would get caught and fired. Then he would move on to the next job.

He had been working at the Mucky Duck when Aubrey and Zander showed up. He recognized Aubrey. During his break, he made a call to Corey's cell phone. They hadn't talked recently. Ignacio thought it best to keep his distance for a while, but this could be some profitable information.

Corey picked up on the first ring.

"Ignacio. I haven't heard from you for some time. What's the reason for the call?" Corey was suspicious. He had never trusted Ignacio, because he was driven by money. He had no idea what the word loyalty meant. Corey believed he would sell out to anyone for a buck.

"I may have some information that might interest you."

"What would that be?"

"I've seen Aubrey, and she's with some dude."

Corey was indeed interested.

"Where?"

"Not so fast, my friend. What is this information worth to you?"

"If it's legit, it might be worth a great deal."

"How much?"

"I don't know, a couple hundred."

"I want a thousand."

Corey didn't like to be held hostage especially by this turncoat. He would be cautious, however. He wanted the information.

"Done. Where is she?"

"She's having lunch at the Mucky Duck with her new lover." Ignacio couldn't help turning the knife a bit.

"Is he a big guy?"

"Tall dude."

Corey thought for a few minutes without saying anything.

"Hey, are you there?" Ignacio asked.

"Yeah. I'm thinking about how I'm going to get to her. I think I may need your help."

Ignacio could feel a new total coming soon.

"I could help, but it's going to cost more."

"Naturally. I wouldn't expect you get involved without being reimbursed."

"What did you have in mind, my friend?"

Corey didn't like his tone of voice, but he chose to ignore it for the time being.

"I'm tied up at the moment and won't be able to move before dark."

"Okay. What do you want me to do?"

"Follow them, but don't let them know it. I want you find where she's staying, and then call me back. I'll let you know what you are to do at that time."

Ignacio was sensing this would involve more than he was originally considering.

"I don't know. This sounds risky."

"How does five grand sound?"

"You've got your man." Ignacio said. There wasn't much he wouldn't do for cash.

"I'll be waiting for your call." Corey hung up.

Ignacio went to the boss and told him he needed the day off. The boss agreed after he fired him on the spot. Ignacio didn't care. The five grand was more than he could scam off the cards in two months, if he was extremely lucky. Besides, all up and down the coast, they needed servers in all kinds of restaurants. Another job would be easy enough to get. He could use the five thousand, and it would get him through a few months of high living.

Ignacio was a patient man. He wanted to follow them into the Timbers and grab a beer, but he thought it might not be a very good idea. Aubrey could easily recognize him. He wasn't concerned when riding his cycle. He always wore a helmet, and no one could recognize anyone through those things.

He followed the couple all over the island, and when they went back to the cabin, he called Corey.

"They are in a resort called Mitchell's Sand Castle Resort."

"What kind of place is it?"

"Looks nice. A bunch of cabins right off the gulf."

"Do you know what cabin she's in?"

"I'm looking at it as we speak."

Just then, Zander exited the cabin and walked over to his pickup.

"Wait, the dude looks like he's leaving," Ignacio said.

"Follow him. Let me know what happens."

Ignacio would follow instructions. He shadowed Zander's pickup until he crossed the last bridge just before the toll. Ignacio took the exit that led under the bridge and back to Sanibel Island. He pulled onto some parking a little later and called Corey.

"He left the island."

Corey was puzzled but didn't have time to figure out what was happening.

"I want you to go back to the cabin. Get Aubrey and meet me at the fishing pier in an hour."

"Hey, how am I supposed to do that? I'm driving my cycle."

"That's your problem. I'm paying you for a service. How you get that service completed for me will dictate what you are worth."

Ignacio didn't like the comment but kept his mouth shut. He never trusted Corey, and now he knew he would have to tread lightly. For a moment he thought about walking away, but the money was just too big of a carrot.

"I'll be there in a hour."

"Don't be late."

"You either." Ignacio hung up.

His mind was already turning over. The cycle was out. He couldn't transport anyone against their will on that. He had a friend working at the Lazy Flamingo not far from the causeway. The guy had a pickup, and maybe he could talk him into borrowing it for a few hours.

Ignacio made his way to the pub and parked the cycle in the back next to his friend's pickup. He made up a good story about having to move his things to another apartment. The pickup owner was hesitant, but when Ignacio handed him his cycle key he folded. Ignacio promised to have the truck back in less than two hours. He had an hour to go across the island to the cabin, pick up the girl and then make his way to the south part of the island near the lighthouse. It would be close.

~

Corey climbed into the stolen boat. He had stashed the boxes containing the drugs into the little shack. He hated to leave all his potential wealth behind, but he couldn't risk getting caught with the drugs on the boat. There was too much to go wrong up at Sanibel. There were just too many people around, and that meant there was too much law enforcement on the water.

It wasn't as dark as he had wished, but he needed to take the risk to make sure he would be at the fishing pier in an hour. If he poured the coals to the big boat, it would be enough time. He was hoping no one was skulking around looking for him and the boat. That just wouldn't do. He put a rifle and a handgun on the seat behind him. He reversed the engines and pulled away from the shore. He would need to be careful until he was in deeper water.

~

Zander made it back to the marina with fifteen minutes to spare. It was a dark night. Thick clouds obscured the moon, and Ed was concerned about a storm. Holata told him the storm wouldn't arrive until their mission was completed. Zander wondered what they were planning but decided to keep his mouth shut. He was just along for the ride, to satisfy his own curiosity and to be able to tell Aubrey what happened.

At 7:00 they headed out. The boat had been loaded with what Ed and Holata decided they needed. Zander looked around and checked the gear on the deck. There were two rifles and a few handguns. Zander also saw a rope, duct tape, and some flashlights and two lanterns. His attention was drawn to the night vision goggles. There were three pairs, and they were different from the field glasses he had used before. He picked up one set and tried them on. Ed walked him through the directions, and soon he was seeing things that would have been unrecognizable with the simple human eye. Zander was unnerved at all the creatures that owned the night.

They rode the rest of the way to the mangrove island in silence. The motor hardly made a sound, and they crept along without disturbing anything. When they reached their hiding spot, the three put on their night vision goggles.

"Zander whispered, "The boat's gone."

"No shit," Holata said, "this one not slow."

Zander felt stupid about stating the obvious.

"Looks like he's cleaned up the mess with all the bodies. I don't see anything," Ed said, looking through the night goggles.

"Covered area with shells," Holata answered.

"Now, what?" he asked.

"Wait," Holata said. He went to the bow and sat cross-legged.

"What if he doesn't come back?" Zander asked Ed.

"He will. He feels safe here. He doesn't have many options. He'll be back long before dawn. Remember, someone will be looking for the boat. He won't risk being caught in daylight."

"I wonder what he thought when he saw the boat from the marina was gone? Maybe that spooked him and he left," Zander said, somewhat worried.

Holata laughed.

"Any boat left out here overnight would be stolen." Ed answered.

"What do you think he's up to?"

"He's pretty stupid, so it could be almost anything. I think he's still trying to make some kind of final big score," Ed said and threw some netting to Zander.

"Still can't use repellent?" Zander asked.

"No. The rules haven't changed. Put it over you. If the mosquitoes don't get you, the no-see-ums will, unless you don't care."

Zander pulled the fabric over himself as completely as possible. He noticed Holata wasn't using any of the netting.

"Why doesn't Holata cover up?"

"The damn things don't seem to bother him. I just can't figure it. Maybe he's immune."

"Maybe he's just so nasty, that they don't like the taste," Zander said.

"Heard you," Holata said.

Ed just laughed.

"Do we keep watch?" Zander asked.

"No. Just get some shut-eye. Holata will let us know if anything happens."

Zander shook his head. "Is he some kind of shaman?"

"Something like that," Ed said, taking a seat behind the boat's wheel.

Zander sat on a cushion in front of the big outboard. He hoped it wouldn't be a long night.

~

Ignacio drove the pickup to the Sand Castles and parked in the same spot Zander had used earlier. He got out of the truck and looked around. The direct approach was always the best. He didn't have time for anything else anyway.

Ignacio climbed the deck steps. The screen door opened and out popped Aubrey.

"You're back. I knew you couldn't live without me for such a long time." When Ignacio came into the light, she stopped. "Who are you?"

About the same time she recognized Ignacio, he rushed her and cracked her on the side of the head with a right cross. Aubrey's eyes rolled up into her head, before she hit the floor, Ignacio caught her. He hadn't meant to hit her quite so hard. He couldn't worry about that now. He needed her incapacitated for transport to the meeting spot with Corey. He didn't have time for second-guessing of any kind.

Ignacio picked her up, threw her over his shoulder and brought her to the pickup. He thought about throwing her in the bed in the back but didn't want to take the risk of her regaining consciousness and escaping. Corey wouldn't like that, and he had no desire to make him angry.

Ignacio placed Aubrey in the passenger seat and pulled the seat belt around her. He paused for a brief second and looked at her. She was truly a beauty. If he had more time, he might have wanted to explore her assets further. It wouldn't have mattered much to him if she were unconscious when he did it.

As it was, he felt both breasts carefully. He liked what he felt. Such a pity it would end with just that.

He drove toward the fishing pier. He found a parking space close enough, so he could see any approaching boats without having to leave the pickup. There was no one else in the parking lot at the time. The beach goers had left for the day. There would be a few more hours before the night shellers came out with their helmet lights looking for their special shells.

Ignacio undid the seat beats and then pulled Aubrey close. If anyone approached, it would look like the two were parking. He took the opportunity to explore more of Audrey's body, and he liked what he was feeling.

He was disappointed to see a boat approaching the fishing pier just as he was in full arousal. Lucky it was dark. Corey wouldn't have wanted to see his pants bulging. It wouldn't be a good thing at all.

He pulled Aubrey out of the truck, and threw her over his shoulder once again. He walked out onto the pier. Aubrey was moaning just a little. It appeared she was coming around. He wanted to get rid of her, get his money and get away from here as soon as possible.

Corey was tying up to the pier on the right side, and as Ignacio approached, he startled. There was a guy fishing of the end of the pier. He hadn't seen him because he was sitting down.

Ignacio motioned toward the fisherman, when he and Corey were close enough to see each other.

Playing a scene, Corey said, "There she is, drunk again. Thanks for looking out for my sister."

"Just a few too many tequilas," Ignacio laughed.

Aubrey moaned again.

"Hey, what's going on over there?"

"Just a little too much to drink," Corey said, as friendly as he could.

"You'll never get away with this," Aubrey said thickly, as she was coming out of her stupor.

"She doesn't sound drunk to me," the fisherman said, and stood.

Corey could never understand why some people had to inject themselves into other people's business when it was no concern of theirs. It pissed him off. He jumped out of the boat and crossed over to the front of the pier. He reached into his waistband and pulled out his pistol and hit the fisherman hard over left side of his head. The guy went down instantly. Corey kicked him off the side of the pier and heard him splash into the water. It was time to leave.

He jumped back into the boat. "Hand her down to me. Go easy. What the hell did you do to her?"

"She needed to be subdued. I hit her."

"Pretty hard the way it looks."

"She needed to be subdued," Ignacio repeated.

When Corey placed Aubrey on the deck, she turned and threw up all over his shoes.

Corey reached up, grabbed Ignacio's shirt and pulled him into the boat. It was almost a four-foot drop and Ignacio hit hard on the deck with both knees. He cried out in pain.

"Damn it, Corey. Why did you have to do that?"

"You hurt her bad. She might have a concussion. I didn't tell you to do that."

"You didn't tell me not to, either. I did what it took. Give me what you owe me for this job, and I'll be gone."

Corey reached back into his back pocket. Ignacio assumed he was reaching for his wallet. He was rubbing both knees.

It wasn't Corey's wallet that he saw. It was Corey's pistol, and it was the last thing Ignacio would ever see.

26

Corey untied the boat and pushed off. He bound Aubrey's hands behind her back with the bow rope. He wrapped some fishing line around her legs tightly and tied it off. If she tried to move her legs too much, the line would cut into her. He liked that idea. He pushed her into the front cabin of the boat. She would be bounced around like a rag doll when he opened up the motor and hit the waves. Aubrey said nothing. She just looked at him. Corey thought she was out of it.

Corey decided not to make a lot of noise, just in case. No sense drawing any more attention. He wasn't thinking about the noise of the gunshot. In fact, he wasn't thinking at all. He was functioning by rote. There wasn't any reason or planning. Corey merely wanted revenge, and that emotion had taken complete control.

When he was far enough away from Sanibel, he opened up the cruiser. The air felt good on his face. He had been sweating, and his face glistened in the lights of the dash. A huge smile crept onto his face. This was going to turn out just fine.

Somewhere off Marco Island, Corey cut the power and got down from the bridge. He found Ignacio's body where he had left it. It had been a close shot to the head. It was quick and economical. He hadn't imagined there would be so much blood, but it would wash away. He smiled as he hoisted the body over the side of the boat and heard the splash.

"Fish food," he said to himself.

~

The trio was staking out the small shell island. Zander thought they made an interesting mix of humanity. All things being normal, they would never have crossed paths. This was far from normal, however. Zander was thankful for the netting. He could hear the constant high whine of mosquitoes trying to get through and suck his blood. It made him shudder.

He never liked mosquitoes. When he went fishing with his father and some relatives in Minnesota as a youngster, he found that for some reason, they liked his blood. He was always the first person to experience the bites and welts before everyone else. When he would return home, he would always be swollen, and his face would puff up. It was just some allergy, but he blamed it on the mosquitoes. It explained why he didn't like fishing. In truth, he hated the sport. He would have died digging the Panama Canal. He was certain of it.

"You'd better try to get some sleep," Ed whispered. "It will be a long night."

"What if he sneaks in and we're all sleeping?"

Ed motioned toward Holata.

"No worries. He's got us covered."

Ed stretched out on his seat behind the wheel and settled down. Zander decided to follow his lead but whispered to Holata first.

"Holata, do you need anything?"

"Quiet," was all he said.

Zander decided it was best not to pursue the rebuke. He turned on his back and stared at the sky. The clouds were beginning to break up, and he could see patches of stars. Zander always felt bad for the city dwellers. Growing up in a small town, and later living in the Colorado Mountains, he had always been able to see the night sky. When competing with city lights, they became invisible.

Since he had been in Florida, he noticed the sky looked different from that of the center of the country. He had a hard time identifying the constellations, because they weren't where he expected them to be. He thought that it would be a good thing to keep his mind occupied, as he lay in waiting for The Jackass. It didn't work out.

There were still too many clouds blocking the full view of the night sky.

At some time, while Zander was trying to spot the Big Dipper, so he could identify the North Star, he fell asleep.

~

Aubrey lay silently in the cabin of the cruiser, while Corey was on the bridge. Her face showed no emotion. Her goal was to appear comatose. She thought she had been doing a good job. Her act had fooled Ignacio. She had almost lost her composure, when he started touching and groping her body. She kept telling herself that she had worse, and it helped her to remain calm. Being with Corey near the end, had been much worse. Most people would have called it rape. Corey would have sex with her whenever he wanted. She had no say in the matter. When he was caught and went to prison, it was a liberation of sorts for Aubrey.

She never expected to be back in his grasp. Yet, here she was. Her mind was scrambling to come up with a plan. She was having some trouble focusing, however. The right cross to the side of her face had created a light concussion. She knew that's why she had gotten sick. It was easier to fake her near-unconscious state because of it. She knew she had to try and focus. She was in trouble, and she feared for her life.

Aubrey knew she had screwed up. She let her guard down. She had no business riding all over Sanibel like that. Corey had friends everywhere. She should have been content to stay back at the cottage. Instead she paraded around like a spaced-out schoolgirl.

"What's done is done," Audrey whispered her father's often-repeated maxim.

The past was the past. No sense blaming yourself for something you no longer controlled. Put your energy into the present. That way, there might be a future.

Aubrey began working on the rope that held her arms behind her back. She had tried to break the fishing line by putting her knees together and moving her ankles outward. All it did was cut into her flesh. She gave that up.

Tin Roof Rusted

The rope around her wrists was a little loose at the knot. It was awkward trying to move her arms when they were behind her back, but she had no choice. Her shoulder joints hurt tremendously, and every time she tried to move her wrists, pain shot down her arms.

The cruiser had been moving through the night water for fifteen minutes. Aubrey figured they were headed back for Everglade City area. It was the area Corey knew best, and he would be comfortable returning there. She hoped that Zander and his friends had a plan that would take care of things, before it would be too late for her. She had no doubt that Corey would end up killing her. She knew he would have to show her that he was in charge again before he did anything too drastic. At least, she was hoping it would go that way.

She felt the knot moving just a little. She worked her wrists despite the pain. She was able to feel the knot with her right index finger. She pushed her finger into the knot and tried to move it around to loosen it a little further. It seemed to be working, but it was painfully slow.

As the knot began to loosen even more, Aubrey was able to get her thumb involved and soon the rope fell away. She brought her arms around to the front of her body and began to rub her shoulders. Her joints ached, and she tried to move her arms in a circle to loosen everything up.

When she felt like moving from her position on the floor, she looked down at the fishing line wrapped around her ankles. It was heavy monofilament and she wouldn't be able to break it. She needed something sharp to make a cut. Looking around the cabin, Aubrey noticed some cupboards near the kitchenette. Certainly there would be something in one of those that would have a sharp edge. She didn't need much. The line was so tight around her ankles that just a little nick would make it spring right off.

She crawled to a window seat and pulled herself up. She would have to jump over to the cupboards. She hoped that Corey wouldn't hear or feel anything above. Just as she positioned herself to make the move, she caught something out of the corner of her eye.

Corey was sitting on the steps that led to the main deck. It appeared he was enjoying the little scene. In her efforts to get free from her restraints, Aubrey failed to notice the boat slowing down. In fact, it had come to a complete stop.

Aubrey stopped and looked over. She knew her little comatose act was over. Corey broke the silence.

"Good to have you back. I was a little concerned that Ignacio's beating had caused your brain to be scrambled. Well, you won't have to worry about him any more. I took care of the problem." Corey smiled.

Aubrey didn't like his smile. As a matter of fact, it pissed her off.

"So, now you'll take care of me as well."

"Well of course. First we're going to have some fun." He took out a knife, and in two steps he was facing Aubrey.

"Get it over with. You're pretty tough when you deal with unarmed people."

Corey hit her on the top of the head with the end of the knife. Aubrey fell to her knees.

"Be careful how you speak to me." Corey grinned

Aubrey said nothing. Her head hurt like hell. She had no idea what Corey had in store for her, but she knew it wouldn't anything she would enjoy. She was beginning to lose hope. She would never show this bastard, however.

"My friend, Zander, calls you The Jackass."

Aubrey could see Corey tighten up for a moment. She had hit a nerve.

"We will see about this idiot you call Zander. I think I'll have you watch, while I kill him slowly in front of you."

Aubrey relaxed when she heard what he said. It didn't sound like she would be dying immediately. There was some hope.

"How are you going to do that? He's bigger than you. I heard he already kicked your ass." Aubrey was baiting Corey. He didn't like it.

"Watch your mouth. I can end it for you right here."

"What? Where would be the fun in that for you?"

Corey thought about it for a moment.

"You're exactly right. I do want to have some fun."

He took the knife and cut the fishing line from her legs.

"Can't have sex with your feet together," Corey said.

Aubrey looked for a way to escape, but there was nowhere to go. He was blocking the way out. Aubrey looked at him and smiled.

"Do what you want. I put up with it before, I guess I can be humiliated again."

Corey took the knife and cut the straps of her camisole. It dropped to her waist. He pushed it to the floor. Aubrey started to unbutton her shorts but Corey stopped her. He took his knife and cut them away on the inseam on both side. They fell to the floor as well. She was standing in her black thong facing him.

"I always liked it when you wore those things."

"Zander likes them too."

Corey didn't wait for the knife to do its work but simply ripped off the thong and threw it to the floor.

"He won't like seeing this one," Corey said, while he was dropping his cargo shorts to the deck.

"I think he likes me with whatever I wear. He's not a pervert like you."

Corey hit her on the top of the head with the knife again. Aubrey thought she would have two huge welts in addition to the concussion.

Corey forced her to her knees and wriggled out of his white briefs. He was aroused, as Aubrey knew he would be. Rough sex was the only way he could maintain an erection.

"Still can't function without being rough, I see. Maybe it's worse since you've been in prison. Were you some guy's little bitch?"

Corey thrust his penis into her mouth. She gagged, and he laughed. Aubrey thought about biting it off, but she felt the knife at her throat and decided against it. She performed the service he was after, until he pulled away. He didn't want to waste his orgasm in her mouth. She was thankful for some small favors.

He turned her over and entered her from behind. She had always hated that, and he knew it quite well. It hurt her, but she wouldn't let him know. Somewhere she had read that even women who were raped sometimes experienced orgasm. It was the body's natural response to stimuli. Aubrey decided she wouldn't be one of those statistics. He could do whatever he wanted. She wouldn't give him the satisfaction.

When Corey was finished, he sat up.

"You could have at least moved a little."

"What for? I figure if I stay still, you won't make me sick."

"Still got that mouth on you. Well, you're in for the long haul. We're just getting started."

"Oh, don't tease a girl like that."

"When I'm through with you, you won't have an ounce of that damn smugness left in you." Corey got up and got dressed.

Aubrey remained on the floor not looking at him.

"I'm not going to tie you up. There's nothing in here for you get your hands on."

"How about some clothes. You pretty much ruined everything I had."

"Sorry, baby. I want you naked."

He climbed the steps and slammed the cabin door. Aubrey heard what sounded like a padlock being snapped on the outside of the door. She was locked in.

Her clothes were ruined. She picked up the camisole. The straps had been cut but she had an idea. She tied the back two straps together and slipped it over her head. She positioned the top just over her breasts and tied the front two straps tightly so it wouldn't slip down. The former top now served as a low cut short dress. It barely covered the necessary parts, but it would do. She decided that if Corey came back down, she would take it off and throw it on the floor. It was all she had and, she didn't what him to destroy it.

All in all, Aubrey had to remove her new piece of clothing three more times before they made port.

27

It was almost five in the morning, when Zander felt a hand on his shoulder. It was Holata.

"Boat coming."

Ed was already digging for the night vision goggles, and Holata went back to the bow.

"Is it them?" Zander asked Ed.

"More than likely. It's too early for fishermen. Could be drug runners but I doubt it. This is his turf."

"What can I do?" Zander asked Holata.

"Need much quiet." Holata was a man of few words, and he liked those around him to follow suit.

The three had on their night scopes. After a few minutes, Zander could hear the soft purr of an outboard motor. Had it been during the day, Zander doubted he would have even heard it. The night had a way of making sounds louder. Maybe it was just that the sense hearing ramped up when sight was diminished.

The cruiser came in slowly. Zander could see The Jackass looking toward the shell island; he shined a spotlight around the small island looking for anything that looked out of place. He was cautious. Zander thought that if he were in his place, he might be cautious as well. He wasn't cautious enough, however. He was so focused on the small island, that he failed to check the surrounding area. If he had, he might have discovered their boat in the mangroves.

Corey bumped his bow into the sandy area in front of the shack. He jumped off the front of the boat with a rope and tied it to a sturdy mangrove. He walked over toward the small structure and looked in. Satisfied, he returned to the stolen boat and disappeared into the boat's cabin. It didn't take long. He emerged carrying something over his shoulder. At first, Zander thought it might be some provisions he was taking into the shack. But when Corey turned, Zander saw two legs on his back. They were the legs of a female. He was quite certain of it.

Corey looked around the boat and made one more turn. Zander saw it was a dark haired woman. Then he stopped. It was Aubrey. He gasped and made a move toward the bow. Ed stopped him.

"Ed, it's Aubrey. He's got her. We've got to do something."

"I know, but you need to be quiet. Holata's got this covered. If you give away our location, her life won't be worth yesterday's newspaper," Ed whispered, never relaxing the bear hug he had placed on Zander.

Zander could do nothing but go along with Ed's instruction. How the hell did The Jackass find her? He had covered his tracks and tried to keep her safely out of his clutches. Everything changed for Zander in those few moments.

Holata moved toward the two men.

"Not good. Woman naked."

Zander almost screamed. He didn't know what to do, but sitting here in the boat being restrained was not his idea of fixing the problem.

"I'm going to let you go. Don't do anything stupid. We need to listen to Holata about how to proceed. Can I trust you not to do anything stupid?" Ed said, softly.

Zander nodded.

"I mean it, Zander. What happens from here might very well be the difference of life and death for Aubrey. Corey has no plans to keep her alive when he's finished with her."

That hit Zander right between the eyes. All the pent-up emotion simply drained away and he went limp in Ed's arms. Ed let him go and placed him on the seat. Both men knelt next to Zander.

"Sleep soon. Then act," Holata said. He returned to the bow.

"I don't know what he's done to her, but we will get her back. Don't lose hope. Holata is the one person you want in a situation like this."

Zander couldn't argue. He couldn't do anything. The fight had just been drained out of him. It was a strange feeling for him. He was always in control. Now he wasn't. He had never felt this helpless before, and he didn't like the feeling at all.

There was a light coming from the shack. Zander watched but couldn't make out any movement. Almost a half hour went by, and then the light went out. It must have been one of those gas lanterns, because there wasn't any electricity on the island.

Zander fit the night scope back on and looked for any movement. He didn't see anything. The three waited forty-five minutes in position just watching. Holata stood and stretched. Then he went over the side of the skiff. Zander couldn't believe his eyes. He couldn't imagine getting into that water at night. There were too many things that could kill you.

He stood and watched Holata make his way over toward the island. Zander could see that he was standing and moving through the shallows. He knew the water hadn't been that deep, but he hadn't realized that it wasn't over four feet in the deepest part.

Holata made no sound, as he moved effortlessly through the dark water. When he reached the stern of the cruiser, he made his way around the blind side of the boat. Zander lost him for a moment, and then he saw him next to where Corey had tied the boat to the mangroves. Holata took out his knife, cut the rope effortlessly, and then he pushed the boat quietly into the deeper part of the canal. He pulled it around with the rope he had just cut and moved the entire boat away from the island. Zander assumed he was taking it around the mangroves to hide it from Corey.

Forty minutes later, Zander jumped when Holata lifted himself from the water into the skiff.

"First part, done," Holata said.

"Now what?" Zander asked.

"Wait."

Zander hated waiting.

"Give netting to Holata." He pointed to the mosquito netting they had been wearing.

Ed and Zander did as they were told. The netting was almost the same color as the boat. Zander wondered what he had in mind. He didn't like mosquitoes and hated to give up the netting, but Aubrey's safety was at stake, and he was in no position to argue.

Holata took out a roll of off-white tape and began wrapping the end of his rifle with it. When he was finished, he arranged the mosquito netting over him and the rifle. The barrel stuck out of the netting but blended right in with the boat. Zander could see what Holata was doing and for the first time that entire morning; he had a glimmer of hope. Holata was going to shoot the sonofabitch.

"Now what?" He asked Ed.

"We wait for morning light. Either Holata will wake The Jackass, or he'll wake on his own. Then he'll play out his hand."

Zander wasn't sure whose hand would actually play out.

"Why didn't he stay on the boat? Why would he stay in that shack when it is much more comfortable in the cabin?" Zander asked.

"Think about it. He's on the run. If he's caught on the boat, he's done. There's one way in and one way out. On the island, he's got an escape route. He's got a johnboat hidden somewhere on the other side of the island," Ed explained, patiently.

Zander panicked. "Shouldn't we take care of that so he doesn't take off on us?"

"Done," Holata said.

"After Holata hid the cruiser, he sunk the johnboat," Ed said, "and he's not going to leave his little trophy before he's finished with her."

Zander realized he couldn't very well leave in his johnboat with Aubrey in toe. There wouldn't be enough room. Aubrey was smart. She would make all kinds of ruckus, if she knew someone was out to rescue her.

There were too many variables for Zander to even consider. He kept turning things over in his mind, and nothing seemed to come out positive. He wanted to jump overboard and kill The Jackass with his bare hands while he was still sleeping. He might have done it if these two weren't here to stop him.

He was still considering the option, when daylight started to creep onto the island. It was a gray haze at first, and then each minute brought more light. The morning birds began their squawking, and the glades started coming alive.

"Now," Holata said from underneath the netting.

"Call out to Aubrey. Tell her you are here, and you'll take care of everything. Tell her to be patient."

Ed and Holata had apparently talked about this plan previously. Zander was happy they hadn't shared it, because he would have been nervous if he had to think about it. Aubrey's life was in the balance.

Zander would do exactly what Ed and Holata told him.

They could hear some movement coming from the shack and then some cursing. Corey came stumbling out, pushing Aubrey in from of him. Zander raised a pair of field glasses and saw a pistol in Corey's right hand. He was holding it in back of her head.

"No shot. Talk." Holata didn't move.

Zander let his anger take over.

"You need a woman to protect you? Not much of a man if you ask me. Pussy comes to mind."

Corey was looking around.

"Show yourself, or I shoot her in the head."

Ed started the skiff and inched out from their hiding spot. Zander went and stood behind Holata in the bow.

"How's this? Can you see us now?"

"Stop where you are."

Ed cut the motor.

"Where do you think you're going? You've got no boat, and your johnboat has been scuttled," Zander said, trying to grin.

Corey noticed for the first time there was no cruiser on the island. Zander thought he saw some panic in his face.

"Maybe I'll just shoot the bitch. I'm pretty much done with her anyway. She isn't much good anymore. After four times last night, she just pretty much lays there." Corey punched her in the back with the pistol just for fun.

Aubrey didn't react. She was standing, but her head was resting on her chest. Zander noticed her top had been fashioned into some kind of dress. He was happy that she didn't have to stand in front of them naked. He knew she would have been horrified being degraded like that.

As if on cue, Corey pulled the makeshift dress off her shoulders and let it drop to the ground. Zander was incensed. His body went rigid.

"Easy Zander. He's trying to get in your head. Ignore it," Ed whispered.

Zander tried his best to relax.

"What do you want?" Zander asked.

"I want your boat."

"We'll trade the girl for the boat. Send her back to the shack and we'll come ashore, and you can take the boat."

"You think I'm stupid?"

Zander thought he was but decided against telling him so.

"Looks like we've got a standoff. We want the girl, so if you hurt her in any way, we'll kill you where you stand. On the other hand, you've got a gun to her head, so it appears like this isn't going to end well unless we have some kind of compromise."

Zander was trying to keep him thinking about his predicament without making things look completely hopeless. If Corey felt there was no way out, he would kill Aubrey. Zander was certain of it. He had dealt with psychopaths before, and they were predictably unpredictable.

Corey was beginning to lose his patience and seemed more erratic. Zander was afraid he would blow at any second and take Aubrey with him.

"Why don't you let her go and take me as your hostage," Zander said, trying to buy more time.

"Sure. You come ashore, and I'll let her go."

Zander knew it was a lie, but he needed to get Holata the shot he needed. He slipped over the side of the boat. As he passed the bow he heard Holata.

"Circle to his left side. He'll keep Aubrey between you and him. Go quickly before he shoots you."

Zander could hardly process the complete sentences he heard coming from Holata, but he listened and followed Holata's direction. He moved quietly through the water even though his flesh was creeping. He walked up on the beach and moved to Corey's left. Corey moved Aubrey in front of him and then placed the gun to her right temple with his arm straight out.

"I'm going to shoot Aubrey in the head, and you can watch her die before I kill you."

It was all Zander heard before a shot rang out. He didn't know what had happened. Aubrey was standing, but Corey was falling in what appeared to be slow motion. Zander thought that maybe he was screaming. He didn't stop to find out but ran over to Aubrey, wrapped his arms around her, and moved them both to the cover of some mangroves.

Ed had pushed the boat up onto the shells and Holata was standing and pulling off the netting. When everything began slowing down to real time, Zander could hear Corey, and he was screaming.

There was blood and tissue surrounding the spot where he had fallen on the ground. Zander didn't know what it meant. He just knew Aubrey was safe in his arms. He found her makeshift dress and helped her into it. When he got it to fit the best he could, he turned her around to look into her eyes. He wondered how much damage Corey had caused. Would she ever be the same? He hoped so but was afraid it might take a great deal of time.

Aubrey looked into his eyes and smiled. "Thanks." It was all she said before turning and walking over to Corey. Aubrey was much stronger than Zander had realized.

She looked at Corey for a long time. He didn't stop screaming. He didn't have a right elbow. Holata had shot it off.

Ed and Holata had joined the party. Aubrey went over and removed Holata's knife from the sheaf on his belt. She leaned over Corey and cut off his shirt in two quick cuts. Then she cut off his jeans. She removed his belt just before the last cut and wrapped it around his arm using it as a tourniquet to slow the bleeding from his limp arm.

"What are you doing?" Zander asked.

"I don't want him to bleed out. He's got to suffer before he dies."

The belt seemed to eliminate some of the pain, and Corey stopped screaming. He just lay on the ground staring at the sky. He was naked except for his underwear. Aubrey cut that off as well. He just looked at her. His eyes were glazed over. Zander wondered if he even knew what had happened to him.

"Now everyone can see you naked. You raped me last night, but you can't do much damage with a little pecker like that. I'll be all right. You won't."

She took the knife made a few small cuts along his flaccid penis. He was beyond screaming.

"What do you want us to do with him?" Ed asked.

"Tie him up." Aubrey said. She was in control now.

Ed did it.

"Aubrey, I apologize. I guess I need some shooting practice. I meant to blow off his bicep but instead I hit him in the elbow. That could have been a real bad ending." Holata said.

"No worries, Holata. The elbow worked better anyway. He dropped the pistol." She walked over, picked up the handgun and threw it into the water.

Zander was staring at Holata.

"What you did today took a lot of courage, and I applaud you for your heroics," Holata said, directly to Zander.

Zander didn't know what to say.

"You can talk," Zander said, finally.

Ed and Aubrey laughed.

"You didn't realize that Holata graduated from Stanford. He is the curator for all the museums in Collier County. He decided to come back here to give back to the indigenous people of Florida. We're glad he's here."

"So am I," Zander said. "I don't understand his routine, however."

"Well, I didn't know if I could trust you to do the right thing. Sometimes, the mystique of an Indian makes people think we've got some kind of power that the average person doesn't possess. It has worked for me countless times. People tend to want to believe in some kind of mystical power. It helps to keep them from moving blindly into situations that need to be planned and well thought out."

"Is that what this was? Planned and well thought out?"

"Not really. We just got lucky," Holata said, and smiled for the first time.

Zander decided he liked this guy.

"Have you forgotten about the principle player here?" Aubrey asked.

Zander felt bad. He went over and put his arm around Aubrey.

"Tell us what you want us to do."

Aubrey turned to Holata. "Call the gators."

"First things first," Holata said.

He walked over to the shack and went inside. Soon he came out with a box of drugs. He put it into the front of the boat.

"I could use a little help. There are three more boxes in there."

Both Ed and Zander helped him with the remaining drugs.

"I'm not very comfortable with all this shit in my boat," Ed said.

"We'll drop them in the bay on the way back."

Ed seemed comfortable with the plan.

Holata walked over to the water's edge to make his call to the gators.

"Just a minute. Before you make that god-awful sound, let us get into the boat." Ed was emphatic.

Aubrey and Zander drug Corey by his ropes down to where Holata was standing. Then she and Zander climbed into the boat next to Ed. Holata began his gator calls. Zander thought it sounded like a rumbling bellow or some kind of deep growl. It almost resembled an echo. Zander was mesmerized, even though the sound grated on him.

"Holata is a gator whisperer. It's the craziest thing you ever saw. If I hadn't seen it with my own eyes, I wouldn't have believed it," Aubrey whispered.

Holata continued his calling, and Zander saw a pair of eyes rise from the water. The eyes were looking at the man on the beach. Holata took the opportunity to move and jump aboard.

"I think we should move away from here. There will be a whole lot more of them in a few moments." Holata was smiling.

Like clockwork, other sets of eyes popped up. They were all looking at Corey.

"Let's go. I don't want to see this," Aubrey said, and sat down.

Zander could understand. She had spent time with the guy, and even though he was crazy, there had been some past memories. He could relate.

Ed put the boat into gear, and they moved away slowly. Zander looked over his shoulder and saw one of the larger gators moving up to the shore. It looked like he was at least fifteen feet long. It wouldn't take him long to make short work of The Jackass.

Somehow it wasn't satisfying. Aubrey could see he was brooding just a bit.

"Remember when you told me you had never killed anyone?"

Zander nodded.

"Well, we could have killed Corey. But if we did that, we would cross the line. Once you cross that line, you can never go back."

Zander nodded again.

"It's better to let nature take over, don't you think?"

"Nature is always the ultimate winner. No matter what we do, nature always figures out a way to make things right," Holata interjected.

"I agree," Zander said, quietly.

"Then, what's the problem?' Aubrey asked.

"I would have preferred one of those big-ass snakes."

28

The unlikely group of seafarers tied the cruiser to the skiff and began the trip back to the marina in Chokoloskee. Ed made a call to the marina and told the owner they had a boat in tow. He agreed to call the Coast Guard about a possible drug deal going down on the shell island. Ed gave him the coordinates but told him to wait for an hour so the gators could get their work done.

Zander was concerned for Aubrey. She had seemed strong before, but now she appeared distracted. It was hard for Zander to fathom what she had gone through. Would it be possible to come out of all this without some damage to her psyche?

"I think I need one of your motel units," Zander said to the marina owner when they arrived, and he put down two twenties.

The owner pushed the money back.

"This is on me. Your money's no good here. You helped get my boat back. I'm just thanking you for that." He gave Zander a key to unit two.

"Thanks. But you should be thanking Ed and Holata. I was just basically along for the ride."

"It was a team effort," Holata said. "We wouldn't have been able to end this without your input and help."

"Hey, what about me?" Ed asked.

"Well, it was your boat. So that's something, I guess." Holata's eyes twinkled, as he turned away.

Jeff Zwagerman

Zander took the opportunity to get Aubrey situated into the motel room.

"I need a shower," Aubrey said, without much emotion.

"Run the hot water until it turns cold. It will help you to feel better," Zander said.

Aubrey nodded and began removing her makeshift dress as she headed to the bathroom. Zander hoped she would be okay.

"You need to sleep. When you are finished with your shower, go to bed. I've got some loose ends to tie up."

"Find me something to wear," Aubrey mumbled from the bathroom.

Zander could barely hear her. But he was happy she was thinking about what she needed. Maybe she was just exhausted, and she would be better after sleeping. He hoped so. He slipped out of the door as quietly as possible.

Zander got into his pickup and went to Mike's house. He was sitting on the deck under an umbrella with a glass of sweet tea in his hands.

"Mike. It's good to see you up and around," Zander said.

"Thanks. It is good to be seen. Can I get you some of this?" Mike held up his glass.

"Looks good, sure."

Mike called out to his wife for another glass. She looked out and saw Zander. She smiled and then ducked back into the house.

"What's the news about Prescott?"

"He won't be bothering anyone any longer," Zander said.

"That's not a story. I want details."

Mike's wife came back out with a glass and placed it in front of Zander. "Enjoy," she said, and went back into the house.

Zander took a drink and started coughing.

"Damn it Mike, I thought this was iced tea."

"Jack Daniels and soda, my friend. We drink adult beverages around here."

"A little early don't you think?" Zander was still trying to clear his throat.

"After what I've been through, I'm never going to pass up the opportunity to drink what I like."

"I can't argue with that logic."

"Wouldn't do you any good if you tried."

They badgered each other and enjoyed each other's company, while Zander told the entire story. Mike liked hearing about Holata's dumb Indian routine.

"He does that shit all the time when someone new comes around. I told him he should start doing some local theatre roles. He seems to enjoy the flair for the dramatic."

"I should think so. He would be good."

"Yeah, but he doesn't think there are that many roles for Indians. Besides, he's pretty darn busy."

"When will you be back to work, Mike?" Zander asked.

"The department said I need to take it easy. I'll need a doctor's go-ahead before they let me back. I'm just enjoying the paid vacation right now. When I quit hurting, I'll go back."

"I may have something that will hasten your recovery," Zander said.

Mike appeared interested, so Zander explained about the money Corey had hidden. Mike looked puzzled.

"I thought you took that money."

"I put it back. It wasn't mine. I took it to force The Jackass's hand. I think I did a pretty good job. That's blood money, and I don't want any part of it. However, if a certain police officer stumbled on some drug money, it might prove to be good for someone's career."

"Wow. I don't know what to say. Thanks, man."

"It's the least I could do. You wouldn't be in this predicament if it weren't for me." Zander was contrite.

"Don't say that. It was Corey Prescott that did all of this. It was just a matter of time. You just happened to be in the right place at the wrong time. It was just a coincidence."

"I don't believe in coincidence," Zander said.

"That's your problem, my friend. That kind of thinking will make you nuts. Let's go get that money."

"I think that should be something you do without me around," Zander said.

"I still can't drive, you drive me and point me in the right direction and we'll go from there."

Zander looked at him. "You aren't thinking about keeping that money, I hope."

"I'd be lying if I told you I hadn't considered it. But I wouldn't be able to live with myself if I took that shit."

Zander was relieved. He liked Mike, and he didn't want to see him lose his way over something stupid like money. He helped Mike up, and together they went to Corey's house. Zander went over and pulled up the money, while Mike waited in the truck.

"Why do I feel like I'm doing all the heavy lifting," Zander said, and grinned at Mike.

"Quit your damn bitching, and get over here with the evidence."

Zander liked hearing the word "evidence." Mike would do the right thing. He took the water bottles filled with cash and literally threw them in Mike's lap.

"Lordy, look at all this. I don't think I've ever seen this much cash all at once, ever."

Zander smiled. He wondered what Mike made in a year. He would remember to do something special for him down the line.

"Take me home. I'll have the wife drive me to the station. This stuff needs to be under lock and key."

"What do you think will happen to it?' Zander asked.

"Not my concern. That's for someone up the food chain to decide."

Zander couldn't help but think the cash would end up in someone's pocket. That was his overall pessimistic attitude, but he hoped he was wrong. It was out of his hands now and no longer concerned him.

They drove back to Mike's, chatting about nothing in particular.

Mike changed the subject. "How is Aubrey doing?"

Zander looked down. "Too early to tell, I think. I've got her down at the marina motel. Hopefully she'll be able to get some sleep."

"What's in your future?"

"I think we need to get away from here. She needs to forget about this Everglade city. Too many bad memories would keep coming up."

"Zander, she's a strong woman. I think she will be fine with your help. You need to be there for her now. Don't leave her alone."

Zander nodded.

"I've got a friend up in northern Florida. I've been thinking about calling him and spend some time up there."

"That sounds like a great idea. Get away from everything, and let her heal. Zander, I don't think she should come back here, ever."

Zander nodded again. "I was thinking the same thing."

"She's someone special. She's taken to you for some odd reason." Mike smiled. "Zander, she's a keeper. Don't do anything to screw this up."

"I hear you. I don't plan on it, but my track record isn't very good."

"Piss on that. What is in the past should stay in the past. It has nothing to do with the here and now. Just tell yourself that you're going to start your life from this moment on. It's easy."

"Good advice. I'll give it a try."

Zander wasn't sure it was even possible, but he was willing to try anything. Mike was right. Aubrey was special, and he would do everything he could to make this relationship work.

Mike grabbed Zander's hand and shook it. "I'll miss your ugly face."

He walked to the house, and Zander drove away. He liked these kinds of goodbyes. The less emotion involved, the better. He looked at his watch and noticed it was almost 11:00. He decided to go to the Rod And Gun Club and explain to the boss what had happened.

It had just opened, and Zander sat in the office explaining what had happened to Aubrey. The boss wasn't surprised when Zander told him they were leaving the area and wouldn't be back. He gave Zander his check and put some cash in the envelope for Aubrey.

"This should pretty much get us even. I hadn't done anything with the hours she still had. I was waiting for her to come back. Tell her I'll miss her," he paused, "I'll miss you, too." He grabbed Zander's hand and then left the office abruptly.

Another successful goodbye, Zander thought.

When Zander pulled into the motel parking lot, he saw the marina owner motioning him to come to the office. Zander resisted the urge to look in on Aubrey and went over to the office.

"I jumped the gun just a little."

Zander looked at him a little puzzled.

"I called the Coast Guard after you left. They just got back to me."

"What did they find?" Zander was interested.

"Not much. They found some clothing and a bloody belt. There was quite a bit of blood on the shell beach, but that was about all."

Zander liked what he was hearing. "So what did they do?"

"Nothing. There was no evidence of drugs. They assumed a deal had happened and it went bad. There was no body to recover so they just wrote it off, I think."

"Well that's good news, anyway. Sounds like Corey Prescott made some gators happy this morning," Zander said.

"They asked me who gave me the information. I told them it was an anonymous phone call. I never told them about the boat. I just didn't see the need."

Zander thanked him and walked back to the motel room. Then he remembered that he had forgotten to get Aubrey some clothes. He got back into his pickup and went to the little general store. Most everything they sold was for tourists. He managed to find a little sundress that he thought would fit her. He found a nice little two-piece swimsuit that would serve as underwear. Zander was quite proud of himself.

As he drove back to the marina, he realized it was a pleasant day. Time was slipping away, and it was after 4:00 when he arrived back at the motel.

He put his ear to the motel door but didn't hear anything. He decided to sit in one of the chairs next to the room. He placed the bag of clothing at his feet and leaned back into the chair. Suddenly he realized he was very tired. He closed his eyes and soon was sound asleep.

About an hour passed, and he woke himself with a snort. It took a few minutes for Zander to realize where he was. He tried to shake the sleep from his foggy brain. Then he heard something.

"Wake up."

Zander looked around and saw the room door was open a crack. Aubrey was trying to speak to him.

"It's about time," she whispered. "Did you bring some clothes?"

Zander held up the bag.

"Well, bring it in here. I'm standing here naked."

"Just the way I like you." Zander hoped it wasn't too soon to joke.

"You." Zander could tell she was smiling however.

He got up and pushed the door open. Aubrey stood in the middle of the room. Zander didn't think he had ever seen anyone as desirable.

"Let's see what you brought." She took out the dress and the swimsuit.

"Remember I didn't have a Sacs Fifth Avenue at my disposal."

"I suppose it will have to do." She slipped everything on. She looked as magnificent to Zander as when she had been standing naked. That surprised him. There was definitely something to this woman. He was looking for signs that the sleep had done her some good.

"I'm hungry," she said simply.

With that, Zander knew things were good.

29

"Where do you want to go?" Zander asked.

"Surprise me," Aubrey said.

Zander wanted to get her away from anything that would remind her of Corey Prescott as soon as possible. He would proceed cautiously, however. He hadn't bounced anything off Aubrey. He didn't want her to think he had made any decisions without her input.

"I would like to take you back to Sanibel, but I'm not sure if Corey's man is still a threat."

"He's dead. Corey shot him in the head. I'm sure he's either floating in the gulf or shark food by now."

Aubrey's comment made Zander uneasy. He thought she was being too cavalier about the whole thing. He hoped things wouldn't manifest themselves later.

"We've still got a few days left on our reservation in Sanibel. Let's go back. You liked it there."

"I did. It's a good idea."

They drove in silence. Aubrey stared at nothing in particular. Zander tried to catch glimpses of her without drawing attention. He was worried.

There was the usual traffic leaving the island when they crossed the causeway. Zander took the back way to the cabin. When he drove into the parking area, Aubrey broke the silence.

"I thought we were going to get something to eat."

"We are. I'm taking you to Traditions. We're going to make a night of it. Why don't you put on something stunning for this evening, and I'll try to look halfway presentable."

Aubrey smiled at the comment and went into the cabin. Zander got out of the pickup and stretched. He looked around, and decided he understood why Aubrey liked the island so much.

He climbed the stairs to the deck and heard the shower running before he even opened the door. He wondered how many showers Aubrey needed before she would finally feel clean. He fought the desire to take off his clothes and join her. He would have to wait to be invited. He didn't want to push Aubrey into doing anything until she was ready. He hoped he would find the patience he needed.

Aubrey took her time in the bathroom. Zander was on his second Yuengling when she emerged. Zander almost dropped his beer. She was in a little black cocktail dress he had never seen before. She looked absolutely stunning. He couldn't take his eyes off her.

Aubrey saw him watching her and did a full turn in front of him.

"What do you think?" she asked, coyly.

Zander was careful. "I don't know how you do it. Every time I think you can't look any better, you go and prove me wrong."

Aubrey blushed at his comment. She went over and put her arms around him.

"You always seem to know the right things to say."

Zander didn't think he knew anything, let alone, the right things to say. So, he decided to stop while he was ahead. He just put his arms around Aubrey and returned the hug. He didn't let go until she did.

"You'd better get ready," Aubrey said.

Zander gave her an easy kiss on the lips and moved into the bathroom. He was ready for their evening together in less than fifteen minutes.

"You men are so lucky. You never have to put on a face to look presentable."

"I can't imagine what you women have to go through. Present company excepted."

"What does that mean?" Aubrey had her hands on her hips.

"You wouldn't have to do anything. You have a natural beauty that just radiates from your entire body."

Aubrey pushed him out of the door, and they were on their way to the Island Inn that boasted the Traditions restaurant. Zander could remember places like Traditions when he was a kid in Iowa. Back in the fifties and sixties, they were called supper clubs. They were places where you went on a Saturday night and spent the entire evening. Maybe you wouldn't even eat until 10:00. The kitchen always stayed open until midnight. People would drink cocktails and dance to whatever live music they had that evening. The tables all had table cloths and candles. It was an experience, not merely someplace to eat dinner. Zander liked places like that. There weren't that many around anymore.

There was a nice table for two, near the windows, that overlooked the beach. A nice combo was playing show tunes and some easy listening. They were great songs for dancers, and the floor was busy.

The waiter had an Italian accent and wanted to know what the lady wanted to drink. He didn't seem to be too concerned with what Zander wanted. Zander understood that feeling perfectly.

Aubrey said she wanted some wine. Zander ordered a nice Zinfandel, and the waiter went to get the wine.

They both looked at the menus. Zander thought the ribs looked interesting. When he mentioned it, Aubrey stopped and looked up.

"We are in Florida and on an island for God's sake. You want to order pork? What's wrong with you?"

Zander thought maybe there was quite a bit wrong. So he put down the menu.

"Why don't you order for us both?" he asked, smiling.

"Do you trust me to order something you might like?"

"Of course."

"It will be fish of some sort."

"Sounds good to me," Zander said.

Aubrey went back to looking at the menu. The waiter returned with the wine, went through all the gyrations with the cork and had Zander sample a bit of the bottle to make sure it was drinkable. Zander always was amused by the little song and dance. He had never turned away a bottle of wine but played the game anyway.

The waiter poured their wine and mentioned that the special for the evening was a sea bass. Aubrey closed the menu.

"We'll take two," she said, with authority.

The waiter nodded and smiled. He looked at Zander when he smiled. Zander knew it was his way of telling him he was a lucky guy. There was no argument.

"Let's dance," Aubrey said, and stood.

Zander wasn't much of a dancer, but he agreed. He wanted the evening to be something memorable for Aubrey.

There was an older gentleman playing the baby grand piano, and he had two female singers working the harmony. They were both knockouts. Zander thought Aubrey would have fit right in between them. She wouldn't even have to sing. She still would be the best-looking woman on the stage.

They were singing "Memory" from the Broadway show *Cats*. It was a showstopper that lent itself well to a slow dance. That was fine with Zander. Slow dancing was about all he knew how to do, and it gave him an excuse to hold Aubrey close without seeming like he wanted her sexually. Of course he did want her sexually, but he needed to be patient.

When the song finished, they returned to their seats. Zander could hear the waves rolling in on the beach. The seas were quite rough that evening, and there were small craft warnings listed.

Zander poured more wine and held up his glass to Aubrey for a toast. She raised her glass.

"Here's to us and to some very fine adventures in our future."

Aubrey clinked her glass with Zander and smiled. They drank and Aubrey set her glass down. She reached over and grabbed Zander's hand.

"I was so worried that you wouldn't want me after what happened with Corey."

The comment took Zander by surprise. He just looked at Aubrey and broke his silence.

"How could you even think something like that? I would have to be pretty shallow to react like that. I have nothing but love in my heart for you."

The comment surprised both Aubrey and Zander. Neither had vocalized the word "love" seriously in the past. Zander had thought about it and wondered if Aubrey had the same feelings. Aubrey, on the other hand, was thinking the same thing.

They both looked at each other wondering what should come next. Aubrey was the first to again break the silence.

"It's just that with the rape and what happened after, I didn't know how you would feel about being with someone so damaged."

Zander took her hand, "We're all damaged, some of us more than others. I'm tired of living that way. You have been the one thing in my life that has taken me out of that repetitive behavior. I can't let you go, because without you, I am nothing."

Aubrey smiled. "You might be more than I deserve. I hope you'll understand if it takes me some time to get over this last experience with Corey."

"The Jackass, you mean."

"Yes, The Jackass."

"You take as much time as you need. I'll just be waiting to give you whatever you need."

Their sea bass came, and they ate in between bits of conversation. Zander didn't think he had ever had fish as tasty. He told Aubrey so a number of times.

She shook her head and said, "Get over it."

Zander couldn't help but kick her lightly under the table. She hooked his foot and pulled it close. Then she rubbed her foot up and down his leg. Zander couldn't ever remember a more sexual act. He was aroused instantly.

"Keep it down, little boy," Aubrey said, knowing full well what she had just done.

"I'll try, but only because you asked me," Zander said, but moved his hand on her leg. He hoped it wouldn't be something he would regret later.

Aubrey pretended not to notice.

"You are such a bad boy," she whispered.

"I am. I just can't help myself around you."

They finished their meal without too much more sexual tension. Aubrey wanted to dance some more, and they danced until their shared dessert of Key lime pie made its appearance.

Aubrey took the first bite, and Zander followed suit.

"They make their own crust here. Most places have a graham cracker crust, but they have real pie dough. That's what makes this so much better," Aubrey said.

Zander had to agree.

They were both too full to do much else.

"Let's go for a walk along the beach," Zander suggested, after he paid the bill.

Aubrey agreed and hooked her arm in his, and together they walked out the beach door past the swimming pool. It was a dark evening without the benefit of the moon. They walked next to the waterline. Aubrey took off her shoes and let the water wash over her feet and legs. Her little black dress was short enough to escape the waves.

"The night sea is so mysterious," she said.

"It's kind of creepy, if you ask me."

"Why do you say that?"

"There's so much you can't see. The ocean is full of things that can kill you. The night just makes it seem more sinister."

"Did you ever swim in the ocean at night?"

"Not on purpose, if I could help it."

"Well, there's no time like the present."

Aubrey was taking her black dress over her head.

"Are you crazy? I'm not going out there in these waves."

"What's the matter with you? Are you afraid of some waves and a little salt water?" Aubrey asked, mockingly.

"I think I might be."

"I hope you're not planning to let me go out there all by myself." Aubrey said, as she placed her dress on the sand and wiggled out of her panties. She wasn't wearing a bra.

If Zander had considered avoiding the water, Aubrey's bare butt changed all that. She ran into the water, and was kicking and screaming just to egg Zander into following her.

Zander removed his pants and shirt and put them with Aubrey's things. He pulled off his white Fruit Of The Looms and ran into the water.

"Shit, this water is cold." Zander almost screamed.

"Worried about shrinkage?" Aubrey asked.

"Damn right. This is ridiculous." Zander pretended to be irritated.

"Swim over to me."

Zander dog paddled over and Aubrey wrapped her legs around him and held on with her arms around his neck. Zander was aroused again.

"Don't tell me to keep it in my pants. I'm not wearing any, and that's your fault."

Aubrey let go and swam away laughing.

"You are such as tease." Zander was laughing as well.

Together, they spent the better part of an hour in the surf and sand. When they got out, they were both tired.

"There are some towels at the pool. Go get a couple. I don't want sand in my things."

"What things are you talking about?"

"Oh, just go get the towels, dirty boy."

"Me? I don't have any clothes on. Why don't you get the towels?"

"I don't have any clothes, either. Besides, I asked you to do it first."

Zander couldn't argue. She did ask him first. He ran up the beach until he had the pool between himself and the restaurant. Keeping an eye out for other beach walkers, he found the pool gate and took four towels and put another around his waist. Then he went back to the stretch of beach where Aubrey was hiding.

"I've got the towels." He called out to Aubrey.

"Bring them over."

"I think you should come and get them. Since I had to do the heavy lifting, it's the least you could do."

Zander was just kidding. His intention was to tease Aubrey, and then deliver the towels when the joke played out. Much to his surprise, however, Aubrey charged out to where he was standing. There was just enough light coming from the resort that Zander got quite an eyeful.

Aubrey stood in front of him not making a move for the towels he was holding.

"Is this what you were waiting for, you pervert?" Aubrey asked.

At first Zander thought she was angry, but then he saw she had a huge smile on her face.

"You are something," Zander said, meaning that she was quite a character. But her naked body was indeed quite something as well.

"Well, I know that. Tell me something I don't know."

"There is nothing you don't know when it concerns what I want to do to you."

"I think it's time we got back to the cabin, don't you?"

Zander wasn't about to argue. He figured Aubrey would be fine. What he hadn't realized was that he was the reason she would get past Corey Prescott.

30

They both woke up later than they had planned. The reason was that they had gone to bed later than they had planned. They had gone to bed early enough, they just didn't have a reason to sleep.

Zander rolled out of bed first and made the coffee. He was still naked, and when he turned around to head back to the bedroom, Aubrey emerged in some sort of spandex outfit. Obviously, she was going for a run on the beach.

"I didn't know you were a runner," Zander said.

"I used to run track in high school. Sprints mostly. I've found that it is a good way to take my mind off the nastier things in life."

Zander looked at her puzzled.

"The Jackass," she said, and went out the door toward the beach.

Zander looked out after her. He was wondering why she didn't invite him along on her run. Then it hit him. He was recently part of Corey Prescott drama. Aubrey needed to be able to work everything out on her own.

Suddenly he had an idea. He found his phone in the bedroom and pushed the number he had programmed for Herbie. Aubrey had put the number in, because Zander still hadn't figured out how the whole phone thing worked. He thought that maybe he would have to be dragged kicking and screaming into this new world of technology. Better yet, he just wouldn't enter it at all.

Herbie answered almost immediately.

"Zander. It's about time I heard from you. Is everything okay?" Herbie always assumed the worst when Zander called him.

"Things have been interesting. Aubrey is safe, and this Prescott asshole won't be bothering her anymore."

Herbie decided that was as much information as he needed.

"Where are you?" Zander asked.

"Ocala and heading north. I've got a few more stops, and then I should be home for a few days."

Herbie still found it strange calling Cedar Key his home. He had always been a Midwestern boy and Florida was a very strange place to him. But he knew that wherever Gail wanted to be, it was enough for him.

"I was just wondering if your offer of having me stay for a while was still on the table?" Zander asked, cautiously.

"No. That ship has sailed. Now the offer is that you can stay, but only if you bring Aubrey along."

Zander smiled. "That was my next question."

"Always one step ahead of you."

"You always had the better wit. I could never argue with that."

"When are you thinking of coming to see us? I need to give Gail a heads-up. You know how women are, she'll want to clean the entire house."

Zander didn't have clue how women were. He was willing to start learning, however.

"Why don't you tell me what works for you and Gail? I've got another day booked here, but I can try to extend our time."

"Nonsense. Let's make it tomorrow night. Be here by 7:00, and we'll have cocktails and then decide where to go to eat."

"I don't want to put Gail out. You call me if she doesn't like that idea," Zander paused, "I haven't run this by Aubrey yet, so if she doesn't take to the idea, I'll call you back."

"It sounds like maybe she needs to get away from that part of the state. You've always been a silver-tongued charmer. Use your skills," Herbie said.

"I don't think I'm as good at the art of persuasion as I used to be."

"What are you rambling on about? I was talking about oral sex." Herbie hung up.

Zander always liked Herbie's sense of humor. That's why they had always been friends. He tended to border on the bizarre at times, and that's what made Zander lose some of his inhibitions. Everyone needed a friend like that.

Zander went back into the kitchen and poured himself a cup of coffee. He decided to walk over to the beach to see if he could spot Aubrey. He put on a tee shirt and some shorts and padded off barefoot.

On his way, he stopped in the office, and found that the entire resort was booked. There would be no chance to extend their stay. Checkout was at 10:00 the next day. That would make his pitch to Aubrey a little easier.

When he reached the beach, Aubrey was returning from the north at a slow jog. Zander waved and she waved back. He could see something in her hand. As she got closer, Zander could see she was holding a huge shell.

"Looks like you've stumbled onto a nice find."

"Almost as good as when I found you." She flashed a toothy grin.

"What the heck is that?" Zander asked.

"It a Horse Conch. It's the state shell."

"Is it dead?"

"Of course it's dead. It's illegal to pick up live shells on Sanibel." Aubrey just looked at him and raised her eyebrows.

Zander figured she knew more about picking up live shells than she was admitting.

"That thing is huge. I've never seen a big shell like that before. Where did you find it?"

"I was running up Bowman's Beach, and this shell was just rolling in the surf right by my feet. It has to be the granddaddy of anything I've ever seen."

"So, the shell found you. I think that may be a good omen."

Aubrey looked out over the gulf.

"I could use a little good luck after what's happened lately."

"Well, this is the start of something big," Zander said, hoping to lighten her sudden change of mood.

Her mood did change. "This thing is full of barnacles, but I think we can clean it up. It will be a striking addition on an end table."

"That thing is so big, we could make a lamp out of it. Hell, it's so big we could plant a medium sized palm tree in it."

"Shut your stupid mouth. This splendid creation needs to be displayed naturally. Lamp my ass." She turned and huffed off, but Zander could see a little grin on the corners of her mouth.

The resort had a place for shellers to clean their finds, and Aubrey was busy at it when Zander caught up. She had some kind of tool and was using it to scrape off the all the nasty little hitchhikers. Zander could see that the shell's outside color was a deep brown. The inside appeared to be shiny beige. It almost looked like it was porcelain.

"Looks like a real treasure, Aubrey." Zander meant it.

"Here take a smell." She held the shell up to Zander's nose.

"Holy shit, that's just awful." Zander coughed.

"Not another smell like it as far as I know. The creature died in here, and after some time, the waves just sucked his carcass right out of the shell."

"How do you get that stink out?" Zander was still trying to get the smell out of his olfactory.

"Bleach works, but you can't put the whole shell into the bleach or you'll lose the dark brown color on the outside. I think I'll put some drain cleaner into it, and let it sit overnight. That should get rid of any remaining tissue that didn't get pulled out."

"Well let's hope that it works. We've got to check out by 10:00 tomorrow morning."

Aubrey stopped her cleaning. "Can't we extend our stay?"

"I tried. This is high season, and they are booked until April."

Aubrey looked at the shell, "Well, if it isn't perfect by tomorrow, we could pack in some fresh coffee grounds. That always works until there's time to really clean it out."

Zander could tell she was disappointed. Aubrey liked Sanibel Island, and that made him sad. Underneath, however, he knew they needed to get away from Southwest Florida. There were just too many memories that would fester for a long time.

"Maybe that shell has brought us more luck than we know."

"What do you mean?"

"I think it's time to make a move. I called my friend Herbie up in Cedar Key. He and Gail have room for us. I think we should go and make plans about where we go from here. You've shown me much about Florida, and I'd like to do the same for you with the Midwest. There's a lot of country that neither of us have seen, and I'd like us to explore it together."

"Will you take me to Colorado?"

"Well, sure. Why wouldn't I?" Zander was puzzled.

"Well, you told me a lot about your history there. I thought it might be too painful."

"It was a long time ago, and I've moved way beyond that. You are the reason for everything good in my life."

"I like that."

"I really would like you to meet my friend Fats and his girlfriend Fran. Well, who knows, she could be his wife by now."

His own comment hit Zander hard. He hadn't talked to Fats in a long time, and he needed to rectify that. He knew Fats would be angry and knew he had every right.

Aubrey took his hands and put them around her waist. "I know why you are doing all this. I know you think it's best that I leave this place of bad memories. I want you to know, I believe you are right. I'm not as strong as I'd like people to believe, so I'll rely on your judgment. I'll do whatever you think is best."

Zander looked into her eyes. Maybe this shell was all they needed to turn their luck around.

"I'll go to maintenance and see if they have some drain cleaner for your shell," Zander said.

"Thanks. I'll go shower. When you put in the drain cleaner, don't let it touch the outside. Just prop it up by the cabin, so we can keep an eye on it."

Zander did as Aubrey suggested. He always enjoyed doing as he was told when the telling came from Aubrey.

By the time he had followed his orders, Aubrey was drinking coffee on the deck. She looked beautiful, but Zander was once again disappointed to see her fully clothed. She had on a small crop top and shorts.

"We have the rest of the day. What do you want to do?" Aubrey asked.

"You decide." Zander was trying to be magnanimous.

"Okay, we'll go biking, and I'll show you the island."

Zander groaned.

"Hey, I gave you the first option. You deferred to me."

Zander didn't argue. He went inside to get dressed for his bike tour. He didn't mind all that much. It was just that his crotch got so sore from the tiny little bike seat. It was the favorite part of his anatomy and wanted it always to be fully operational.

When he came back out, Aubrey had wheeled both bikes near the door and was waiting patiently straddling hers.

"Lunch at Traders, and then off to the south end, to see the lighthouse and fishing pier. We'll have beers at the Lazy Flamingo and cocktails later at Casa Ybel or the Sundial."

"Well, it sounds like at least I'll be able to rest my ass now and again."

"If you keep up and stop whining, maybe I'll let you rest with my ass later." Aubrey took off, and Zander did everything he could to keep up with her.

~

Herbie dialed Gail's phone after his last stop. She was working in one of the art store co-ops, but it wasn't busy so she could talk.

"I invited Zander to stay with us beginning tomorrow evening at 7:00. I hope that's okay with you." Herbie always wanted to get out all the potential questionable decisions as soon as possible. He found it worked for him quite well. If all the bad news came out quickly, then the problems didn't compound themselves.

"How long do you think they'll stay?"

Herbie had forgotten about that piece of information, and he felt bad.

"I don't know. Does it matter?"

"Of course not. He's your friend. He can stay as long as he likes."

Herbie was always amazed at Gail's flexibility in dealing with everyday life. Nothing ever seemed to rattle her.

"One other thing, he's bringing Aubrey."

"I'll be anxious to meet her. If Zander thinks enough of her to introduce her to us, I believe we'll be well on our way to a great friendship."

"You always know what to say. I don't deserve any part of you."

"No, but I deserve you."

Herbie was still trying to figure that out on the rest of his way home.

31

By 8:00 the next morning, Zander and Aubrey had the pickup loaded. Aubrey wanted to take one last stroll on the beach, and Zander went willingly. Neither one saw the black SUV drive into the parking area. While Zander and Aubrey walked along the water's edge, the man walked to Zander's vehicle with something in his hand. When he stepped away, his hands were empty and he walked back to his black vehicle and sped away.

Zander and Aubrey strolled the beach for over an hour before they returned. There was nothing left to eat in the cabin, so they decided to go out for breakfast. Zander went over to the office to check out, while Aubrey did the once-over in the cabin to make sure they left nothing behind.

When Zander returned, Aubrey was already waiting in the pickup.

"Where do you want to go for breakfast?" Zander asked.

Aubrey looked at the clock on the dash. It was 10:30.

"Let's skip breakfast and do an early lunch somewhere."

"Any suggestions?"

"Surprise me."

"I wish you would quit telling me to do that."

"I trust your judgment."

"That could be a big mistake."

"Let's take one last ride around the island. I want to imprint it into my mind."

"What are you, some sort of computer?" Zander asked.

"Something like that," Aubrey said, and sat back.

They drove around for the better part of an hour. Aubrey was directing Zander the entire time. Zander didn't mind her front seat driving. He thought about offering to let her drive, but he wasn't quite ready to deal with something like that. He needed to be in control even if it was merely steering the vehicle to Aubrey's commands.

Aubrey made a few suggestions concerning lunch. Zander ignored all of them. After all, she had told him to surprise her, and that's what he planned to do.

When he turned the pickup onto the causeway, he could tell Aubrey was disappointed. She wanted one last meal on the island, but since she had given up the choice, Zander decided to make the decision. He thought that this might cure that "surprise me" phrase of hers. If that were the case, her minor disappointment would be worth it.

"Where are you taking me?"

"It's a surprise."

Aubrey turned, trying to pout, knowing she asked for what was about to happen.

Zander made his way off the island and then took a right turn on Old McGregor Road. Aubrey took notice. She hadn't been on this road before, and she was interested in the different businesses. There was a strip mall on their right hand side about a mile beyond the turn. Zander drove into it and parked in front of a bar called Buster's.

"We're going to a bar?" Aubrey asked, sternly.

"Sure. But it's not just any bar. Wait before you make judgments."

"Anything else, preacher?"

Zander laughed. He went around to her door and helped her out of the pickup.

"This way, madam."

"Oh, please. No matter how you shine it up and try to make it look pretty, a turd is still a turd."

"Well, this turd has an entire lobster as their special today."

"How much?"

"14.99."

Aubrey grabbed his hand, "Let's go." She led him into the front door.

The seating area was huge. There were lots of tables, booths and a larger circular bar that appeared to be filled with locals. Of course locals around here meant snowbirds.

"This is an Ohio State bar. All the fans come here on game days and watch their team."

Aubrey looked around and noticed a huge sign on the wall. It read, "Muck Fichigan."

"I like that sign, so I must like Busters."

"Well, it's not an Iowa Hawkeye bar, but it's okay. Where do you want to sit?"

Aubrey pointed to the bar. "I want to get the local flavor."

They found two seats in the middle of the morning crowd. Most of them were drinking beer, and most of them were men. A few older woman were sitting next to what Zander thought might be their husbands. They were by far the youngest people in the bar. They were the center of attention. It was Aubrey who had turned the heads. If she noticed, she never let on. Zander was enjoying the whole scene because Aubrey was enjoying herself. He knew she no longer cared about missing out on some Sanibel eatery.

The server came over and spoke to Zander.

"Welcome to Buster's. I'm Barb, and I'll be serving you today. Can I get you something to drink?"

"Barb, get us a couple of Yuenglings. We want your special as well."

"Do you want to split it with the pretty woman?"

"No. Two orders please."

"I don't want to lose a sale, but you should know that it's a lot of food."

"Don't let her size fool you. She could outeat the both of us."

Aubrey turned from her conversation, "I heard that. He's right, I want that lobster all to myself."

"I'll get right on it." The server smiled and left.

Zander was always amazed at how Aubrey could be in a conversation and still know what was being said around her. Maybe she just keyed into what Zander was saying, but he couldn't be sure. He just knew it was a talent he didn't possess. Too much information coming his way made Zander's head spin.

Their drinks were delivered, and Zander was almost ready to order another, when their food came. He had lost Aubrey to the attention of the other men. A pretty girl in a bar always gets the attention of the older patrons. Maybe they were reliving their youth, or maybe they just appreciated a young pretty woman. Zander had talked to Jasper about that, when he tended bar at the Glass Onion. Jasper told him that aging was a dirty bastard.

"Your body gets old. Your hair gets gray. It's harder to take a leak. You get aches and pains in places you never knew existed. Your skin gets thin. You get age spots and your hair gets thin or goes away altogether. You can't see, and you can't hear. But here's the kicker. In your mind, you're still that 21-year-old virile stud you always were."

Zander could see that in these guys in the bar. It made him sad somehow. Maybe because he knew it would happen to him someday. Some mornings he felt it was already happening.

Zander tapped Aubrey on the shoulder.

"Your lobster's here. Do you want another beer?"

She had taken a few sips from the first one, so she declined. She excused herself from her admirers, and they took the hint gracefully.

"You seem to be quite the sensation," Zander said, while trying to crack his lobster. He wasn't having much luck.

"You brought me here, remember? I can't help it if these guys are in love with me." She smiled at Zander.

"It's okay. I'm not threatened."

"Shoot. Here I was hoping to make you jealous." Aubrey took the plastic bibs that came with the special and tied one around Zander's neck.

"Why do we need these?"

"Have you never eaten lobster before?"

"Well sure. I mean I've had lobster tail."

"Not the same thing at all. You'll be a buttered mess when you finish this. Help me with my bib."

Zander tied the straps around her neck.

They finished their shellfish and after giving hugs to her

newfound friends, Zander and Aubrey left Buster's at 1:00.

"Did you have to hug every one of those guys?" Zander asked.

"They were all so sweet. It didn't hurt to give them just a little thrill for their day."

Zander marveled at Aubrey's ability to work a room. She seemed to make friends wherever she went. Zander was more aloof. He didn't want to invest a large amount of time into relationships that would end with no chance of any future. He knew that it gave him the appearance of being arrogant. It just wasn't how he was brought up. The Dutch always kept everything close to the vest. Sharing feelings and being outgoing with strangers just wasn't part of the culture. He envied Aubrey. It was one of the many things that attracted him to her. He had no idea what she saw in him. Maybe it was just that opposites attract. Whatever the reason, he knew he was a lucky man.

"We should make our way to Cedar Key. It's a good five-hour drive from here. That should get us there after 6:00. It will be just enough time to show you around the island before we meet Herbie and Gail at 7:00."

Aubrey's eyes opened wide, "Cedar Key is an island?"

Zander had forgotten that Aubrey had never been there.

"Well sort of. It's hard to explain. You'll just need to see it."

"I like the area already, and I've never even been there. This should be a great adventure."

"Don't get your hopes up. I may have oversold it, so you would agree to go. It's pretty laid back. It's not a Sanibel by any means."

"I think I could use some laid-back time. Don't you agree?"

Zander agreed wholeheartedly, and he nodded his head.

By the time they made I-75, Aubrey was napping with her head resting on Zander's right arm. She woke up, when they were about to cross the Sunshine Bridge at Tampa.

"I've never seen such a huge bridge," Aubrey said, almost childlike.

"Wait until we get to the top. You'll love the view."

Crossing the bridge always made Zander feel good. He had no idea why, but it was just a freeing feeling he got when he crossed huge man-made expanses. The only time he didn't like this particular bridge was when it was windy. He was always afraid some vehicle would be traveling too fast and swerve into his lane when the wind gusted. Luckily, today was calm, so he enjoyed the ride with Aubrey.

They took the toll road out of St. Pete and headed toward Cedar Key. Zander figured there would be less traffic, and the few tolls wouldn't add up to much anyway.

They stopped for gas in Crystal River. Aubrey noticed all the signs advertising tours for manatee watching. She was disappointed that they didn't have time to take a tour. Apparently, Crystal River had a large population of manatees.

"We will need to come back here. I want to see some of these creatures. I've heard so much about them, but I've never been even close to seeing one."

"That can be done. It's about an hour-and-a-half to Cedar Key from here. In fact, we can see the power plant towers from the island. We'll come back and do whatever you want. We've got the time."

Aubrey nodded. She knew Zander was still walking on eggshells, trying to get her to forget Corey Prescott. She loved him for that. She didn't have the heart to tell him that she was stronger than he was giving her credit.

They rolled into Cedar Key at 6:30. Aubrey could see what Zander was trying to tell her about the island after they crossed the fourth bridge. The island was at the end of the causeway and surrounded by water.

"This place is fascinating," Aubrey said.

"The tide is in. Just wait until tomorrow when it goes out."

"Then what?"

"You'll just have to wait and see," Zander said, as they drove toward the wharf area.

"Stop the truck," Aubrey commanded.

"What?"

"I want to buy a tee shirt. There's a shop right there."

Zander pulled into the first available parking spot. They both got out and found the shop. It was right below the restaurant called Steamers that Zander had visited before.

Aubrey tried on a number of shirts before she was satisfied with two that didn't make her look fat. Zander just shook his head. He would never understand women.

Zander paid for the items, they walked over to the fishing pier, climbed up the steps and found a bench to sit on. It was a pleasant evening even though darkness had set in.

Seven o'clock was just a few minutes away. It would be okay to be a few minutes late, but Zander couldn't abide being anything over five minutes past the agreed time. He hated to disturb Aubrey, but his friends were waiting.

"We need to get moving. We will be late otherwise."

Aubrey knew of Zander's time fetish and didn't want to agitate him. She had never been overly concerned with time. Zander had been good for her in that respect.

"Is their home far from here?"

"Nothing in Cedar Key is far from here." He pointed toward the northwest. "You can see the house from here."

Aubrey followed his arm to where it pointed. She could see the four-level house he had indicated.

"That looks like a really nice place."

"It is. I'm sure Gail has made it even nicer since the last time I was here."

They talked about Gail and Herbie on the two-block drive to their home. Zander explained how she had embraced the artist community since they had moved here. Aubrey found that very interesting.

Before Zander could park the pickup under the house, Gail and Herbie were opening their doors. The welcome impressed Zander. He couldn't have asked for anything better for Aubrey's introduction.

The usual hugs were given all around. Gail took Aubrey's hand.

"Come along, hon. You need to see the house. The boys can bring the luggage to your room. I suppose we can find another room for Zander to stay," Gail said, and looked over her shoulder at Zander.

"Damn funny, Gail. You are just hilarious."

The girls laughed and went into the house.

Herbie grabbed Zander by the shoulders and looked into his eyes.

"It good to see you again, old friend."

"Easy on that old friend shit, Herbie. I'm starting to think that way, and I don't like it one bit."

Herbie just looked at Zander. Zander thought there was something in his eyes that he hadn't noticed before.

"What's wrong? Is everything all right?"

"Everything's perfect. It just couldn't be any better."

Herbie wasn't necessarily that convincing, however.

32

Herbie and Gail had been having an argument prior to Zander and Aubrey's arrival. It wasn't much of an argument by most people's standards, but it was as close to a fight that the two had ever experienced. It had almost made Herbie sick. He hated the feeling. Gail was everything to him, and he didn't want anything to ever come between them. He agreed to do as she had asked.

The conflict had arisen when Herbie asked if he should tell Zander about Jayne. Gail had been forceful.

"You stay out of this. He's your friend, and nothing good would come of it. You don't know how he would react. He might even blame you."

"I don't think he would."

"Don't think. Just keep your mouth shut. If this woman thinks he should know, she will tell him. Besides, this is all conjecture anyway. You don't have all the facts."

"Well, I would want to know if the tables were turned."

"Lucky for you, you'll never have to worry about that. You're stuck with me."

That's when all the wind went out of Herbie's sails.

He just couldn't get rid of that nagging feeling that he should be doing something, however. Maybe he just needed to talk to Fats. At least he might feel better. Somehow, he felt he was selling out his good friend, and that made him miserable. The last thing he wanted was to drive a wedge between Gail and him. It was a predicament that Herbie had tried to avoid his entire life.

He was thinking about calling Fats when they drove up. Gail saw them first.

"Are you okay? Are you going to be able to pull this off?" she asked Herbie.

"I'll be fine," Herbie said, but didn't sound convinced.

"I've been thinking about this, and I've decided to share something that will take everyone's mind off this Jayne woman."

"That would be a blessing, but it would have to be something huge."

"Trust me. It will blow your socks off."

Herbie doubted it, but he hadn't been disappointed by anything Gail had done previously. He would just have to wait and see.

They met their friends at the foot of the stairs. After hugs and introductions involving Aubrey, the girls went upstairs. Zander went to the back of the pickup to get their luggage. Herbie couldn't help notice that there was quite a bit of stuff in the pickup bed.

"Traveling a little heavy, don't you think?"

"That's all Aubrey's stuff. I'm taking her away from Southern Florida?"

"Where are you planning to go?"

"That's why we're here. We need to make some decisions."

Herbie's eyes must have shown some panic. Zander smiled at him.

"Don't worry, we won't be staying long. We'll try not to put you out."

"It's not that." Herbie was about to say more when Gail called down.

"Hey, you two, get up here. There are a couple of girls who are thirsty and need a good bartender. But I guess one of you will have to do."

Herbie laughed and helped Zander with the luggage.

After they got Zander and Aubrey settled into their third-floor bedroom, the four returned to the bar area in the kitchen. Herbie mixed up a drink he called a pea picker. It contained a can of limeade and four cans of water. He mixed in a can of Sailor Jerry white rum and filled four glasses with ice. It was his answer to an easy tropical drink. Most people liked them. He liked making them because it didn't take much work. Herbie decided early on that he wasn't much of a bartender.

They had finished their second pitcher of pea pickers, and Herbie was mixing a third.

"Jeez, I didn't know you were all such lushes. I'll need to go back to the market for more limeade if you keep this up."

"Looks like you could use more rum as well," Zander said.

"We were thirsty. But, I think we'll slow down now," Gail said.

"If we don't, you'll have to pour me into bed," Aubrey added.

Zander liked that idea. Going to bed with Aubrey was always something foremost in his mind.

"I've got something to tell everyone. I think it will come as quite a shock to both Herbie and Zander. Aubrey, you'll just enjoy the irony," Gail said.

Zander and Herbie just looked at her.

"Oh, I do love a good mystery, especially if it involves Zander," Aubrey said, and sat on the edge of her chair.

"I have a question for Zander and Herbie. What do you remember about the businesses on the main street in your hometown? It would have to be while you were growing up. Can you name them?"

Zander and Herbie looked at each other for a moment. They both liked this game.

"Let's start at the statue on the west end and work east," Zander said.

"Let me get some paper, so we can write this down." Herbie went to the drawer and came back with a notepad and an ink pen. He had taken both from a Holiday Inn on one of his overnight trips.

"South side of the street first," Zander said.

Together, they listed everything on the block's south side. When they followed with the north side, Gail stopped them when they mentioned John and Jo's Market.

"What was that you just said?"

"It was a little grocery on the north side of the street," Herbie told her.

"Did you know the people who ran it?" Gail asked.

"Not very well. We were young, and they left town before we were in junior high, I think."

"Say, wasn't there a girl in our class? I remember seeing a skinny little thing in the store when I went in there with my parents."

"I believe that's right," Zander agreed.

"Why the interest in the market?" Herbie asked.

"I just wanted to see what you remembered. That skinny little thing was me."

Zander and Herbie's mouths dropped open in unison. Aubrey started laughing when she saw them.

"What a great story. You two must have had your heads up each other butts."

"We were kids. We didn't care about girls, unless they wanted to play ball at recess," Zander said, seeing the humor himself.

Herbie just looked at Gail. His face looked like he had just witnessed a bad accident.

"Herbie, what wrong with you?" Gail wanted to know.

He just shook his head for a few moments before he spoke quietly.

"You knew me when I was fat. I don't understand. Did you know right away when we met?"

"Not immediately, but it didn't take long. I knew for sure when you talked about Zander."

"Why didn't you say anything? I can't believe you agreed to be with me knowing what a dipshit I'd been."

"That was a long time ago. Besides, I was a skinny little thing, and you were a fat big thing. Neither of us are those things anymore."

"I've spent my whole life running away from what I was in the past. Then, when I find someone who takes me beyond all that, I find out she was still a part of the history." He dropped his head.

Gail got up and put her arms around Herbie.

"That's the ironical part don't you think? Here you were trying to run away from your past, because you were miserable there. So was I, until I found you. I told you this because I wanted you to know that none of that matters. The past is the past. None of us can do anything about it. The future will be what we make it. I thought you might enjoy all that irony."

"I guess I just never wanted anyone to know the former me."

"Zander is sitting right here. He knows all about your past, and yet, you are still friends."

"Well, yeah, but he's not a woman, and I'm not interested in marrying him."

Gail pulled back.

"Holy shit. This is better than a movie," Aubrey said.

Gail almost threw herself into Herbie's lap and grabbed him around the neck.

"That's the most romantic thing I've ever heard anyone say." She buried her face into his chest.

Herbie didn't know what to do. He looked up at Zander. Zander just shrugged. Aubrey got Herbie's attention and mimed for him to embrace her. She pretended to show him kissing her as well.

Zander liked what he was seeing, and to help the situation, he grabbed Aubrey and kissed her in a tight embrace. Herbie took the cue and followed suit.

Finally, Zander broke away.

"Before this turns into a love fest, we need to go out and celebrate. This will be on me, and we're going to make a night of it. You two decide where you want to go."

Both Herbie and Gail didn't have to think twice. They decided on the hotel.

"Let's make this a real celebration. We need to dress for the occasion," Aubrey said.

Both Herbie and Zander groaned.

"It's a fine idea, Aubrey," Gail said, "Let's go Herbie. I'll find something for you to wear."

"Same for you, Mister." Aubrey said to Zander.

In fifteen minutes, they were ready and making their way to the hotel. They decided to walk because it was a flawless evening. Zander thought the women might have wanted to show off their evening dresses, but that was all right. They looked beautiful. Both Zander and Herbie were proud to walk the few blocks up the street, showing off the best things that had ever happened to either of them.

They had two bottles of wine with dinner, and after-dinner cocktails followed. When they returned home, the four were just a bit tipsy. There was much laughter and song. They walked to the pier on the way home. At first the intention was to stop off at one of the bars for a nightcap, but everyone was filled to the top, so they sat on the fishing pier and tried to harmonize to Peter, Paul and Mary. They thought they were spectacular. Other passersby probably didn't share that opinion, but they smiled nevertheless.

~

The black SUV found some parking near Gail and Herbie's house. The driver shut off the motor and got out to stretch. The passenger made a call on his cell phone. After a few minutes of conversation, he told the driver to get back in. They would need to find a somewhere to stay for a few days and keep an eye on these two. After that, there would be other orders.

~

The next few weeks were a time of exploration for Aubrey and Zander. They both wanted to see everything in the area. Zander showed her what he had already seen. They explored the Lower Suwannee River and Wildlife Refuge. They did all the tidewater tours and hiked in Fanning Springs State Park. There were kayak trips that Zander particularly liked. They got to see places that couldn't be accessed by car or boat. He felt like an explorer, and Aubrey was ready for everything and anything. After such excursions, they would return to Herbie and Gail's exhausted. Many evenings saw them both in bed and sleeping before 8:00. It was without a doubt the most fun Zander had ever experienced with a friend. What made it even more special was that this friend was a woman that he loved. Part of him thought he should quit trying to be this lovesick goofball, but the other part just couldn't help being silly.

They chartered an all-day fishing excursion and somehow stumbled into some redfish. Aubrey always seemed to catch the biggest fish. It was a little factoid that she never got tired of telling

Zander.

As Zander had promised on the way to Cedar Key, they went back to Crystal River and did the manatee tour. Aubrey found the courage to swim with them. Zander didn't have the same desire. He was happy to just watch the gentle giants lumber around in the warm waters coming from the power plant.

Despite all the fun and relaxation, they both knew they had some decisions to make. Herbie and Gail had already been putting pressure on them to find something on the island to buy. They wanted them to stay in the worst way.

Aubrey had told Zander that she would be happy to do whatever he decided. He didn't like that very well and told her so. Zander needed Aubrey to be fully vested in all their decisions. He knew it would be the only way their relationship could possibly last. That was the most important thing to him.

"I can't see us staying here. We've almost seen everything there is to be seen. What would we do, then?" Zander asked.

"I suppose we could get a job tending bar. Looks like they could always use help in that area."

"I don't feel like working like that any more," Zander said.

"Then we'll need to move on. I want to see things. You could be my tour guide. We could go until the money runs out, and then we could work for a while."

Zander didn't tell her that he had enough money. They wouldn't need to work at all, unless they did something stupid like buying an expensive property on an island like Sanibel.

"I think I like that idea," Zander agreed.

"Besides, I want to see where you grew up after hearing all about your background with Herbie and Gail."

Zander shook his head and smiled. "I suppose stranger things have happened, but that was an unusual story, don't you think?"

"It was a nice turn of events. Both Gail and Herbie need an explanation if you don't take up their offer to stay."

"I know. I'm dreading that."

"They'll understand. They are good people. Besides, they have each other. I think that's all the two of them need."

"Like us?' Zander asked.

"Exactly like us."

In another week, plans would be made, and Herbie and Gail would be saddened to see them go.

There would be one other piece of business that would put Zander back on high alert, however.

33

Two days before their scheduled departure, Zander decided to get the pickup serviced. He had exceeded the recommended three thousand miles, and he didn't want to take the time for an oil change down the road. He had asked Herbie where he serviced his vehicle. Herbie had pointed him to a little business across the street from the market. The name on the sign said "John's Service." There was a John's Service in almost every little town, and Zander loved the folksy living of small communities.

Zander dropped off his pickup and walked across the street to the market. He was purchasing steaks for dinner that evening. The little market had almost everything anyone needed. Zander was filling his basket with items he thought they needed for a great meal. He bought two porterhouse steaks for the guys, and the girls got some nice bacon wrapped filets. He found some fresh green beans. He decided to get a lemon and some fresh dill for the beans. Some lettuce, spinach, and a few bottles of a red-blend wine rounded out his purchase.

Just as the clerk was ringing up the total, Zander remembered the key lime pie. He had her include the pie in the total, while he went to the cooler to retrieve it.

Zander was just putting his billfold back into his rear pocket, when a young boy rushed into the market.

"Are you Zander?"

"That's me."

"My dad needs to see you about your pickup. I think it's really important."

"I'll follow you." Zander was hoping it was nothing serious. He didn't want have to waste any more time now that Herbie and Gail knew they weren't staying.

When Zander crossed the street, he noticed his pickup was still on the rack and in the air. He was concerned.

"This doesn't look good," Zander said, to a man he assumed was John.

"I want you to see something," John said, and walked over to the driver's door.

He pointed to something under the running board, and Zander let his eyes adjust to the darker undercarriage. It was a square black metal box with a piece of black electrical tape hiding something on the face.

"I scratched off some of that tape just to try and see what this thing was about."

Zander looked at the small opening and saw a red light was flashing underneath.

"What the hell is this thing?" Zander asked, but he already knew.

"At first I wondered if it was a bomb. That scared me a bunch, I can tell you. But after I studied it, I think it's some kind of GPS. Looks like someone is tracking you."

"That's what it appears to me, also."

"Any ideas?"

"None whatsoever."

"You want me to remove it? I could put it on one of my loaners and see what happens."

"Thanks, but I don't want to involve you, especially if it becomes dangerous," Zander said, although he thought the idea of the loaner was a good one.

"Suit yourself. But have Herbie let me know what comes of all this. I enjoy a bit of intrigue now and then. We don't get much of that around here."

Zander thought he could have as much of his as he wanted. This was something that made him nervous, because he had no idea where it was coming from.

John lowered Zander's pickup. Zander deposited his groceries into the passenger's seat and paid his bill. He thanked John for his vigilance and backed out of the bay.

A black SUV sat in the parking lot of Annie's café, and the two suits were having a late breakfast. One of them had a handheld GPS tracker and was watching as the red dot moved out of the service station.

"Looks like he's heading back to the house."

The other shrugged and went back to eating his gigantic omelet.

When Zander reached his friend's house, he parked the pickup, took the grocery bag and climbed the stairs. He wasn't thinking much about dinner. He put the bag on the counter and turned to face his friends.

Aubrey could see something was wrong.

"Zander, what happened?" She moved to his side.

"I don't know. You need to come with me. I need to show you something." He led them down to his pickup.

Before anyone could say anything, Zander dropped to the concrete and slid himself under the truck. A few moments later he came back out from under and had something in his hand.

"What the hell is that?" Herbie asked, loudly.

"That's what I asked, after John showed it to me."

"It's a GPS," Aubrey said quietly.

Zander, Herbie and Gail all turned to look at Aubrey.

"Did you know about this?" Zander had been taken totally off-guard.

"No, but I've seen others like it."

"Where did it come from?" Zander's question was a bit more forceful than he had intended.

"I can't be totally sure, but it looks like the something from the State Department."

"Why would they be tracking Zander?" Herbie asked.

"They're not. They're tracking me." Aubrey said.

"But why?" Zander asked.

"I don't know. If I had to guess, something is happening in Cuba. I've done some translation work for them in the past. I've heard rumors that Castro is in poor health. Maybe they are planning something. I just don't know."

Zander looked at her for a moment. He knew there was more than she was telling them. No one went to this much trouble to track a translator.

"What should we do?" Zander asked Aubrey.

"I've told them, time and time again, that I'm finished working for the government. I don't want any part of anything they might be planning."

Herbie and Gail sat on the steps. Zander opened the driver's door and placed the GPS gently under the seat.

"Tell us what you want to do." Zander said, as gently as he could.

"I don't know. Chances are there are two guys in a black SUV hanging around here someplace."

"How about I throw that thing in the muck off bridge number three." Zander blurted out the first number that came to his mind.

Aubrey smiled. "I think bridge number one or two might be better."

Her little joke served to cut the tension.

Gail was the first to speak. "Would that really solve anything?"

"Probably not, but it would make us all feel better," Aubrey replied.

"What are you thinking, Herbie?" Zander asked.

"I think I've got a good idea, but it's going to hasten your departure."

"What devious thing are you planning?" Gail asked, good-naturedly.

"It will be business as usual in case we're being watched. We'll have dinner like we planned. You're grilling the steaks, Zander."

Zander agreed.

"Then what?" Gail asked.

"These two will pack their bags in the dark, and I'll put that box thing under my truck. At 3:00 tomorrow morning, I'll take off for Everglade City. I just so happen to have a delivery scheduled for the day after tomorrow. I'll just be a day early."

Zander wasn't getting the plan.

"How will this help us?"

"You need to leave right after I take off. By the time they figure out what happened, you'd be long gone. What will they do to me? They'll assume you found the GPS when you had your oil changed."

Zander tried to find fault with Herbie's idea, but it seemed sound. Since he had nothing to counter, he agreed.

"You can't tell me where you're going, in case they try to sweat me."

Zander thought Herbie might be a bit overdramatic, but he knew he was right. He even thought about Mr. Sparky. He hadn't been carrying it lately, but he would be putting it back in his cargo shorts.

"This is way beyond anything I could ask you to do for us, Herbie." Aubrey said, and gave him a hug.

Herbie reddened, and he looked over at Gail. She hid a smile. Herbie was embarrassed at being hugged, and that's what drew Gail to him. In so many ways, he was just a boy, trying to find his way around women. Gail was just happy he had chosen her. It would be a lasting relationship.

"There's something you're not thinking about," Gail said to Herbie.

"What?"

"Their phones. You'll need to take them and get rid of them just in case they have some sort of trace on them." Gail was firm.

"Damn, I never thought about the phones. Good call, Gail." He stood and put out his hand. "Give me your phones."

Zander groaned. "Not again. These things are a pain in the ass. It's no wonder I hate technology."

They both handed over their phones.

"You can buy new ones at some Wal-Mart down the road. Wait, on second thought, why don't you copy down the relevant numbers so you can put them in the new phones. We don't want to lose contact with you totally."

"Already done," Aubrey said.

Zander glanced at her. "You don't have mine."

"Of course I do. In my purse, there's a little black book. It's just something I always do. I made sure to take down your numbers just in case something happened to your phone."

Zander was confused. He wondered why she would be interested in his phone. Aubrey could see he was bothered by her actions.

"It's what couples do, isn't it?"

Suddenly, Zander didn't care what prompted all his confusion. All he wanted was to continue being with Aubrey, whatever the consequences might be

Herbie put the phones in his pocket. They would end up in the bay between Everglade City and Chokoloskee.

"I'll grill the steaks, but that's it. There's green beans, salad, wine, and key lime pie that needs attention."

"I'll cut the pie," Herbie volunteered.

"More like you'll cut the cheese," Zander joked.

Herbie's cheeks turned red.

Gail took him by the arm. "You open the wine. Let's celebrate good friends tonight. We don't know when we'll see each other again."

Zander wondered if they would ever see these two again. He hoped so. He looked over at Aubrey and could tell she was thinking the same thing. It took him by surprise. How could he know what she was thinking? Yet, he did. Her needs had just become the most significant thing in his life.

Dinner was filled with laughter and four bottles of wine. Gail was ready to open another bottle, but both Herbie and Zander stopped her.

"We don't need a hangover to start this adventure," Herbie said.

"It might be too late for that." Zander was joking, but thought he might have had more than his limit.

"I just don't want this evening to end," Gail said, with disappointment in her voice.

They did a group hug and then staggered up to bed. It was 10:30, and 3:00 a.m. would come all too soon.

Herbie opened Zander and Aubrey's door at 2:45. "Fifteen minutes, and I'm gone. You wait until 3:30 and head north. Take the back roads. Stay off 75 and 10."

"Herbie?" Zander asked.

"Yeah?"

"Thanks, man. I love you."

Herbie closed the door. There was a little smile on his face. No guy ever told him he loved him in his entire life, not even his father.

Truth was, it seemed quite natural coming from Zander.

Zander heard Herbie's truck start and begin moving away from the house. There was one little short honk, and the truck moved out of earshot.

Zander would remember that little horn honk for a long time. It was totally appropriate for Herbie. It was his way of saying goodbye.

34

Aubrey and Zander got up and showered together in the dark. It was too risky to put on any lights. They had all agreed on that fact the night before. They also got dressed in the dark. Their clothes had been laid out the night before, and their bags were packed. Zander took both bags down to the pickup and saw Gail busy doing something at the counter as he passed through.

When his pickup was loaded and secure, he went back into the house. Gail had put together some food in a small fabric cooler. She handed it to Zander.

"This is for the road. Put some miles behind you before you stop. It will be harder for them to trace your movements."

"Thanks, Gail. I don't know how to thank you guys for all this."

"Nonsense. It's what friends do for each other." She gave him a hug and a quick kiss on the lips.

By that time, Aubrey had come down. Gail handed them both an insulated coffee mug. They were the kind that had a top and no handle, so they would fit in the cup holders.

"Now, get out of here before I start crying."

Zander went back down the stairs toward the pickup, and Aubrey gave Gail one last hug.

"Come back to us, promise," Gail whispered in her ear.

"I promise." Aubrey said.

It was 3:30 on the button, and Zander would follow Herbie's

advice and stay on the back roads. He followed 341 to Chiefland and then turned onto 19/98. Zander figured it would take under two hours to reach Perry.

He didn't know that he would have his own ironical situation that would almost rival Herbie's. When they made the city limits, Zander would be within three hundred yards of Sara Jane. Of course, neither of them knew the other was in the area. So, the irony would have been saved just for Herbie, who already knew of Sara Jane's new address.

They blew right through town and continued west on 98. It was almost 5:30 in the morning. Aubrey had been dozing on and off because there wasn't much to see. She did wake when they went through Perry.

"This looks like a nice community," she said, rubbing her eyes. "We should come back here sometime."

Zander said nothing, and Aubrey went back to her dream world.

They pulled into Mexico Beach, Florida, at 8:00. Zander found a gas station and paid cash. He was used to not leaving a trail and only used his credit card in extreme emergencies. By that time, Aubrey was wide awake.

"I'm hungry."

"Why don't you see what Gail packed us?" Zander asked.

"Looks like ham and cheese sandwiches." She turned up her nose.

Zander didn't want to take the risk of stopping at a restaurant. They were a little over four hours from Cedar Key. He felt it was too close.

"Gail went to all the trouble to do this for us, so let's go and find a spot on the beach. I promise, they will taste great out in the sand and surf."

Aubrey wasn't so sure, but she agreed anyway. Zander had picked up two bottles of flavored water at the convenience store, and Aubrey put them into the little cooler with the sandwiches.

Zander found some public parking next to a restaurant called Killer Seafood. It wasn't open. It was just open for dinner, so it wouldn't tempt Aubrey.

The two got out of the pickup and took the boardwalk to the beach. There were a few portable toilets right on the beach, so they both used one.

"I hate these things," Aubrey said, as she slammed the door behind her. "They are so gross."

"Better than peeing in your shorts," Zander joked.

Aubrey couldn't argue with his down-home logic, so she just took off down the beach. They walked a few blocks and found a lone picnic table. Zander unpacked the cooler, while Aubrey went to the water's edge and waded into the surf almost knee deep.

Zander called to her to come back and eat her food. She came back reluctantly.

"Have you seen how white this sand is and how emerald green the water looks?"

"I have. Mexico Beach is one of a kind, I'm thinking."

Zander liked small laid-back places like this. There wasn't even a stop light in the whole community. It was a place where one could get lost in the everyday wonders of life.

Aubrey tore into her sandwich. It was gone in almost three bites.

"I guess you were hungry," Zander said.

"This salt air makes you ravenous," Aubrey said, breathing in deeply.

"Ravenous for something," Zander said, watching her chest rise and fall as she breathed in.

Aubrey punched him in the arm and then sprinted off for the gulf again, taking her water bottle along. Zander watched her play in the surf as he finished his sandwich. He could only marvel at her beauty and wonder why he was lucky enough to have her. He realized he was happy. He hadn't been happy for a very long time. In fact, he couldn't remember the last time he had been truly happy. He had buried that part of his life away in some deep, black hole.

When he was finished eating, he joined Aubrey. They walked the beach hand-in-hand, until Zander knew he had to end it. Besides, Aubrey was starting to pick up shells again. He didn't need that.

"It's time to head out," he said, quietly.

"I know," Aubrey said, but Zander could see her disappointment.

"I'll grab the cooler, and we'll go back to the pickup. You find the Florida map and choose our next stop."

That seemed to lift Aubrey's spirit, and she wrapped her arm around Zander's. Together, they made their way through the sand and back to the pickup.

"Knock that sand off your legs and feet. I don't want it in the mats," Zander ordered.

"You are such a putz. This sand will remind us of Mexico Beach." She hopped right into the passenger's seat.

Zander just shook his head, as he knocked the sand from his sandals. By the time he was able to take his spot behind the wheel, Aubrey already had their route decided.

"I've heard a lot about Destin, so I want to stop there for lunch and look around. After that, we'll go to Pensacola and stay there for the night. I'll be sick of riding by that time."

"Let it be said, let it be written," Zander said, as he took the map from Aubrey.

He looked at the route and was happy with it. They would stay on highway 98. Zander knew that anyone looking for them would assume they would take the fastest route away from Florida, and that would be the interstates. They would be far enough from Cedar Key, and maybe if they liked Pensacola, they might even stay for a while. That wouldn't be something anyone would expect.

Where the road would take them from there would be anyone's guess. They would go north or west depending on Aubrey's whim at the moment. He wanted to show her around the Midwest, and he would lobby hard for that direction, but Aubrey would have the final say. That's the way it had to be.

He put out that idea to Aubrey, and he could tell she was pleased. He knew he needed to be honest with her always. There was still one thing nagging at him, however. He decided to bring up the subject after they had driven through Panama City.

"Why don't you tell me what's really happening with these state department guys, if that's what they are."

Aubrey eyes flashed for a moment, and then she settled back into her seat.

"Oh, they are state department, don't ever be confused about that."

"What do they want with you? I know it's way more than some translation problem."

"I wanted to keep you out of all this."

"We've had this conversation. We agreed to be honest with each other, or this relationship will never work."

Aubrey sat still for a few moments and then turned toward Zander.

"You are right, and I apologize. I'll never keep anything from you again." Aubrey's eyes were watering.

"I know you thought it might be something I shouldn't know, but you've heard all about my past. I'm no lily-white guy, so never be afraid I can't handle any truth you might have out there."

Aubrey began her confession.

"I've worked for the state department in many capacities. So did my parents. I guess you could call us spies for the government. Everything we did involved Cuba and what Fidel was doing to his people. My parents were involved with the Cuban missile crisis. I was just a kid then. They never talked much about it, but I knew."

"Wow. I remember seeing all that on television. The U2 plane caught the Russians assembling the missiles, and it looked like they were aiming them at us. It was a pretty frightening time in America. I remember all those silly air-raid drills we did in school. We would go into the hallways and put books over our heads."

"Like that would protect us from the bomb and the radiation."

"I suppose it made everyone feel better. We were being proactive, no matter how stupid it appeared to be," Zander said. "Some people even converted their storm shelters, on their farms in Iowa, to bomb shelters."

"What did that mean?'

"I have no idea. I suppose they stocked it with things they needed to stay underground for a long period of time."

"I'm afraid if they dropped the bomb, no one would have to worry about it."

"We're a little off subject," Zander said, trying to refocus.

"What do you want to know?" Aubrey asked.

"Everything. What did you do for these guys?"

"Not a whole lot. I went over to Cuba to keep an eye on things for them. Since I had Cuban blood and still had some relatives over there, I went as a university professor on a cultural exchange."

"Did you run into any problems?"

"Sure. I was tailed wherever I went. I got to see more of Cuba than most and always had a great deal of protection. It was just that the guards were watching to see that I didn't cross any lines."

"Did you?"

"Did I what?"

"Cross any lines?"

The question made her stop and think. She looked over at Zander.

"I'm pretty skilled at small firearms, so yes, I crossed some lines. Maybe I'll tell you about it sometime."

Zander didn't like her response at all, but he decided not to pursue it at the moment. It would be better to let the subject cool down, before he found out the truth. He sat back and drove on toward Destin. It was silent in the pickup, and Zander noticed that it was making Aubrey nervous. She couldn't seem to sit still. Zander pretended not to notice.

"These guys aren't stopping until they find me."

"I would assume that to be a certain. But, I guess I need to know why."

"If you've paid attention to the news lately, you would have noticed that Fidel Castro is supposedly quite ill, at least that's the latest rumor."

"I've seen something on the news about it."

"Well, I'm sure they want me to go back and keep and eye on things. This might be the start of a regime change, and someone needs eyes on the ground. Since I've never been compromised, they are looking at me again."

"And you don't want to go back?"

"No. I told them I was through, but you're never finished unless they say you are."

"I don't like the sound of that."

"Now you are beginning to understand. That's why I took up with Corey in the beginning. I thought that if I was with someone from a prominent family, they might leave me alone. It didn't quite work out like I had planned."

"I thought I was taking you away from some bad memories. Now I see that I'm helping you to run away from the government."

Aubrey grabbed his arm. "Zander, it's not what I had planned. You need to believe me. I would never use you like that."

"Whoa. I think it's a fine idea. This will be very interesting and actually test how smart the two of us really are."

"You're not upset?"

"It would be the exact opposite. It's like a game, isn't it?"

"It has some pretty high stakes if you ask me." Aubrey said, and grimaced.

"What's the worst thing that can happen? They catch us and try to make you go to Cuba."

Aubrey turned and looked out the window for a long time. Then she turned and looked at Zander.

"Yes, and they could very well kill you."

35

The two suits woke up around 7:00. The driver of the SUV rolled out of bed and went to check the handheld GPS. The passenger was still laying in his double.

"Get up. They're on the move," the driver said.

"What? Where are they?"

"Looks like they're headed back to Everglade City. They just passed Naples on I-75."

"Shit. They must have left in the middle of the night."

"Get dressed, we've got to move."

"Let me take a shower first."

"No time. We've got to tie this up right now."

"They've got a pretty good head start on us, wouldn't you say? Another fifteen or twenty minutes won't matter."

The driver threw his phone over to his partner.

"Go ahead. You call the director, and tell him that."

They were on the road in three minutes.

~

Herbie took his time. He had a few deliveries before he needed to head back to Immokalee to reload. He stopped at the Island Café for breakfast and wasted more time. He figured the GPS boys wouldn't get there until almost noon. After an hour-and-a-half breakfast, he paid the bill and went back to his truck. He didn't want to hang around just waiting to be caught by some governmental agency. He suppressed a desire to remove the tracking device and put it on some local's vehicle. There was an old rusted-out Pontiac next to his truck that would have been ideal. He knew he couldn't play that card, because he needed to have these guys find him. He would need to have a convincing story, so they would think he and Gail had nothing to do with his friend's disappearance.

He made four stops, at various restaurants, and took extra time to talk to the proprietors. Life was slower down in the Everglades. People still talked to one another, and Herbie knew if he didn't reside in Cedar Key he would live down here.

It was almost noon when he made his final stop at the Rod And Gun Club. Zander had asked him to let the owner know that he and Aubrey were safe. Herbie did as he was asked. He also explained what was happening, and he expected to be interrogated by two men in suits within the hour. If it was okay, he would have lunch and let them find him right there.

"Do you want me to remove these assholes? I don't have much time for government men."

"No, it's part of the plan. I draw them back down here to give Aubrey and Zander a head start."

"Where are they going?"

"I seriously don't know. They didn't tell me, and I didn't want to know. That way I won't be lying to these guys."

"Smart. Maybe you should sit in the bar area. That way the rest of my customers won't be bothered by this," the owner said.

Herbie found a seat in the bar at a corner table. There was no one else around. It appeared that they didn't need a bartender over the lunch shift. If someone needed a drink, the server would take care of it.

Herbie liked being alone. He had lived most of his life alone. Well, he and Mr. Peabody had been together, but even that had changed. Mr. Peabody had become Gail's dog. He no longer wanted to go on road trips with Herbie. Gail took him to the art gallery when she worked her shift, and Mr. Peabody was a hit at the business. The artists and patrons seemed to be attracted to animals, which made perfect sense to Herbie. People with artistic talent seemed to have a passion for all things in nature. Gail thought Mr. Peabody helped to increase sales, and Herbie didn't mind the loss of his dog's loyalty. He had given it to Gail, and that was important. It made them a family.

A server saw Herbie after some time had passed. Herbie hadn't minded. He had nothing better to do until this situation resolved itself. The longer it took, the more distance Zander and Gail would put between them and these guys.

Zander was finishing his Cuban sandwich, when he caught sight of the two men. He pretended not to notice. He finished his glass of iced coffee and pushed his plate away. The two men walked through the entire restaurant, before they spotted Herbie sitting alone in the bar.

The taller of the two walked over and showed Herbie some credentials and a badge of some sort. Herbie pretended to be confused, as he looked everything over.

"You need to come with us," the shorter man said.

Herbie thought he might had seen too many cop shows on television.

"What's this all about?"

The guy took out a notebook trying to look official. It amused Herbie, but he tried not to show it.

"Do you know an Aubrey Moreno?"

"Well, sure, she's my best friend's girl."

"We've been following her, and now we find you where she should be."

"What the hell did she do?"

"You need to come with us."

"Sure, but I need to pay my ticket first."

"We'll go with you."

Herbie went to the cashier, paid the bill and left a twenty percent tip on top.

"Where are we going, boys?" Herbie asked loudly, and the owner looked out of his office.

The suits didn't like being conspicuous.

"Out to your truck, right now."

"Easy guys. I'm not the bad guy here."

"Just move." The taller suit pushed Herbie.

Herbie's temper instantly flashed. "I don't need you to lay hands on me," he said loudly.

The owner came rushing out of his office. "What's the problem here?"

The pair flashed their badges. "This is none of your business."

"The hell it ain't. This is my place. I know the guy you are shoving around, and I don't know either of you from nowhere. I've got the cops on speed dial. We can make this a real cluster fuck if that's what you want."

The two government men decided that it wasn't in their best interest and softened their demeanors.

"We just want to ask him some questions about some people he associates with. That's it. He'll be free to go, but right now we need to have him at his truck."

"It will be fine. If anything goes south, I'll holler," Herbie said.

"Maybe you guys should try not to be such assholes. I'm going to get some of the boys together, and we'll be watching you both."

"Are you threatening us?" The taller of the two was tired of listening.

"Damn right I am. What are you going to do about it?"

The shorter guy knew it was a no-win situation and pushed his friend out the door. Herbie smiled at the owner and gave him a thumbs-up. Then, he turned and followed the pair out the door. By the time Herbie reached his truck, the owner and five of his friends were on the back porch overlooking the parking lot. Herbie knew the owner would make good on his threat.

The suits were already waiting for him at the truck. One of them had the tracker in his hand.

"What can you tell me about this?" He thrust it at Herbie.

"What is it?" Herbie took the gadget and turned it over in his hands a few times.

"It's a GPS tracker, and it was on your truck."

"How the hell did it get there?" Herbie threw it back to the tall guy.

"You tell us."

"I have no idea. Why would I have something like that on my

vehicle?"

"It was on your buddy's pickup."

"Why?"

"We were using it to track Aubrey Moreno."

"Why?"

"None of your business."

"Looks like you're making it my business." Herbie was playing his game.

The pair looked at each other. The shorter one spoke.

"She's a government asset."

Herbie laughed. "Apparently, she doesn't want to be one."

"How did this tracker get on your truck?"

"Well, if I was the one trying to reason this out, I would say that my friend found your device and put it on my truck as a diversion."

"So you think your friend was using you as bait? It would piss me off if my friend used me like that."

"Do you have any friends?" Herbie asked.

"You're a funny guy. We'll see how funny you are when we take you into custody for aiding and abetting." The tall suit was getting angry again.

Herbie decide not to push it any further.

"I think that if you two thought I had anything to do with this, I'd be in cuffs already."

"Enough of this. Now you will cooperate, or we will take you in."

"What do you want me to do?" Herbie asked.

"Call your friend, and find out where he and Aubrey are right now."

Herbie did as directed, knowing full well that both phones were resting at the bottom of the bay between Everglade City and Chokoloskee. The phone continued to ring until Herbie handed it to the shorter guy. He listened and then handed it back.

"Why don't you call Aubrey's phone?"

"Already have. Same deal. Now what?"

"Call your wife. Find out if they are still at your house. Tell her you want to speak to your friend. Don't let her know we are looking for Aubrey."

Herbie made the call.

"Hi Gail. Would you put Zander on the phone? He's not answering his cell."

Herbie waited and listened.

"When did he leave? Both of them?"

Herbie looked over at the two. "They seem to have left sometime in the night. When Gail got up at 7:00 this morning, they were gone."

"Give me the phone." The big guy grabbed the phone out of Herbie's hand.

"I want you to listen to me, and make no mistake. If you are lying about this, you'll be spending time in a facility of our choice. You won't like it."

He listened for a few seconds and then returned the phone to Herbie.

"What?" the short guy asked.

"She told me to stick it up my ass."

Herbie laughed out loud. "That's my Gail. Trust me, you'd rather deal with me than try to take that tiger by the tail."

The pair seemed unsure of their next move. Herbie decided to expose all of his cards.

"Listen, I didn't know anything about any of this. My friend never mentioned anything to me. I never met Aubrey until recently. It looks like she wants to escape whatever it is that you want from her. My friend is head-over-heels in love with her, so he's going to do anything she wants. Doesn't your agency have other ways of locating missing persons?"

Herbie stopped and answered his own question silently. He didn't like what he was thinking. They hadn't thought about Zander's pickup and the license plate number. He was sure these guys had all that information.

He hoped that Zander would get a new phone soon. Herbie decided he would call Zander's answering service and leave a message with all that information. Zander would need to return any calls to Herbie's landline. Herbie was quite sure these guys had the ability to trace any calls coming into his phone. He was almost certain they already had his information. He had a new appreciation for Zander's loathing of all things technological.

"If either of these two people contact you, you will let us know."

The short one handed over his card.

Herbie looked at it. "Fat chance. I'm not going to do your work for you. These two aren't criminals, so I have no real reason to help you."

"Your country could use your help."

"Already served my country. Keep that bullshit to yourself." Herbie was finished. He walked back into The Rod And Gun Club.

The two agents got into their car and sped off. If they had waited a few more minutes, they would have heard a huge round of applause, as Herbie walked back into the club.

36

Zander and Aubrey pulled into Pensacola late in the afternoon. They had spent more time in Destin than expected because they both liked what they saw. Pensacola was larger than either of them had anticipated. Zander stopped for gas and asked the attendant where he could recommend a place to stay. He told them to go to the Holiday Inn on Pensacola Beach. Zander was surprised to see that Pensacola Beach and Gulf Breeze were two separate locations and not part of Pensacola. He had to cross the causeway to get to Gulf Breeze. Then there was another bridge to cross to arrive at Pensacola Beach.

Both he and Aubrey were stunned at the sugar-sand beaches. They had thought Mexico Beach and Panama City had great beaches, but both paled by comparison. Aubrey wanted to run down to the beach the minute Zander stopped the pickup.

"Go ahead. I'll see if they've got a room," Zander said, and watched her run barefoot to the edge of the water.

Since it was off-season in the panhandle, Zander could have his pick of rooms. As he was signing in, Zander marveled at how areas of Florida differed. The panhandle was in high season in the summer months. Spring breakers found some of the areas in March, but otherwise people came to the beaches to escape the summer heat. Southern Florida was opposite. High season there started in January and ran until the first part of May. It was because the snowbirds were escaping the winters up north.

All the rooms faced the ocean; so Zander selected a king room on the upper half of the hotel. He brought up their bags and opened up the slider to their small deck overlooking the ocean. Zander could see Aubrey on the beach. It looked like she was writing something in the sand with a large stick. Zander couldn't make it out. Their room was too far up. He tried to call down to Aubrey, but she couldn't hear him over the surf.

He was tired from driving, but he knew he had to go down and let Aubrey know they had a room. He needed to find some place for dinner as well. The elevators were quick, and he was in the lobby almost instantly. He asked the desk clerk for a recommendation for dinner. She was a pretty young thing, and Zander felt she might be flirting with him. There seemed to be a generous amount of eyelash-fluttering.

"I think you might be happy with Peg-Leg Pete's. It's known for their oysters. They have them on the half-shell of course, but they also have three different kinds of baked oysters." She smiled. "You know what they say about eating oysters."

Zander knew, but he wasn't about to let her know. He played dumb, and she was almost ready to make her move when Aubrey walked in. She walked over and put her arm through Zander's and smiled. The clerk was intimidated. Zander was amused. He couldn't help but think that almost anyone would be intimidated by Aubrey's beauty.

"Do they have a room for us?" Aubrey asked.

"We're already checked in, and our bags are in the room. I was just asking this striking young woman where she would suggest we go for dinner."

"And?"

"You're going to love it. The young lady tells me it is known for their oysters."

"Oh, my God. Not again. I don't think I can take it."

The desk clerk smiled a bit, as she realized she had been taken in with their little act. Zander smiled at her.

"Thanks for the information. You've been very helpful."

"Don't let his height fool you. He's not all that virile. He needs every oyster he can get his hands on."

The clerk had to smile again. She was laughing to herself when the couple walked out of the lobby into the parking lot.

"Isn't it a bit early for dinner?" Aubrey asked.

"I wanted to get you out of there before you completely destroyed my ego," Zander said, looking at her cross-eyed.

"You are an idiot."

"But I'm your idiot. Never forget it."

"How could I? You never tire of letting me know," Aubrey said, trying to sound cross.

"Actually, I wanted to find someplace where we can get a couple of burner phones. I think we should let people know where we are and what we have planned."

"What do we have planned?"

"I was hoping you'd tell me."

"Well, I hope it's something better than flirting with hotel desk clerks."

"Hey, she was flirting with me."

"I know. I was watching you both. You shouldn't tease these poor young things. If I weren't quite so understanding, I'd just give you the old heave-ho and see how long you'd last with someone half your age."

"You might be surprised."

Aubrey knocked him hard in the shoulder. They got into the pickup and went to find a drug store or a Wal-Mart. Zander wasn't picky.

They found some phones at a Walgreens. Zander spotted an Irish pub and after some convincing, he got Aubrey to go in with him. Both were amazed at all the dollar bills attached to the ceiling. People wrote their names on them and the waitresses would staple them to the ceiling. The server said they had well over a million dollar bills up there. It was Zander's kind of place.

They decided to drink some Irish beers and programmed both phones with the numbers Aubrey had written down previously. By the time they were finished with their second sixteen-ounce draw, Zander decided it was time to find the oyster bar, and they left. Zander wanted to come back and try the food. Irish food always reminded him of growing up. It seemed the Dutch and Irish ate many of the same items, and Zander always found it comforting.

The desk clerk had been right. Peg-Leg Pete's was a huge success. People were friendly, and the couple had a great time. There was a band playing on the deck outside. The night had turned a bit cool, and the restaurant had clear plastic curtains to block the wind. Zander noticed a few propane heaters as well.

Aubrey was having a great time. The beers she had been drinking seemed to be having an effect. She simply oozed sexuality and hung on Zander the entire evening.

They didn't get back to the hotel until after midnight. Zander knew he would need to rely on every oyster he had eaten that entire evening.

~

Fats woke up with a bad feeling. He had been fielding some threats from the biker gang he had taken on previously. But that wasn't what he was feeling. He didn't know what it was, but he knew something was in the wind. He had a sense for things like that. Fats had always been aware that he was clairvoyant. He had tried to tell others about his gift, but no one ever seemed very interested. It didn't matter to Fats. He knew his gifts were sometimes a curse, and that was why people avoided the subject.

Today might be one of those curse days. He didn't know, but he figured he would find out soon. He wasn't wrong. He received three phone calls within fifty minutes. They all concerned his friend Zander. Coincidences be damned, this was serious.

The first call came from Sheila, Sara Jane's sister. The minute Fats heard her voice, something started to burn in his stomach.

"Hello Fats. This is Sheila, I don't know if you remember me."

"Of course I do. Has something happened? Is Zander in trouble?"

"You might say that. I think you're going to get a call from a family member of mine, and I just wanted to prepare you."

Fats was worried, and he had dropped his usual hippie lingo he used so often. He waited for Sheila to continue.

"Are you still there?" Sheila asked.

"Depends what you plan to tell me."

"She's pregnant, Fats."

"Don't tell me that," he growled.

"There's no other way to say it."

"I suppose you're telling me that you know for certain that it's his."

"Of course I do. I wouldn't be telling you this otherwise. You know you can say anything you want to me, but I want you to be careful how you speak to my aunt."

"What's her name?" Fats was being short.

"She'll just call herself Millie. I told her not to call you, but she's not used to being told 'no' by anyone."

"Then she hasn't met me."

"That's why I'm calling. Fats, please just hear her out, and then tell her you'll take it under consideration. She'll want to give you her phone number."

"Why would I want that?"

There was a pause on Sheila's end. "My sister is staying with her. She will be asking you for a way to contact Zander. I lied and told her I didn't know. Somehow, she must have got something out of Sara Jane, because she just called and asked for your number."

"That makes no sense. She's got Zander's answering service number."

"Maybe not, or she doesn't want to contact him. I don't know. I'm just calling you to let you know what I know."

Fats softened. "Well, thanks. I do appreciate the information. I know this isn't your fault. It's just that every time that stupid shit gets involved with her, things go south."

"You can say her name."

"No, I can't. She's no good. How Zander could have been so stupid is beyond me. He just can't think clearly around her."

"I have no idea how all this is going to end."

"It won't end well at all," Fats said.

"Well, thanks for hearing me out anyway. I knew this wouldn't be an easy call."

"It's the last thing I ever wanted to hear."

"I'm sorry to have put this on you. I know it will be a burden to someone as sensitive as you."

Fats liked what she was saying. "Thanks. Give me your number, and I'll try to keep you somewhat in the loop."

"Good luck." She gave him her number, and then hung up.

He hardly had time to put the phone down when it rang again. He was dreading the call. He didn't know what he would say to this woman whom he had never met, and yet was a relative of the woman he most disliked at the moment.

"Hello. Branchwater, Fats speaking. How can I help you?"

"You don't know me, but I believe you know my niece." Millie's conversations were always short and to the point.

"Who might that be?" Fats wasn't about to let this woman know he had been warned by her other niece.

"Right now she goes by the name, Jayne Grafton. You might have also known her as Sara Jane De Graff."

Fats couldn't hide the loathing in his voice. "'Oh yeah, I know the woman."

"I have a need to get in touch with your friend, Zander. I have some important information for him."

"Is she dying?"

"Not hardly."

"That's a disappointment." Fats wasn't following Sheila's wishes, but he couldn't help himself.

"I realize that she's had a checkered past, and you may not like her very much," Millie said, trying to keep the conversation on point.

"What do you need from me?"

"Do you know where he is, and can you give me a way to contact him?"

"I truly don't. He had a cell phone at one time, but it's out of service."

"Can I give you my phone number? If you would hear from him, I would appreciate a call. This is very important."

"I'll consider it." He wrote down her number after she repeated it twice. "Why isn't Sara Jane contacting me?"

"She doesn't know I'm doing this. She doesn't want me to be involved in her affairs."

"Were you planning to tell me why you have such a pressing need to contact Zander?"

"Oh, I think you know already. If I know my family, my niece,

Sheila has already told you everything. If you can find it in your heart to help, I would appreciate it. Every child should know his father."

Fats couldn't argue and was about to say something when he realized she had already hung up.

Fran walked in to start her shift, and she knew that something was wrong by the look on Fats' face.

"Who kicked you in the gut?" she asked.

"You are not going to believe this." He began to tell her what had just transpired when his phone rang again. He looked at the number and stopped talking.

"It's Herbie."

"You'd better take it. I'm sure it has to do with all of this mysterious stuff. Go out the back. I'll watch the bar."

Fats went out the back door.

"Herbie. I was wondering when I would hear from you."

"She's pregnant, Fats. I saw her in the Piggly Wiggly down here."

"Did she make you?"

"No. I got away before she knew I was there."

"So what should we do?"

"I don't know. Gail won't let me talk to Zander. Besides, I couldn't if I wanted to. His cell phone is dead, and he hasn't contacted me with his new number."

"You want to contact him?"

"Yeah, but don't tell Gail. She would kill me. She says it's not our business and bad things would happen if we get involved."

"So, you just call and lay everything on me?"

"Pretty much. I figured if anyone would know what to do, it would be you."

Fats liked the flattery. It made him feel less like throwing up.

"This whole thing will probably blow up in all our faces, but I've decided not to tell Zander. It should be coming from the woman."

"Do you think that's wise? Wouldn't you want to know if you were in his shoes?" Herbie asked.

"There's that, certainly, but why is this our problem?"

"He's our friend."

"Sure, but he was a dumbass. He had no business screwing that bitch."

"Did you know he's with someone?"

"I think you might have mentioned it."

"This is the real deal. Gail thinks so anyway. I have never seen Zander pay as much attention to any female as he does with Aubrey."

"Nice name. That cuts it. I'm not going to be the one to destroy his happiness. I couldn't if I wanted because he doesn't have a phone."

"He's got that answering service."

"Damn it all, Herbie, work with me here. You need to swear you won't do anything you'll regret later. Swear that you won't tell Zander."

"I swear but…"

"No buts. If anyone tells him anything, it will need to be me. If I need your help at that time, I'll involve you."

"That's a lot of pressure on you."

"The story of my life."

The two friends said goodbye, and Fats returned to the bar and put the phone on the counter.

"If that thing rings again, I'm not going to answer it."

Then it rang again.

The caller ID read Jasper. "Damn that Herbie, did he go and tell the whole world?"

Fats answered the phone.

Epilogue

Leugens Hebben Korte Benen
A Lie Has Short Legs.
— Dutch Proverb

Jayne had become friendly with Hector's wife. They spent a few evenings each week, sitting together. Millie called her Mexicali Rose, but her name was actually Rosita. Jayne called her Rose because she thought the name fit her.

They would sit in front of the carriage house, out of the evening sun, and talk about life. Rose was always positive, even though Jayne knew her life hadn't been easy. She was raising her two boys with love and concern. Jayne was trying to take lessons.

Sometimes they would drink tea. Other times it would be lemonade. It was always nice watching the sun go down. It seemed that everyday it took a little longer and dinner would come a few minutes later.

"The winter days are getting longer," Rose commented one evening.

"It's hard for me to fathom that winter in Florida generally sees temperatures of 70 degrees."

"It's my favorite time of the year. The summer, well, she just gets too hot."

"That's why I always liked summer in the mountains," Jayne said.

"I've never been to the mountains. Have you decided to talk to the father?"

Rose was like that. Jayne thought she was intuitive or maybe something even more. She knew things before they happened. One evening she asked if Jayne knew what she was having, a boy or girl?

Jayne hadn't had an ultra-sound and didn't know if she wanted to know. Rose brought out a button on some thread and held it over Jayne's wrist. After a few minutes, she put it away.

"You will have a girl."

Jayne went to the doctor the next week and found that she was indeed having a girl. Jayne decided she should listen to whatever Rose wanted to share.

One evening, just before Millie called for dinner, Jayne decided to broach the subject of Zander with Rose.

"Rose, do you think I should involve the father?"

"That should be your decision. I cannot say what is right or what is wrong. You are a strong woman, and you could raise your daughter here without many problems. Miss Millie will be someone you can rely upon."

"You didn't answer the question."

"Yes, I did. If you want my opinion, that's another thing."

"I do."

Rose sat still for a few minutes. Jayne wondered if she planned to reply. Finally, she spoke.

"Fathers are important. If they want to be in the family, it gives perspective. What is this man's role in your life?"

Rose always asked the hard questions.

"I don't know. He loved me for a very long time. I'm quite sure of that. I think I ruined that, however. Our last meeting didn't go very well."

"And yet he made you pregnant," Rose said.

"Yes, but it wasn't out of love. I believe it came about because of anger. There was no passion, it was just an animal act."

Rose shuddered. "Then a decision must be made. If you believe when he learns he has a child, it will change his feelings, you must tell him. If you believe that his involvement with this daughter will lead to more trouble and heartache, you must keep the secret."

Jayne nodded just as Millie rang the dinner bell. They both got up and made their way to dinner.

All through the meal, Jayne wrestled with what decision to make. She weighed both the pros and cons and just couldn't see a clear-cut way out of the mess. She would need much more time to come to a conclusion. She thought about Zander's answering service. She had gotten rid of all of his numbers, but she would always know that one by heart. If the time came, she could always get in touch with him. She even thought about Fats at the Branchwater in Frisco. She could always talk to him.

Little did Jayne know, that Sheila, Millie and Herbie had already been in communication with Fats. If she had known that the people closest to her had possibly sold her out, it would have made her crazy.

~

Zander and Aubrey decided to hang out around the southern states until at least May. Zander suggested they explore places they hadn't been before. It was always more interesting discovering things together. There was a lot to see in Alabama, Mississippi, and Louisiana. Texas was a huge state and too big to give it justice in three months. Zander always thought New Mexico would be interesting but had no desire to even enter Arizona. There were just too many people to suit him. Aubrey agreed. She was happy to let Zander plan out an itinerary. It was nice having someone else in charge for a change. She had lived most of her life being the one to make the decisions. She liked just being along for the ride. Especially when that ride was Zander.

So, the plans were made. Sometime in May, they would venture north and Zander would show her the Midwest. He was excited to share his youth with her and wanted her to experience everything

Iowa, Minnesota, South Dakota, and Nebraska had to offer a little southern girl.

Somewhere down the line, Zander's life would be altered forever. That meant Aubrey's life would change as well. Time would tell if they would be ready for such a change or even if they could survive it. Lies and secrets were a test to anyone's relationship.

The Skinny

By Jeff Zwagerman

Prologue

Wie zijn billen brandt, moet op de blaren zitten
When you burn your butt, you need to sit on the blisters.
---Dutch Proverb

Fats went by his nickname. He figured no one else other than his good friend Zander, knew his actual nomenclature. He could hardly remember it himself. It had been so long ago. Roland Sinning really didn't fit his personality, at least that's what he always told himself.

Fats sat with his elbows on the bar and his head resting on his fists. He had done a fairly good job of putting Zander out of his mind. The bar had been busy over the holidays and the ski season, but now

March had come and he could see the tail end of it. Fats had lost track of Zander and his new girlfriend. He tried to remember her name but Audrey was the only thing that came to mind. He knew that wasn't right.

Fran, Fats' ladylove, was sitting on the other side of the bar drinking some lousy coffee. She looked up at Fats meaning to say something about his bad coffee, but she noticed the puzzled look on his face.

"What the matter with you? This shitty coffee freaking you out?"

Fats ignored the comment.

"What was the name of Zander's new romantic companion?"

"His significant other's name is Aubrey. Don't use the word 'was' when referring to her." Fran didn't like it when Fats spoke in past tense. It always signified that he was unhappy with what was happening in the present.

"You know Zander's track record with women. He may already have screwed everything up," Fats said, still resting his head on his fists.

"What's really bothering you?" Fran asked, losing the sarcasm.

"Those two have fallen off the face of the earth."

"And?"

"And I think Zander should have the common decency to at least check in regularly, so we don't have to worry."

"He's a big boy, and he's with a woman he might very well be in love with for a change. Why don't you just let everything work itself out?"

"It's not in my nature, my dear inamorata." Fats was back.

"Don't try to vocabulary me to death. I was an English major in college. I can spiral circuits around your circuitous babble."

Fats knew it was the truth. Fran was the only woman he had ever met who understood him. She could cut through all his bullshit and get him back on point before he even realized what she had done.

"You know what is really bothering me?" Fats finally asked.

"Of course I do. We've had this conversation more times than I'd like to remember. I'll tell you what I've always told you, 'mind your own business.' Sara Jane and her child are of no concern of yours."

She was talking about Zander's girlfriend from his youth and the fact that she was pregnant with his child. Every time Fats heard her name he would wince. It was the reason he never used it. He generally found an appropriate moniker that better fit a woman of her lack of talent and inabilities.

"But he's my friend. If the tables were turned, I would want to know." Fats sounded like a scolded child.

"Grow up. Not everything is under your control. This thing will work itself out without your meddling." Fran emphasized the last word.

Fats realized what she was talking about immediately. If it hadn't been for his meddling, Sara Jane would never have become pregnant with Zander's child. He was the one who sent Mona to follow Sara Jane and when that went south, he talked Zander in following them to Key West. It seemed like a bad dream, but it didn't go away during his waking hours.

Someone once said, "No good deed ever goes unpunished." Fats knew it was a basic truth. He also knew he just couldn't help himself. He was one of those "Rainey day people."

"I'm going to Wal-Mart to get some supplies for the bar. Do you need anything?" Fran asked.

"A kind word?"

Fran went around the bar and took his face into her hands and kissed him squarely on the lips.

"The bar opens in an hour. Are you ready for the day?" Fran asked.

"I think so."

"Then get off your dead butt and get to work. Make some fresh coffee and don't be using the soft water from the bar sink. Go in the back and use the hard water from the tap. Hard water is the key to good coffee." Fran said.

"Why haven't you told me that before?"

"I have. You just refuse to listen." Fran's voice sounded a bit frustrated, but she was smiling.

Fats smiled back. They sounded like an old married couple, and that gave him a warm feeling somewhere down in his gut. He thought that was a strange place for a warm feeling. Most of the time his warm feelings went quite a bit lower. He wondered if he was getting sick.

"Marry me woman. Let me put you in the midst of all these good things." Fats swung his arm around and indicated the entire bar.

"I'm already here. Don't ask me again. I don't need a scrap of paper to tell me that we are a couple," Fran said, and walked briskly out the back door.

Fats watched her leave. He must have asked her to marry him a thousand times. She always turned him down. Once she told him that she didn't want to jinx their relationship. He had no idea what that meant. Something probably happened to her before they met. Fats figured she'd tell him about it when she was ready. In truth, Fats didn't know if he was the marrying type, either.

He went back to his thinking pose with his head on his fists. Many things had happened to him, since he met Zander at Ole's Big Game Bar in Paxton, Nebraska. Most of them were good, and even the crappy things had made their friendship stronger.

Fats began to think of his time before Zander. His life had taken many twists and turns that would have devastated a weaker person. He wondered if his desire to mend other people's lives came from his inability to reconstruct his own.

View other Black Rose Writing titles at www.blackrosewriting.com/books and use promo code **PRINT** to receive a **20% discount** when purchasing.

BLACK ROSE
writing™